# RAINBOW PLAGUE

# RAINBOW PLAGUE

LIA ATHENA

*For Uncle Nicholas, who loved regardless of gender.*
*I never got to meet him, but his love will forever be*
*in my heart*

# ONE

# Bang!

# Sunday, June 28, 2026: The Night after the Pride March

# I

I see their rainbows dim in the darkness, and I long to hug them and tell them that everything is going to be all right; but I can't because my hands are tied behind my back, and if I were to speak, the guards at the front of the school bus would bark at me to shut up.

I breathe in and out, letting the stale bus air fill my lungs.

I hear the bus door open, and a clatter of footsteps getting louder and louder. Several stop next to me, in the back of the bus.

A small boy, maybe twelve years old, stands next to me, hands tied behind his back. Wet, thick, tears are scattered all over his innocent pale face. Grey and green snot sticks out of his nose. His chin trembles, a small bruise spreads on his right cheek. Blood spatters his blue elephant patterned pajamas.

I dart my eyes at the soldiers standing behind him with slight smirks on their faces. "What did you do to him?" I want to yell. "How could you hurt a little boy?" But I'm afraid of them. Of their Tasers and guns and big fists. I don't want to be like my parents, tased to the point of fainting and falling to the ground. Heads thudding on the floorboard, red oozing. They were still breathing, still *alive*, but. . . clearly in pain.

I'm mad my parents got tased to the point of almost not being.

But I'm enraged that my younger sister Janice had to find their bodies on the floor and see me dragged by the other soldiers—

I don't get it.

This shouldn't have happened. But it did.

"What's your name?" the boy whispers as he sits next to me.

"Maia. . ." I bite my lip. "What's yours?"

He shakes his head, his eyes wet, "I don't remember."

# 2

As the seconds tick by, as the minutes creep past, more and more people around my age are forced onto the bus. Most of them have their hands tied behind their backs, some of them have bruised lips and black eyes.

It's still night out. There are no stars in the sky and the moon seems to have disappeared—she probably doesn't want to witness the scene unfold.

The boy asks if he can sit next to the window, I'm not sure why, maybe he feels safer there, or wants to see if his parents are running out the building to try and save him.

We quickly and quietly shuffle around each other, switching places.

The soldiers eye us, but once they realize what we're doing, they don't seem to care anymore. I notice that the soldiers all have this weird patch on their uniforms, over their left arms. It's bright red, with a blue cross inside (like the Red Cross logo, but blue) crossed diagonally by a gold sword, and underneath, the letters USMG in gold. What this means, I have no clue.

Soon the bus is packed, but there isn't the usual chattering that fills a packed bus. It is quiet. A couple more soldiers clamber aboard, sitting in the front, and then a man, a normal-looking man with jeans and a black t-shirt, gets in the driver's seat, enters a destination in his phone, and places it in front of him so he knows where to go. And the bus rumbles off.

The boy looks out the window and eventually falls asleep, leaning against the glass.

I think he lives in my building. I don't know who he is. . . I hope to God that he eventually remembers his name.

Outside, we pass by some concrete and brick buildings. I don't know what street we're on, and it's too dark to tell. There are some people out there lingering on their phones, some with their mouths moving, some filming the bus as we pass by

The bus rolls on, and I feel sleep hitting me.

Why does sleep come now?

I need to stay awake. I have to see where we're going.

But my body takes control. All the exhaustion of the parade and the soldiers and my parents and my. . . sister. . . I really do hope she's okay. She's ten years old. She can't possibly understand what just happened, and I hope. . . I hope she's doing okay. Our parents will wake up; they have to, and she, she's smart. She'll be okay.

She *has* to be.

And I wonder, *where is Aimee?*

And bam, sleep. Just. Hits—

\* \* \*

I wake up.

But not the usual way I wake up. Where on weekends the sunlight wakes me up and on high school days, my phone alarm wakes me up.

I wake up to shouts and yells.

Several people, braver than me, are up and attacking the soldiers.

And it is working; there are more of us than of them.

I just watch. . . because I'm not brave.

More people get up and join in the melee.

The bus jolts to a stop. The driver seems unsure what to do, he flicks a couple of switches and the lights in the bus grow brighter, and the soldiers are tasing people and punching, but others are tackling them.

More are standing and are prepared to fight. But one soldier takes out his pistol and shoots it at the riled-up crowd.

Bang!

Bang!

Bang!

Three figures fall down, blood pouring from their foreheads, and everyone hurries to any empty seat, stumbling over the bodies, not wanting to die.

The three bodies are right there. A foot is right next to me, and I start to smell the blood, which is somehow worse than the red pouring and pouring. And their eyes, their eyes, are cold and still. Their faces frozen in fear.

They are so innocent.

And I recognize one of them: an Asian girl, dead as night.

Fear shudders through me and I can't seem to breathe.

Long, wavy brown and purple hair cascades around her face. Her piercing brown eyes void of all emotion. Her beautiful soft lips, her small nose that perks upward just the right way, her long beautiful neck, her small orange rose tattoo on her left shoulder. She wears a white t-shirt. Her rainbow bra is see-through, and her long purple leggings match her hair. I look at her bare feet, covered in scrapes and cuts. Her fingertips, each nail a different color from the other, all the colors of the rainbow.

And I scream, and my tears start falling down hard and hard, and I fall on top of her body. . .

I didn't even know Aimee was on the bus. I don't think she knew I was on the bus.

And... now... she... is... just....

I bawl, I shriek and yell so loud. I can't move my arms; they are stuck behind my back, and I don't know what to do. My whole world shatters, and the blood from her forehead is on my feet, and I don't know what to do.

I look into her cold, dead eyes, and I want to close her eyes with my fingers, but I can't because I'm stuck.

The soldiers are pulling me away, but I'm still now, and everyone is just watching... they are too afraid. Fear does things to people. It freezes your soul, takes hold of your brain...

I feel the Taser shock me. It burns, stings, and sends a million shivers of nerves rushing all over my body pricking and prodding me, and shockwaves collide into me and collapse, and I feel like just fainting, but something in me keeps me awake.

I can't seem to look away from my beautiful girlfriend, Aimee, from the woman I love.

She is the rushing blood that pumps my heart, she's the electricity that keeps my brain alive... she is my whole world.

And now... she's... gone, and I can't do anything but weep and whimper, and I push the soldiers with my shoulders, but they slam me back, and they pull me by the hair to the front of the bus, where there is some space next to a soldier, and I'm thrown next to the soldier, and I'm crying and they keep tasing me, because I am so awake and so angry and then the soldier takes out his gun and bangs my head and spots dot my vision, and everything becomes a mosaic. Where the tiles are tiny dots and they blot my vision, and blackness takes over me.

\* \* \*

Someone is slapping me. It hurts and bright sunlight hits my face. I open my eyes and taste blood in my mouth. I feel so tired even though I slept, how long did I sleep? I look at my wrist to check my watch but realize I don't have it. I wasn't wearing it when they kid-napped me.

I look around and see the soldier who was slapping me. He has a small face and very tiny eyes, and he looks at me with so much ag-gression on his face. And my arms ache from being held behind my back. I look out the window and see green and the bright sun shin-ing through.

I look behind me and the whole bus is emptied out.

I look in front at the driver's seat and a different guy is sleeping, his head lolled to the side of the seat, drool seeping down his chin.

The soldier grumbles, "Let's go, Ling-Ling."

*Ling-Ling.* I shudder. Ever since President Miller came to power, racists have been more violent, committing more hate crimes than ever before. Being half Korean, half white, I'm used to all kinds of slurs, but hearing him say it, in a school bus, with my hands tied behind my back, I can't help but feel a cold hand grab my soul and wring it dry.

"Where. . ." My voice is hoarse, my throat aches, and I remember, I remember Aimee. I look at the aisle behind me, and the bodies are gone, but the blood still lingers on the bus floor. There are foot-prints in the blood; people must have stepped on the blood. And I'm about to cry all over again, but the soldier stands up and pulls me up, and I have no time to say anything because he pushes me down the steps and I can't catch myself because my hands are tied behind my back and I'm stumbling through the open door, and my head hits the ground with a huge thud, and it hurts.

The soldier rushes down the steps and pulls me up, and he pushes me, and the sun shines, and I can kind of see where I am.

The bus I was on is parked behind a whole line of other buses. And behind it, there are several more buses pulling in and lines of people with their hands tied behind their backs exiting the buses. They look torn and exhausted. And by this road of long school buses are several large houses and to the right of that, there is a beautiful grassy meadow that is so large, and there is a beautiful blue lake and along the sides of the lake are a scatter of little cabins.

A dock stands in the lake, it's worn down, the wood chipped, it looks like once upon a time sailboats would land there, with cheering people in lifejackets jumping from the boats and tying ropes with special knots to the dock—but now, it's empty, deserted.

On the other side of the lake, I see little cabins next to one another, surrounded by pine trees that look almost dead.

There are some wooden poles with outdoor speakers attached to them.

On the other side of the meadow several large tents have been erected, like the ones you see at a wedding reception, white and pointy.

And the people from the buses are being herded to the tents. The soldiers who are herding them all have that same red patch on their arms, with the blue cross and the gold sword.

Pine and spruce trees surround the tents. The sky is so beautiful.

But the soldier pushes me toward one of the large houses. It is a pretty building on a low hill, walled with smooth logs and ornamented with intricate carvings around the windows and doors. There is a wooden patio in front, raised on poles.

He's carrying some papers and there's something familiar about the one on top, horribly familiar. And I realize it's a printed screenshot of a photo I posted on Instagram just the other day—the one with. . . I can't think of her. I can't. I am numb. Maybe she didn't die; maybe the bullet didn't hit the critical part of her brain. . . or. . . I don't know what to do. . . I have. . . I have to figure out how the fuck to get out of here.

But my hands are tied, and I'm so tired, and the soldier has his Taser and gun in his holster.

My bare feet hit the wet grass, and it feels so nice. The mud squishes around my feet and under my toenails, but I don't care. I don't fucking care anymore.

I ignore the blood on my shirt and the blood in my mouth.

Soon we are at the large house, and we go up the patio stairs and there is a wooden sign that is covered with a piece of laminated paper taped to it. It says: "Headquarters."

The front door opens and another soldier appears. She is very tall, white, appears to be in her late thirties, with silky black hair in a bun, and her uniform looks crisper and more official than the others I've seen so far. It, too, has one of those red patches on the left arm.

"I'll take it from here, soldier."

The man nods. "Yes ma'm, General!" he barks. He hands her the papers and leaves. And I'm just standing there.

The General peers at me intently, like I'm a specimen in her butterfly collection, and gestures for me to enter. I step through the door.

I'm in an old-fashioned house. To the right is a nice living room with a light blue carpet patterned with pink circles and a grey couch that is overused and covered with dust. On the far side, there is a bulletin board on the wall; they must have forgotten about it, because there are photos pinned to it, of smiling kids like they are at camp. . .

I stop and realize. This *is* a camp, a sleepaway camp, somewhere, in New York, on the East Coast? This used to be a sleepaway camp, with kids. . . but. . . now it's. . . "Where am I? What is this? What the fuck is going on?"

I came out to social media and the world declaring that I'm gay. My girlfriend came out as bisexual. We declared our love on Instagram and Facebook, for all the world to see.

I went to the Pride March yesterday with Aimee, to protest President Miller's new orders banning gay marriage. . .

When I get home, my parents are watching CNN. A church is on fire, the big one on Fifth Avenue that we passed on the March. The familiar anchor on CNN is looking serious. There was a bomb. The police say it was planted by "gay liberationists." That makes no sense to me, no fucking sense at all, but that's what the cops are saying, according to the sad-faced CNN man. There have been arrests, he says, and confessions. The program cuts to President Miller, sitting at his desk in the Oval Office, looking solemn. "Our nation's Godly values are at risk," he is saying, "and those who threaten our blessed way of life have shown today that they will stop at nothing. . ." I lunge forward and switch off the TV. I've been hearing this shit more and more, since Miller was elected, and I really don't want to hear it right now, not after my beautiful day at the Pride March, with Aimee.

That was yesterday.

In a different world.

Before the soldiers came knocking on our doors at midnight and dragged me, Aimee, my neighbors, and my friends from our homes because of who we are. . . because we are different.

"Language," the General says.

Because I said "fuck."

She takes my arm and guides me past the living room and into a hallway with several doors; the floor is cool under my feet. It's dark oak or something.

She moves ahead of me and opens a door at the end of the hallway, beckoning for me to enter. A soldier is standing by the door who looks at me like I'm dirt and looks at her like she's God.

Inside, there is a window in the back, an office chair in front of the window, with a desk in front of it, and a rickety, old chair in front of the desk. There's a painting on the right side of the wall with an orange-red sun and people of all shapes and colors swimming in a lake beneath the sun, glowing in the vicious light.

She goes to the office chair and sits down, then gestures for me to sit. And I sit, scared, and tired, and hungry and thirsty. My mouth is so dry like it's filled with sand.

She nods at the soldier by the door, and he leaves, shutting the door behind him.

She looks at me. "I'm General Wilson."

She inspects the papers the soldier gave her, smoothing them out with her fingers on the desk. "Maia. Anna. Robinson. Correct?"

I nod and sniff. "Where. . ."

"You're in a safe place."

"Safe? *Safe?* What are you *talking* about?"

She looks at the papers, clasps her hands, and looks at me. "You caused some disturbance on the bus. I wanted to talk to you about that before you join the others in orientation."

I close my eyes and then open them wide. "You killed *my girl-friend!*" I stand up. "Your fucking men killed her. . ." I want to climb over the desk and punch her face, and I'm about to, but she stands up, about to slap me.

I kick the chair behind me and run toward the door, but my hands are tied, so I put my back to the door to open it, and. . .

The General yells something, and the soldier from before opens the door and pushes me to the wall.

He drags me to the chair and holds my body down on it.

I thrash about, trying to get up, but I can't. The soldier is too strong. My seventeen-year-old body is too weak.

The General sits back down and looks at me, her eyes steel and greedy. "First, what occurred was an unfortunate accident. The soldier acted in what he thought was the correct manner to deal with a dispute, but he was in error. He is being reprimanded as we speak."

She puts her hands together. "Second, that person was not your girlfriend, she was your girl. Period. Friend. There's a huge difference, which you will soon learn to understand here."

"What are you talking about? She was my girlfriend! Nothing you say can deny that."

"You are confused. Maia. This wretched society and sinful media have turned your innocent brain into an abode of sickness."

"I am not sick," I spit, "you are!"

She leans close to me and slaps me hard on the cheek. I taste more blood.

"You are angry, I know. You are confused. But soon you will realize why you have those sinful thoughts and thus, you will then be freed of them. . . Soon, your mind will be cleaned."

"Fuck you."

"You're going to thank me later. Once you're done with this program, you're going to thank me for inviting you to participate."

I take a deep breath and exhale slowly. "Tell yourself whatever you want to hear," I say, "but I know the truth. You fucking religious homophobes are trying to control us and belittle us, but nothing you say or do is going to work. I was born gay, and I will always be gay, and there's nothing you can do to change it."

The General sighs and takes out a pen from her desk drawer and writes something on a pad of paper. "You don't understand what you're saying, Maia. You don't understand that you're under an illusion. Of love or whatever. You don't know what love is. You don't even know what pain is. *Not yet.* You're just a privileged freak that needs to be taught her place."

There's still blood in my mouth and I swallow it. "I know what love is. I know it in my heart."

She slams her pen down. "You're going to be late for the orientation. You better get going."

"I loved her," I shout. "I loved her so much!"

The General stares at me and says in even, steely tones: "You may have loved her like sisters would or how best friends loved each other, but you never loved her like a married couple would. You never loved her how a man and a woman love each other. You are delusional, which makes you *blind* to what you are doing to yourself and to others. The things you do with your *friend*, the sins you perform on each other, the way you unclothe yourself, and. . . You are a disgusting animal, Maia."

She is breathing heavily now and abruptly she stops and nods at the soldier holding me. She hands him the paper she was writing on, and he puts it in his pocket. He pulls me up. He forces me toward the door. He opens the door, one hand gripping my arm behind my back, and the other gripping the knob tight.

I turn around before he has a chance to push me out, and I look at the General. "You only say those things because *you* don't know what true love is. *You* will never know what true love is. I can guarantee that." Her face falters for a fraction of a second, but she puts her mask back up and makes herself look like she wasn't affected by my words. But I know the truth. I know she was.

# 3

The soldier pushes me outside, and it's hotter now. I can hear birds chirping in the distance, and bugs clickercackling about.

The soldier pushes me toward the tents where the others were headed before. There are lines of people snaking toward them.

I take a couple of gulps of air. Things happened so quickly. . . there is just so much to feel, I don't know *what* to feel anymore. It's like all my emotions except happiness were thrown in a blender, and the high button was flicked, and everything is just being churned into mush now, and I can't tell which emotion is which. I cannot tell them apart. I cannot tell if this is sadness or anger or how much of each I feel. . .

We head to the nearest tent.

I see everyone on the line. Their faces are filled with gloom and confusion. Hands are tied behind their backs, and they look so exhausted that they might just collapse at any moment. They are all around my age. They are of all shapes, sizes, and colors, and they all wear whatever they had on at the moment the soldiers came for them: pajamas, or jeans and t-shirts with rainbow designs, or party costumes, or just bathrobes, whatever. They are all holding papers with their tied hands. The papers appear to be printouts of social media posts, emails, health records, and other documents that look official. Everyone on the line has a large red X on the back of their left hand.

Suddenly I remember the same red X that they wrote on my hand before I was loaded onto the bus, as if I were some farm animal being tagged and about to be slaughtered.

When they wrote the red X's, they also took away everyone's phones.

The soldier holding me pulls me to the end of the line. He takes some papers out of his pocket and checks them, as if to make sure they're the right ones. I see an Instagram printout among them, it's the one where we declared our love to the world, and I see the note the General scribbled when she was lecturing me. He puts them in my tired hands behind my back. He peers at me strangely and then walks away.

I start to think that maybe I can take my chances and run, but I see so many soldiers around the tents all watching us, guns and Tasers ready.

The line moves slowly. I look at the person in front of me. He is tall, white, skinny, with very short blond hair that kinda spikes up like a mohawk, and he wears a bright blue tank top with white shorts. He wears camouflage slip-on sneakers. I look at the paper in his hands and I read the name "Ozzy."

We are in a tent, and I see many lines and many white plastic tables and gray metal chairs with ordinary-looking civilians sitting on them. There are laptops, papers, pens, and other devices I can't put a name to.

The line we are on goes to the closest table, where two people sit with stern faces. They cut the plastic handcuffs with scissors and then the prisoners hand them the papers.

They take the papers and put some sort of bracelet on the left wrists of the prisoners. And then those people are ushered to another line that leads to a table deeper in the tent. They write stuff down in their computers, ask questions, treat us as unhuman.

The line moves and the guy in front of me goes to the desk with the civilians and their bracelets. These people look so very ordinary. The woman, mid-thirties, brown-haired, is wearing a light orange silk blouse and black jeans. The guy, a little older, balding, is in a white button-down shirt with black pants. His shirt is folded to his elbows, and he wears a watch which says. . . 8:15. . . 8:16. . . I would be sleeping in my home now if none of this shit happened.

"My name is Ozzy," the guy in front of me says to the ordinary people.

The man sighs and looks at the paper that Ozzy gave them a couple of seconds before. "But your birth name is Thomas."

"Yeah, but I changed it."

The woman rolls her eyes and remarks as if Ozzy wasn't even there: "*He* is one of *those*."

"*They*," Ozzy corrects her. "Not *he*."

The woman rolls her eyes again and taps several things on her laptop while looking at the piece of paper. She takes out one of those bracelets, and now that I get a closer look at it, it looks more humiliating than I thought. It's a tight metal thing with snaps at both ends, and on it is a sort of barcode with a couple of numbers on it.

She picks up a scanning device that seems to be connected to her laptop and types several things and then puts the scanner to the barcode. There's a beep. "Give me your left hand."

"What is that?" Ozzy says, still frustrated and angry that they are not being respected with their pronoun.

"Don't make me say it again."

"Fuck you and fuck—" A soldier appears out of nowhere and stares at Ozzy. And Ozzy glares back at him.

Ozzy is about to punch him, but the soldier is too quick and hits them on the side of the head with the butt of his pistol. And they fall to the ground, and the woman clambers over them and snaps the metal bracelet around their left wrist. And then she goes back to her seat. The soldier drags them out of the tent, to somewhere, somewhere, I don't know where.

The ordinary people at the desk continue as if nothing bad happened. They look at the next person in the line—me.

I look around and see more soldiers in the tent.

I step forward, my legs shaking and gulp.

"Turn around."

I turn around, and they cut off my plastic handcuffs, which fall to the ground. I look at the ground; I didn't realize it was covered with broken plastic.

The woman takes my papers, and I turn back, rubbing my wrists. She notices the General's note, and her eyes widen. She looks at me again and then types some things on her laptop.

The guy looks at my papers. "Maia. That's a pretty name."

I don't respond.

He looks me up and down and smirks. I feel so humiliated; I feel like meat. He clucks his tongue and then taps several things on his laptop.

The woman reaches into a box for another barcode bracelet and then looks at me. "Give me your left hand."

I eye the soldiers. I don't want to get on their bad side. I give her my left hand.

She clasps the metal bracelet above my wrist. It is tight and, weirdly, it fits perfectly. But it's uncomfortable.

"Okay, off you go," she says. The papers I've been holding stay with them.

I go to what I assume is the next line. And wait, and wait, and wait, and they ask me questions, ask about medical concerns, medications that I need to take. I tell them I take vitamins in the morning and they laugh as if I had told them a joke.

At another desk, they hand me some more papers, some simple clothes, undergarments, boring old people shoes (they guessed my sizes), simple white sneakers, a toothbrush, a bed sheet, and a pillow cover.

And now, I'm with a group of others.

There are boys and girls. We just stand with our stuff, waiting for the next instruction. We don't talk to each other because two people who were whispering got dragged away to who knows where.

I look at my feet. They are so dirty.

\* \* \*

Finally, after what feels like an hour, our group, which is about twelve people, are herded toward the cabins by the lake. We pass several that are filled with people. At the very end of the row we come to a rickety old cabin, brown and splintery, dark brown paint peeling on the sides, with a sign that once said something else but now has a piece of white laminated paper taped to it. It says: "Housing 15."

It must have been named something cool like Wolf Den. I have a feeling that is what this camp was like.

I lift my hand to my neck, to feel for a necklace Aimee gave me, one with a red chain and a large red heart at the center, but I realize it's gone. I left it at home.

I wore it every day since Aimee got it for me on our one-year anniversary. I always felt naked without it.

And. . . that necklace. . . the only things that's left of her. . . gone . . . gone just like her.

I start to shake, but I don't have time to grieve.

They push us in. There are six bunk beds. Three bunks on each side of the room.

Each bed has an old pillow and a thin wool blanket on top. There are windows along the side of the wall, but they are boarded up.

Above the doorway, is a plaque with the quote:

*"Do not practice homosexuality, having sex with another man as with a woman. It is a detestable sin."*

LEVITICUS 18:22

Ugh.

It's musty inside, and the only light comes from a single lightbulb that hangs from the center of the ceiling. The light is already on. There is a chair in the back of the cabin, facing all the bunks.

One of the soldiers looks at all at us as if we are rats, but clearly he's enjoying looking at us like that. He starts assigning who goes to which bunk bed.

I am assigned to the one in the back. A bottom bunk.

He did it so cleverly that that no one is sleeping next to a person of their own sex. And no one is sleeping under or above the same sex. It was like he mastered a logic puzzle. But he didn't consider the bunk beds opposite each other. It's same sex there. But they are so far apart, I'm sure he doesn't care.

"Make your bed and come out in two minutes."

We all quickly make our beds. We don't talk to each other because the soldiers are here, and we are scared.

One boy, the one above me, looks like he is about to cry. He has makeup on his face and his clothes seem very feminine. Could he—she be a trans woman?

The soldier barks something and we all hurry outside.

* * *

Orientation. All lies, so boring, and I can't believe the fucking government did all this.

The fact that the President is Doug Miller, and that most of the House and Senate are extreme rightwing Republicans, and that the Supreme Court majority are also rightwing Republicans—all that should have made us realize what was coming.

A bunch of us, all from different cabins, are sitting in a large house, in an area that serves as a sort of auditorium. There's a screen in the front of the room and rows of chairs facing it. Some sort if educational video is playing. The footage is kind of fuzzy like this TV was made in the early 2000's, and everything they are saying is such bullshit.

A lady in a bright blue dress is looking at the camera in a very ordinary-looking house: "Welcome," she is saying. "I know you are all scared, I know you are all confused, but you are all here because we, the American people, we, the concerned government, we, the army, all care for you. You all have been plagued by a disease, by a mental disease that ravishes souls and spreads to innocent people like you."

She smiles.

"Luckily, there is a cure. There are steps we can take to help your lost souls and rid you of this disease. And afterward, you can go about your normal lives, get married properly, have children of your own, and never, ever again will you have those sinful urges, and never, ever, again will you spread those sinful urges to the younger generation."

She claps her hands, and a gentleman enters. He is in a tux, hair groomed, and he looks so perfect. He speaks to the camera: "You will stay here for six months." There are some groans from the crowd. "The President has initiated an executive order whereby all of you will stay here, participate, follow the program's rules, and get cured.

. . If you are not cured at the end of six months, you will be sent to a more demanding camp and be required to stay there until you are cured, and I can tell you that is not what you want. We have strict rules; we put you in this environment for a very good reason; we all do this for you because all we care about is *you*." I roll my eyes. "We care about *you*. I know things will seem tough, but it's for the greater good."

The lady walks to the gentleman and turns to him. He turns to her. "We are a happy married couple," they say at the same time.

The lady looks at the camera: "I used to be sick. I did so *many* vulgar things. It disgusted my family and my friends, and it was a disgrace to God. I was so, so, so sad, and depressed because of the things I did. And then, the Lord be praised, I was cured! I checked myself into a *voluntary government program* for people like me and I met him there as well!"

The gentleman looks at the camera. "It's been seven months, and we are both so happy, cured of the disease, and—" he looks at her as she looks at him— "we are expecting twins!"

I'd heard about this government program on the news. People would voluntary commit themselves to a six-month course that Miller created, led by hack psychologists and religious freaks.

I used to just laugh at those people.

But now I get it. That was a trial run. What none of us realized was that once the program appeared to be successful, they were ready to force everyone who is "sick" to join.

The video clip switches to a weird white room containing a metal table with large hooks attached to it.

A man in a doctor's lab coat enters.

And a soldier enters.

Some words come on the TV screen. A set of rules. The people on the screen say these rules, and when they say each one, that rule is highlighted.

Here's what the rules are:

1. Participate in all activities.
2. Do not disobey us.
3. Curfew: 21:30
4. Use of any technology, books, and any other form of mass communication is prohibited unless a person in charge gives you permission.
5. Do not form any sexual relationships.
6. Do not participate in any sexual activities.
7. Do not flirt, look at each other sexually, touch each other sexually, or do anything sexual whatsoever. Do not even think about it.
8. Do not attempt to escape this camp and/or cause any harm to the soldiers or the people in charge.

The man in the lab coat looks at the camera intently: "If you break *any* of these rules, you will be punished *severely*."

And then I kinda space out because what they are saying, and what they're trying to say, and what they're saying underneath and in between the lines, is such total bullshit and lies.

Some more people talk about these metal bracelets that are forever clamped around our wrists.

Apparently the bracelet has three purposes.

1. It's identification. The barcode carries information on who we are and where we're supposed to be and how many more "chances" we have. Break a rule, lose a chance. Break three rules and the punishment is very bad.
2. There is a GPS tracker inside, always on, that gives our location every five minutes. It's waterproof, shockproof, and at the very cutting edge of surveillance technology. Now I know where my parents' tax money went.

3. It has a chip in it that—if it passes over a metal band under the ground that surrounds the whole camp, supposedly—it rings and alerts the soldiers and people in charge. So, apparently, there is no way we can escape.

More useless rules, more obligations etc. etc. etc. etc. etc. etc. and I just don't fucking care. I just don't want to listen anymore. . .

My mind wanders to a time when Aimee was alive. We were just two girls in the concrete jungle, and we stumbled upon this cute little park that I forgotten the name of, and we were kissing on a bench in broad daylight, because we could. And a guy, a Wall Street man in a suit, came up to us with his hot cup of coffee and poured it all over the two of us. I remember the burning feeling, harsher than the splash of butter from a hot pan, and Aimee and I were angry. . . but we didn't do anything. He left right away, and once we were dried up, we didn't call the police or tell anyone.

Because it was just one incident. We didn't get seriously injured; it wasn't sexual assault. It was just hot coffee. . . It was nothing, really.

We should have never let him off the hook.

We should have tried our best to get him arrested, indicted, and hopefully do jail time. Even if it would have cost a lot of money and time, we should have done so, anyway. Because maybe *if* we did, he wouldn't think he could get away with things like that, and maybe he wouldn't support a President that thinks about sending everyone in America who is part of a certain community to be sent to camps to be "fixed."

Maybe we should have tried harder. Maybe we should have fought harder. Maybe, maybe, maybe. . .

"And everyone should know this!" I look up and there is that woman, the General from earlier, in the front of the room, and she is looking at all of us. She must have spoken, but I was not paying attention. "My soldiers are specially trained. Every one of them has *volunteered* for the *special* mission that we have begun to carry out today. They wear this emblem with pride, as do I!" She points to the red patch on her arm. "The emblem of the United States Morality Guard! A blue cross for purity, a golden sword for strength, and the red . . . the red, what that signifies I shall leave to your imagination. For they will use force when necessary! They will act by whatever means necessary to *help* you as they have selflessly sworn to do. They won't sympathize with your notions, your delusional opinions, so *don't* try and talk to them." Her eyes are steel and fire. "Any questions?"

A kid in the front, probably thirteen years old, raises his hand. His hand shakes.

The General calls on him. "Yes?"

"What. . . about. . . our parents. . . and family. . . and school?"

"Your families are all aware of this situation." She smiles broadly. "Right now, the President is speaking to America, and to the whole world, letting everyone know of this situation." She smiles again, teeth gleaming. "And let me tell you something even better. Those people you call *friends*, those people who are made in the right way and do things the right way, who marched and protested with you and *supported* you, who all called themselves *allies*, are living their normal lives now. They have forgotten about you; they have put your lives in our hands because life moves on. Today's news about what's happening to you will be old news. And life *will* move on. . ."

"What about the dead?" a girl shouts from the middle of a row near the back of the room. "How is that *helping*? How can you *seriously* tell yourselves that you're doing the right thing?" She must have been on the same bus I was and. . .

"That was an unfortunate accident. We have notified the families and reimbursed them for their loss."

There should never be a price on a child.

I want to scream, I want to yell, I want to, I want to, I want to just. . . I don't know what to do. My legs are shaking, and I want to do something.

And everything comes crashing into me.

She is dead.

She is dead.

She is not living.

She is not alive.

She is no longer in this world.

Her body is forever trash; her soul has wandered off; her mind has. . . I don't know where she is. I never even *got* to say goodbye.

She is in hell, or heaven, or reincarnation. Or something. I don't believe that you go somewhere when you die. I just believe that you vanish, you just become nothing.

And now, she is just nothing. Only remaining in our memories and. . . I never got to grieve, and there is just boiling anger in my stomach, and there is a ravaging spirt fueling me, and I feel like the blood in my veins turns redder than it usually is. It becomes a dark, dark, dark orange that you only see when your eyes are closed or when you wake up from a nightmare, and. . . .

I stand up. "Their lives aren't worth just a couple of dollars from the government!" I yell. I bring my hand back to my neck, realizing again the necklace's absence, and my heart tugs.

Everyone in the room turns to look at me, surprised by my yelling, but I continue because I don't know what else to do.

I couldn't fight for her life. I couldn't save her. I couldn't grieve for her. I couldn't say goodbye. I can't do anything but yell and scream and try to turn my anger into fuel to do something, to prevent another innocent death, or—I don't know.

"There is no price for life. You killed them. You killed her!"

The General sighs. "Please return to your seat, Maia."

I feel so exhausted and sitting sounds so wonderful, but I can't stop.

I look around at everyone else. "They killed my girlfriend. They killed her and two others when they weren't even doing anything wrong." I look at the General. "One of your men shot them." Tears start falling, and I can't control myself. My sadness turns into anger and my anger turns into rage and my rage turns into something that I have never felt before.

The monster inside of me has finally been unleashed.

Others are standing up and yelling at the General, and I feel my body moving, my legs and feet moving toward the front, to the General, and I crash into her and my momentum knocks her to the ground and I am on top of her, punching her and punching her and punching her, and my hand feels like it's breaking, the muscles feel like they're burning, and my bones feel like they are being splintered, and I don't care. My rage is a storm inside me, a madness. I enjoy the pain that she is feeling. I can feel her pain through my pain. I can feel what she feels.

She is defenseless. I want to hit her harder. And she is shouting and trying to hit me back, but I'm on top of her, and I'm not alone. The soldiers are shouting and blowing whistles, but others are coming to my help, and soon everyone in the room is attacking them. It's a glorious rage, a necessary rage. I feel that maybe we have a fighting chance. That maybe we didn't lose our chance to fight.

We can fight back.

We can fight for those we love; we can fight, we can fight.

. . . but then. . .

A soldier pushes me away from *her*, and I hit the floor. Pain shoots through my back. I look at the soldier and try to get up, but he pulls a black device from his pocket, and he presses a glowing red button, and then—

I feel a punch of electricity spark from the bracelet around my left wrist, and it sends a bolt of pain through my body and attacks my brain, and I shut down, like a computer when it's switched off. There's nothing I can do but just fall and fall and fall into a pit of pain and twirling colors, and I can't even think . . . I can't even. . .

# 4

## THE WHITE HOUSE: ONE YEAR AGO

President Doug Miller, in a perfectly fit navy-blue suit and radiant red tie, stares at himself in the mirror, gazing at his hazel brown eyes, his finely combed white hair, his pointed chin. . . His tie is crooked, he fixes it, making sure it is not crooked.

*Crooked appearance, crooked mind.*

"My mind is clean, my mind is straight, my mind is right," he says to himself, his midwestern accent twanging.

He clears his throat. "My mind is clean, my mind is straight, my mind is right," he repeats and smiles, satisfied.

He twirls around in his suit, feeling the crispness tingle his tender skin.

"My mind is clean, my mind is straight, my mind is right," he says again.

The door opens and Karen Miller, his beautiful wife with her clean white pearl necklace, comes tiptoeing in. "Hey bunny, you ready for that special meeting?" she purrs, leaning against the bed frame and taking one of her feet from her pointy red high heels and massaging her ankle with her thimble fingers.

Doug looks at her feet. "Mother," he says in a stern voice, like a teacher to a child, "your shoes."

"Bunny, my ankles, these shoes are killing me."

"You have to wear them," he says. He goes to his dresser and takes out his favorite American flag pin and goes back to his mirror and places the pin perfectly on his suit. He smiles and looks back at his wife, her shoes are where they should be, he smiles again and heads to the door, passing by his famous plaque above the doorway reading:

*And don't forget Sodom and Gomorrah and their neighboring towns, which were filled with immorality and every kind of sexual perversion. Those cities were destroyed by fire and serve as a warning of the eternal fire of God's judgment.*

JUDE 7

*What a great quote.*

His wife follows a few inches behind him.

And his Secret Service guards follow close behind them. He hears one of them murmuring into a mike: "Lion and Llama leaving Master Bedroom."

He smiles. When he became President of the United States of America, he chose his and his wife's code names, making them something great. Lion is masculine and mighty. Llamas. . . llamas are social and get along with everyone.

His servants are waiting for him, all along the wall, in their perfect black and white outfits. Just like how they should be. Most of their faces are brown and black. *So what,* Doug thinks to himself, *I'm giving them jobs, they should be grateful.*

Sometimes Doug has dreams of back when slavery was legal, of drinking a nice cool beverage on his verandah, gazing off into the distance. . . seeing his slaves laboring in the fields, the sweat on the backs of these strong, black men, the muscles thickening, those long, sturdy legs, how his gaze would linger below the hips, how his fingers would graze—

*No.*

He shudders, those devilish dreams are all part of God's test. To tempt him with sinister desires, which he'd have to resist and kill in his sleep.

He heads to the Yellow Oval Room, the doors open before him, like he is a king. He looks at Karen and shakes his head.

Normally, his wife is his equal, his partner in everything. But the matters he is about to discuss are not healthy for a woman's mind.

She nods obediently and heads to the dining room, probably to ask one of the chefs to prepare her a tasty snack.

He heads inside the Yellow Oval Room, and instantly waves of pleasure enter his mind. *Ahhhh.*

His colleagues are sitting around on the plush couches, the velvet chairs, of course not sitting on his particular throne chair behind the wooden desk in front of the window overlooking the Washington Monument, that glorious shaft, which kind of. . . looks like. . . Doug shakes his head. No, no impurity thoughts today.

The doors close, his Secret Service no longer in his presence. *Good, can't let anything get out. Not until it's time.*

He sniffs the air, smells the light softener of the quilts draped over the sofa cushions, the fresh scent of sunflowers in the transparent glass vase, and. . . he sniffs again. One of his colleagues is wearing a new type of deodorant, more minty flavored.

He has always liked having his secret meetings here.It's "the room where it happened."

He sits on his almost like throne and looks at his colleagues.

The Secretary of Defense, with his peak lapel dark grey suit and red and blue stripped tie, his small nose and scattered acne along his chin line.

Vice President Naomi Howard, with her straight black hair and star and palm tree necklace.

His trusty attorney in a blood red puffy blouse, a long, velvet red wavy skirt, with her bright dark red lipstick.

A constitutional lawyer, with polished shoes and a sly smile.

"So, Mr. President," his trusty attorney slithers and uncrosses and crosses her legs, "why'd you call us here today?"

Doug straightens his tie again, his palm sweaty.

He has never actually said his plan out loud before. Yes, he has said it to God, but not to anyone who could possibly stab him in the back, he has never uttered those words before. He swallows his saliva. He is hungry, actually. He kinda feels like a hot dog.

Doug smiles. "It has been more than a year since I became President of the United States."

They all nod, like they had no idea.

"I made a promise to the American people." He nods, thinking back to those beautiful times when he was campaigning for his presidency.

*It was easy to win.*

Doug gleams. *America was a disaster. And he was their savior. Their prophet. Their hero.*

"You saved us all. You saved us!" Naomi Howard exclaims like a dedicated nun at a church.

"I made a promise to cleanse America of its sins. To bring back the traditional family values, to bring peace and prosperity."

Everyone nods.

The Secretary of Defense smiles. "You have done so much for the good of America. What's the new plan, Mr. President?"

"The next thing we must do is take care of those infidel *rats*."

"Infidel *rats?*" the lawyer questions.

"Those that feel the need to show off their sins, parading around in their clown outfits, holding up 'rainbow' flags," Doug spits. "You know, the gays, the bis, trans, all that tapestry. It's time for a real cleanup.It's time to take care of them once and for all!"

The lawyer chokes on his words, "You. . . the. . . you want to *take care* of these people? You mean, like, *liquidate* them?"

"Liquidate? Oh, you mean . . . Oh, heavens no! No, of course not." Doug smiles. "Fix them, is what we must do; cure them, put them on the right path. I care about these people, I really do! I want to *take care* of them, as God wishes!"

And the President lifts his eyes toward the ceiling, calm now, with a beatific smile. "I only want to save them from perdition, those poor, poor lost souls."

# 5

I feel the ground underneath my body. No. It's not the ground. It's a metal thing. I look up at the ceiling and there is such a bright light coming from the ceiling that flickers orange and yellow. I close my eyes again because it makes me so dizzy and nauseous.

I open them again and look to my right. There is a wooden cabinet. And a door. I look to my left. Just a wall.

I try to move around, but I realize that I'm stuck on this table. My hands, covered in bandages, and my feet are tied down with some sort of Velcro thing that is attached to these large hooks in the table. I realize where I am. It's the room, or one just like it, where the doctor and the soldier appeared in the video.

I try to lift my neck but there is a strap across my neck that attaches to more hooks or something.

I hear a door opening. I look there. A doctor—not the one on the screen but another with that same scary aura—looks at me and smiles. "Hello, Maia."

I don't respond.

"How are you feeling?"

He acts like he's concerned, but I know he's faking. He's the kind of guy who enjoys watching others suffer.

"Where. . ." Ah my throat burns, but I continue talking. "Where the fuck am I?"

"You don't need to worry about that."

I struggle under my bonds, but it burns, and I stop. I feel so tired.

"Why. . . why am I here?" I know that's a stupid question, but I ask it anyway. What am I supposed to do in a situation like this? I'm too tired to be angry, and I'm too sad to be some kind of hero or somebody that says the right thing at just the right exact time, and I don't know.

"You caused a ruckus back there, Maia. You broke several rules. And you know what happens to rule breakers. We were pretty clear on that."

"This is inhumane. All of you are ignoring so many of our rights as citizens, as human beings, you are doing the same thing they did in Nazi—"

"The government has to do what they can do for the good of America. We are simply curing a disease, so it does not *continue* to spread. We have every right to protect the American people."

"You know this isn't a disease. You know it. You're just using it as a cover up. You are trying to change us, when we have the freedom to—"

"Maia, Maia, Maia, you have no idea what you're talking about. You're just a *spoiled* teenager who thinks you are doing things according to your own *free will*. But you are—"

"—under the illusion of thinking that I'm doing what I want," I finish for him, "when really the disease is making me do these things. Go fuck yourself."

He sighs. He goes to the cabinet and opens it.

He takes something out of the cabinet; I can't see what it is.

I look up at the ceiling, my eyes watering. I don't know what's happening. I don't know what will happen. "What. . ."

I close my eyes and feel several tears drop, and I look at him again.

He holds an alcohol wipe package in one hand, and in the other, a small, thin syringe with some kind of musky liquid inside.

He tears the package open and wipes a part of my shoulder. It's cool and feels refreshing.

He puts the wrapper in his lab coat pocket and looks at me. "You broke many rules, Maia." He sucks his lips. "I hope this will teach you to *follow* the rules. Because I really do wish the best for you, Maia. . . I hope I won't see you again."

I am shivering and try to move my limbs, but nothing works. I am stuck. I am trapped.

The syringe looks so scary. I mean, I've had shots before, vaccines and such, but this is the first time I'm held down like this and a needle holding an unknown drug is going to pierce my skin. "What is that?!"

He doesn't answer. He just puts the needle to my shoulder, and I feel a sharp pinch of pain, and he pushes the liquid into my veins.

He puts the syringe in a pocket of his lab coat and pulls out a Band-Aid from another. He places the Band-Aid over the tiny wound and from the corner of my eye, I see that it's a kid Band-Aid. The one with a smiling SpongeBob.

All of a sudden, everything gets very blurry, and I feel dizzy, but weirdly awake. I feel like vomiting. I feel the insides of my body roll around as if my organs are changing places and sending bursts of distress, pain, shattering through my nerves. "What. . ." I try to say.

"It's my special cocktail." He laughs. "It'll weaken your body, but keep you awake for a while. . ." He smiles at the thought.

He's gone, and several soldiers are taking off my bonds and I can't fight back because my body feels so sluggish and slow, but weirdly, I feel their rough hands grip me hard. I feel everything, yet I cannot control anything.

I'm being dragged through a door, and everything is so fuzzy, and I feel my feet going down some stairs, and I hear a door opening and closing. And the soldiers are still there. And I feel electricity go through my veins, and it hurts so much, like I've been shot up with lightning. I've had pain before—I broke my ankle once; I had my appendix out—but nothing like this. This is pain, this is so much pain.

I feel a harsh sizzle, and everything happens so fast. The inside of my body is being pierced with sharp knives that burn, and everything hurts so much, and I just want to pass out, but I can't, and I don't know what's happening. I feel my arms over my head and my hands tied to the ceiling, I think?

I'm standing on my weak feet, and I feel the burn creep up on my armpits and travel to my wrists and my fingers become numb, and I can't see anything, but I feel everything, and I feel so exposed. More sparks shoot through me, and the pain keeps on pulling at me; it keeps soaring through me.

Something plastic, like a plastic bag, goes on my head, and suddenly it is around my head, and something is pulled, and then all of a sudden, I can't breathe, and my body just thrashes. I'm dying.

I'm suffocating, and I'm suffocating, and my legs kick underneath me but hit nothing. I don't know who's holding me, and I can't breathe, and the struggle is real, and the pain—my lungs are being squeezed with a large fist, and my head is splintering into a million pieces, and I just can't...

The pain...

I am losing myself and

I can't even think...

I feel myself breathe again, and I suck large gulps of air and my head clears, but the pain is still there...

The process repeats over and over again, the electricity, the burning of the lungs, the piercing of the skin, the strain of my whole body.

A million years pass, and I don't know. . . I don't know. . . I don't know. . .

And I pray to God, I pray to all the Gods. . . to die.

Because death would be much better than this.

Just to leave this world, let my body no longer feel anything, let my soul wander away. . . and perhaps, in death, find Aimee?

Dying sounds perfect. It sounds so wonderful to go away from the pain and never come back to it.

But they don't hear my prayers.

Something else happens, though. . .

The torture stops.

I fall asleep and fall deeper asleep, and my mind just wanders away, and I just feel myself soar into bliss and bliss and cushions and. . .

# TWO

A girl who is lost,
and forever broken.

# 6

I wake up. My arms burn. They burn like they are on fire, no, worse than fire—fire that is on fire. If that's even possible.

I have such a huge headache. A dark immensity is shattering on my head, roaring through my ringing ears, and soaking through my wet, crusted eyes.

I taste metal in my mouth and feel the warmth of blood all over my cheeks, and I smell, I just smell sweat and piss. . . and oh, fuck. I know where the piss came from.

The side of my leg is wet, wet, and smelling, and I feel so humiliated, my cheeks burn red. And I know no one is looking at me. . . *where am I?*

I look around the room.

There is a chair in the corner, and a wooden door next to it, and there is one of those security cameras high in the corner, like the ones you see in airports. I haven't noticed them before, but they are probably in every room, following us and watching us like hungry hawks.

I look up. My wrists are bleeding. They are wrapped by harsh metal that attaches to some rubber thing that connects to the ceiling somehow. Also that techno GPS bracelet thing is still on my left wrist.

I look down. My toes, my poor toes are red and scraped, and the nails are raggedy with uneven edges. I realize I don't feel anything—my feet, my toes especially, are so numb. I don't feel anything at all. It's worse than pins and needles; it's like they don't exist.

I try to cry, but no tears come out. . . I'm completely out of water. My mouth is so dry, and I'm so hungry.

I try to shout, but my voice doesn't come out. Just a croak, like I'm some frog on drugs. And I look at the camera, and I plead with that red dot that blinks on the front of it like the fluttering wings of a butterfly. The lens is a black pool of nothingness. . . and I don't blink, I just stare, my eyes feel so dry, and I feel my exhaustion creeping in and. . . . . . . . .

\* \* \*

I hear the sound of the door opening and my eyes slowly open. I see several soldiers and that *doctor*. . . that doctor from before. . . I don't know how much time has passed, but my torture must have lasted several days. Things feel. . . different. My wrists have stopped bleeding.

I feel worse than I did before. Sleeping did nothing but pass the time.

The doctor smirks at me, and the soldiers chuckle when they notice that I've wet my pants.

"Did you learn your lesson?" the doctor says, his eyes glistening with pride.

I look at him and squeeze my eyes shut. I want to say something back at him, make him feel tinier than he appears to be, but I feel so tired and so hungry, and pain just racks my entire body. Fear overrides my pride and anger brews in the gap of my heart that my Aimee filled.

I look at my feet and nod. A small nod, but it says enough.

They approach and untie my bonds and I fall to the ground. I feel like a puppet.

The doctor looks down at me. "What lesson did you learn?"

I feel like a kid that had a tantrum, and they are teaching me the right way to behave.

I try to remember what I did wrong. And really, I didn't do anything wrong. I was just speaking up in this unlawful place they call camp; I was trying to rile up the crowd or something. I just wanted the truth to be heard. . . I don't know. This grief period where I don't have time to grieve has been messing with my brain.

I haven't even *accepted* that Aimee is dead.

I've. . . just. . . I don't know.

She's dead. But she's not dead. That news that burns in my brain has not reached my heart and soul.

I just want to eat, drink water, clean up, sleep in a bed, and wake up in my bed *at home*, smiling because this was all a scary, nightmarish dream.

"I disrupted orientation. . ."

The doctor sighs and looks at the soldiers. "Clean her up and then send her to have dinner with the others."

He leaves, and the soldiers pull me up, through the door and down a hall, push me into a tiny bathroom. I hear the door lock from the outside. I hear one of them bark, "You have four minutes."

I look around: a small oval mirror above a small turquoise sink, the toilet and bathtub with a shower head, all the same color. There is a cheap plastic shower curtain bunched on one side of the shower/tub.

I quickly use the toilet and wet a light blue towel and wash my legs and try to get the pee out from my clothes, but I can't get it all out. I still stink.

I look in the mirror. My once-neat short dark brown hair is a mess, strands are all over the place, there's a huge knot on top of my head. My light brown eyes a faded color, my light pink lips dry and cracked.

My face is oily and dirty, and I look so exhausted, and my whole body aches. There are bruises and scrapes, bandages over my arms and feet, and that stupid SpongeBob Band-Aid, but there is no serious injury. They did enough damage, but it won't kill me.

I rip off the childish Band-Aid. It stings for a second. I stick it to the mirror.

The door is unlocked and opened.

I am pulled up some stairs and outside and dragged along the wet grass. I see others, other prisoners, and it's so weird.

They wear such simple clothes, grey or beige. Loose, very loose, collared shirts. The boys wear loose pants. The girls wear skirts that go past their ankles. All wear the shoes we were given. I study them carefully; they are slip-ons that only old people wear. I don't even know what they are called. Like there is a bow made of string near the toes, and it's made of leather or something, but it looks handmade, as if it was sewed with simple strings on the sides.

The girls' hair is tied in a ponytail with a red ribbon, and if it's too short, there is a stupid headband bow that is placed on their heads, pushing the hair off of their foreheads. They look like dolls.

The boys' hair is combed clean and sleek like it's the fifties.

Their faces are so clean and boring, and their eyes are so lost.

They have lost hope of leaving this place.

They have lost the will to resist.

*But they can't be broken already. They just can't.*

They head to one of the large houses by the lake, and they are looking at me as I'm dragged there.

There is pity in their eyes. I don't want their fucking pity, but they give it anyway.

I feel like crying, but I don't.

I see the young boy from the bus, he nods at me. He seems calmer now.

I look at the lake. I see the orange from the sunset flick across the top layer of the water, and it's so beautiful, it's *so gorgeous* that it makes me almost forget about this shitty place.

But then the soldiers are pulling me, and pulling me, and my eyes slide away from the beautiful sight.

I look at the house. As we get closer to it, it gets bigger and bigger, which is normal but it's bigger than that; it shouldn't be so big. It has several stories and a shingled roof, and the windows are surrounded by white trim, and I don't know. I look past the house, and I notice there's something behind it that I didn't notice before.

A fence.

It's not high, but it's there. It probably signifies where we are not allowed to pass. Probably there is metal underneath the ground and if it detects our GPS tracker bracelet, it notifies everyone, that's my guess, but I don't know how it works. I don't fucking care how it works.

I see the fence stretching behind all the other houses, and I look behind me. I can't see that far, but I'm going to guess that the fence encompasses the whole camp.

How long was I out?

They drag me through the doors of the big house and through a hallway. On one side is a living room with a shabby carpet, a sad-looking set of old wooden chairs with green plastic cushions, the kind with foam inside, an old TV, and some board games piled neatly beside it.

I'm pushed through another door, and I hear the chatter of talking and the clatter of metal across metal.

I see a huge cafeteria that reminds me of the one back in high school. A high ceiling, with bright ceiling lights every few feet, and dark brown wood plank flooring.

There is a line forming.

There is a long counter, and on one side are people behind a sneeze guard who are our age, wearing the same stupid uniforms, serving food with their large serving spoons onto the plates of the people who are holding out their plastic trays with metal spoons on them.

I smell the food; it smells really good, but I know that it only smells good because I am *starving*. I haven't eaten in days.

The food looks disgusting, just grey and green globs, and what looks like bread. . .

Soldiers are standing along the wall, watching intently, as if we are—well, we *are* prisoners, so—I'm not sure what I'm saying. My mind is becoming foggier by the minute.

The rest of this very large cafeteria is full of long beige tables with benches attached to them on both sides. There are ten tables, with lots of people sitting at them already. And the soldiers aren't holding me anymore.

One of them, an old man with a graying beard, leans next to my ear and whispers with a disgusting garlic smell, "Don't do anything stupid. We are watching you."

Then they are gone, and I'm not sure if they joined the guards along the walls or left the area. Because all of these soldiers kind of look the same, all wearing the same uniform, with the same red arm patch, and the same weapons attached to their belts.

The enemy always looks the same.

I join the line, and people stare at me, and the whole room is quieter than before. But I look at my feet, and they stop staring and keep to each other quietly. And the line moves quickly. I get a plastic tray and a spoon and get the food. I'm so hungry.

I linger, trying to figure out where to sit.

A girl with long, long, brown hair tied in the same simple ponytail with the red ribbon, who looks to be South Asian, approaches me. I notice a scar next to her large, soft lips. And she smiles at me.

"Maia? Right?"

I nod.

"I'm Penelope. Sit with us, yeah?" She gestures to a table in the back.

"I'll get your tray." Her long, slender fingers take my tray, and she does it so carefully that she does not touch me at all. And that sudden gesture sends shivers down my spine. Even if we aren't attracted to each other, she would still do that, because she does not want it to look like she's flirting with me.

We are always being watched. By the soldiers and by the cameras that are everywhere.

Cameras don't belong in a sleepaway camp, but they do here, attached to the ceiling with metal brackets and black cords.

Penelope takes the tray from me and turns toward the table she was gesturing at. And I see her back, and I see the curve of her butt, and her ankles, and I glance away, ashamed. Not because I am not allowed to look but because Aimee just died a couple of days ago. . . or however long ago it was.

I shake my head. I have to focus on food. I follow Penelope to the table, and she sets the tray on it, next to a white girl with bright blue eyes and long, silky, blonde hair in a ponytail, and a black girl with a shaved head.

I look around. I notice there are several people with shaved heads, and I don't know what to think of that.

The girl with the shaved head notices my puzzlement and smiles slightly. "My hair was pink." She chuckles. "Too bright for them, I suppose."

"That's fucked up," I whisper.

I sit down, swinging my legs over the bench and under the table, and all the other girls are staring at me.

The girl with bright blue eyes looks at me. "You're famous around here."

I shake my head and pick up my spoon. I scoop up a spoonful of food and place it in my mouth. It tastes like grits, but grits without the butter and without any texture. I swallow, and it drops down my aching throat.

I feel so tired. That simple action of eating exhausts me. My mouth feels like sandpaper. I look around and notice everyone has a plastic cup of water next to their trays. Penelope seems to read my thoughts and jumps up. "I'll get it," she murmurs in my ear.

I look at everyone, at no one in particular. "How long has. . . it been?"

"Since we were all gathered here?" the bald girl asks.

I nod.

"About two days," she says.

My eyes widen. "What?"

The bald girl says, "It's been sucky."

"Why hasn't anyone rescued us? Where are. . ." I try to think of who can save us, but I stop short, because I can't think of anyone.

The army and the police work for the government, so *who* can really save us? Our families? Who know nothing of fighting?

I touch around my neck for the necklace out of habit and am reminded again of my last piece of Aimee—away from my grasp.

"What about the other countries, Canada, Europe, there must have been *somebody* that got involved."

Another girl, Asian, who looks like she had a ring on her nose, but now has only small red holes, looks at me. "All this. . ." she gestures to everything and everyone around her, "it's all ordered by the President and the whole entire government. He is backed by the most powerful people in the House and Senate. No one wants to get involved. Other countries don't want to get involved either. They don't want a war with America. I eavesdropped on some doctors and they said that some other countries are even thinking of following us, adopting similar laws, because the governments there also think we are *diseased* and the *cure* works."

"That's fucked up, that's so fucked up," I mutter. I take another bite of my food. I remember everything that happened that night. . . the night of the Pride March. "The church bombing!" I say with my mouth full. "Do people really believe that it was us that bombed it?" I shake my head. "Is that why no one's helping us?"

"I doubt *anyone* believes that we bombed anything," the bald girl says. "But it's what the President says, and any excuse to be angry at a group of minorities is going to satisfy them." She shakes her head; her eyes are drained of energy.

"Not everyone. . . what about organizations like the ACLU, or. . . what about our families?"

"Even if there are protests nationwide, and people are going to court, trying to free us, the government is too strong," says the girl who used to have a nose ring. "They have too much power and money. I bet Miller's been planning this whole thing for years. . . and I don't think it will stop with queer people. We are only the beginning of his crusade towards a *pure America*."

"What about the Supreme Court?" I don't remember exactly what they do, but I know they wear those weird outfits and serve till they drop dead.

"The majority of the Supreme Court are Republicans, so of course Miller will win."

"It's so fucked up. And they are also getting away with the government committing forgery," the bald one says.

"What?"

"Some of us already got these documents that say your parents gave them permission to treat you, but that's just another way of them messing with everyone. They'll fool the media, citizens, even you if you're not careful enough."

"This. . . can't. This can't be happening." I swallow my half-chewed food. It gets stuck in my throat. I need water.

Penelope returns with my water and I take it and swallow some, savoring the rush of coolness seeping down my throat. "What are we talking about?" she asks.

"A way out," one girl mutters. She's Hispanic, with short black hair and a rough voice.

"Only if you can prove that you aren't a U.S. citizen," Penelope says gloomily.

"What?"

"I was sitting next to someone on the bus who had an accent, and when he started complaining, they took him somewhere. Haven't seen him since. I'm going to guess he was taken by mistake, and they let him go because if they didn't, they would be assaulting a citizen of wherever he came from."

I eat more.

"What about. . ." I think back to history class, I barely paid attention, but one thing stands out, a thing that was used. . . "people use it if they are wrongly imprisoned. . . habus something? Can't we do that?"

"You mean Habeas Corpus?" the one with short black hair says.

"Yes," I nod rapidly, "that one. Can't we try that?"

She points at a table behind her, at a boy with ginger hair who has bandages wrapped around his arm. "You see that poor kid over there?" I nod. "His parents are lawyers, so he knew all the right terms and what to say, like also how this is a violation of the. . . the. . ." She thinks for a second.

"The Universal Declaration of Human Rights," the one who used to have a nose ring says.

"Yes, the *Universal Declaration of Human Rights*. Universal, that means everywhere, even here. So he demanded to see the person in charge."

I shudder.

"That General."

"Yeah, he saw her. And she told him that those rights got suspended by the President, and then she punished him for even thinking of ways he could possibly get out."

I suppose news travels fast around here. I drop my spoon on the table, it clatters. There. . . seems to be no way to get out of this. I don't know. . . I don't have any more ideas. "This can't be happening."

"It's hard at first," says the girl with the bright blue eyes, "but even if your mind doesn't get used to things, your body will."

"I don't. . ." I look at her and then look at everyone, I mumble, "I'm sorry, guys, I'm not really brave or anything. What you saw back there—I was just angry. . . but now. . . it was just a one-time thing." I shrug.

"You went against the people with the bigger muscles who carried guns. That is definitely an act of bravery. And I know that won't be the last time you rebel," says Penelope, her eyes shining.

I smile at her. "Thanks."

"No problem."

"By the way," says the girl with bright blue eyes, "I'm Crystal." I am about to shake her hand, but realize she is not trying to shake mine, because it's *not allowed*, so I wipe my hand on my pants instead.

"You're looking at Yola," the bald one says.

My eyes widen. "Yola? I, like, watch your show all the time." She is the one and only Yola, the famous vlogger. She gives advice on boys and how to pick a lock and is adored by thousands. She came out as bisexual a couple of months ago.

She nods.

I didn't even recognize her without her bright flamingo-pink hair.

"I'm Jade," the one that used to have a ring in her nose says.

"I'm Diana," the one with short black hair says. I nod. "Well, officially I am Santiago, according to those fucked-up freaks."

"Were all of you on social media. . . or did they find out you were part of the community another way?" I question. They must have found out about Aimee and me on social media.

"Young people," Jade says, "were mostly found out through social media."

"One guy told me that his gay parents never used social media. They were very secretive about their private lives," Yola says, "but they had put in the Census back in 2020 that they were a gay couple with children."

My mouth drops open. That Census. . . it was supposed to *help* people. It was supposed to provide people and organizations enough funding. But instead, it was used to find out who's part of the gay community and who's not. I shake my head and sigh.

I just want. . . I want to wake up from this nightmare, I want to go to an alternate reality where Miller never got elected. I wish I could travel to a time where people like me could live happily and peacefully. . . Tears well in my eyes, but I can't cry. I can't keep crying. Because crying never made my problems go away.

I look at what's left of the food. I don't have the appetite, but I know I need the strength just to get through the rest of the day.

I continue eating and they tell me things and give advice on how to "blend in" and where everything is and what they have to do here to "get by" and things that we are not allowed to do and/or have.

Penelope says she heard that most of the guards here, other than the top officers, are not actually real soldiers. They are people who used to be in the regular armed forces but got busted for infractions like assault, drug-dealing, and prostitution. Miller's genius idea was to offer all these *sinners* a path to forgiveness and rehabilitation if they would agree to undergo special training and join the US Morality Guard, and battle against the *greater sinners*.

"That's us," Penelope says, "the *greater sinners*. Makes a lot of sense, huh?"

I look at Penelope as she speaks. She talks fast like she's a teacher who is trying to get in the last couple of sentences before the bell rings, and she's kinda pretty, and I can't believe I am staring at her and noticing that she bites her lips slightly. And that reminds me of how Aimee would bite her lips like that, and when we would make out, she would bite my lips lightly, and it was so sexy when she did it. And I remember. . . I run my tongue over the area where she bit last, where there is a tiny bump. . . and. . . it was, I guess, our last kiss. . .

*We have just reached the end of the Pride March, and confetti explodes in the air, and "Dancing Queen" is blaring from speakers all over the street and the parade cars, and we want to stand there and celebrate, but we have to keep moving. Even if the March is done for us, it isn't done for the people behind us and the people behind them.*

*So she grabs my hand, and we go to the sidewalk and in front of a store. It has a bright rainbow flag in the window, but it's closed. Maybe the owners are celebrating as well.*

*She brings me to the window, and my back leans against the window and she is in front of me, her hips close to my hips, her toes touching my toes, and her arms are leaning against the window, on both sides of my head, and she looks at me. She's a bit shorter than me and she is smiling, and she is so hot and so beautiful.*

*"I have to go soon," she says.*

*I frown. "Can't you stay with me longer?"*

*"My parents are going to kill me if I'm out any longer." The sun is setting, hitting the glass windows of the many skyscrapers that tower over us.*

*She has summer school, and she has to study. So, her parents are being hard ass on her.*

*I purse my lips. "I wish I could help you study."*

"Me too, Seven."

Seven. Her nickname for me. It took me seven weeks to mutter back that I like her too. I kept avoiding her the whole time because I was scared of what liking her meant to me, meant to us. And she kept thinking that I didn't like her, but we somehow met, and I admitted that I liked her. . .and yeah. It's been history ever since.

I sigh.

"I'll give you a kiss, how about that?"

I smile. "Better than nothing." And she places her lips on my lips, and we both close our eyes, and I can taste the orange melon taste of the gum she's chewing. We separate for a second as she puts the gum back in its wrapper and into her pocket, and then we are kissing again. And my hands are on her hips, and her hands are cradling my cheeks, and I taste her orange, and her tongue drags itself across my tongue and over my teeth and across the inside of my cheek.

There is so much passion, so much, so much, so much, so much, I just can't describe it in words. And I smile and she smiles. And her teeth are there, and she bites over my bottom lip, and it hurts slightly, but she does it in such a kind way that birds fly from the center of my stomach to my brain and back, and I taste a bit of blood, but I continue kissing her, pursing my lips, and feeling my lips all over her lips. And so much electricity is between us, and I don't know what to do with my hands. But somehow, my hands are squeezing her hips a bit tighter and bringing her hips closer to my hips.

And I drag my fingers along her stomach, and she shivers and moans slightly, and like my fingers are feathers, I bring them over her breasts and twirl them around where her nipple should be under this cloth, and I moan and she puts her fingers in my hair, and she pulls my hair toward her fingers, and I moan louder. And we don't even care about the pedestrians around us or the onlookers or the creeps that are taking a couple of photos for their private time. And I squeeze my eyes tighter.

And this memory is so real that I can't seem to awake from it. . .

But I do, I must. My mind snaps out of the beautiful past and I wake up to reality. And I hate myself for it. Why the fuck did I have to wake up from this memory?

I want to kiss her. I want that more than anything in the whole entire world. In my imagination I stretch the length of the universe and squeeze the corners of the world, and I try in vain to use my make-believe superpowers to wind time backward, go back to the point before she was shot and stop her from standing up and going against the soldiers.

I still feel the bump on my lips where she bit.

I want to say that I love her. That I love her so much. Because I never got to say those words. She didn't even get to say those words, but I know she would have wanted me to hear those words from her.

But love does not require words. It does not even require action. It just requires emotion and the connection between people. Between the way they look at each other and what they think of when they are thinking of that person. I saw it in the way her beautiful chocolate brown eyes looked at me. They were wet and meaningful, and she squinted slightly, and one eye was a bit larger than the other.

I remember her face so clearly, and the way she looked at me was a million shooting stars gliding across the night sky.

One thought just hits me hard, harder than any other thought in my whole entire life. The fact that I will never see those beautiful eyes look at me, that she will never love me the way she always did, that I will never be loved by her ever again—it just splits an atom and creates a nuclear bomb in my brain, and my whole world just shatters and shatters and shatters.

She is dead.

I will never see her again.

She will never live again.

Her last memory of this earth will be of pain piercing her head and a thump on the dirty bus floor.

She will never feel loved or love again.

She will never breathe again.

She will never eat again.

She will never sleep again.

She will never wake up again.

She will never. . .she will never feel again.

She will never feel pleasure again.

She will never give pleasure again.

She will never never never never never never never never never never the list goes on and on and on and on. It's a list made of a million points.

I can't live without her.

But I am alive.

I am still breathing, I am still here, I am barely living in this wrecked world that we only thought could happen in movies and novels, but apparently it was closer to us then we ever expected.

This was a near-future scenario that unveiled before our very eyes.

I will never. . . I will never. . . I will never. . .

She will never. . . live. . . ever. . .a gain. . .

She is gone.

I should be gone.

She.

Is.

*Dead.*

\* \* \*

I'm spacing out more than I should.

The others show me around, how things work, but I can't focus. Everything around me is just a blur, and I really don't know what to think anymore. I don't know what to do or feel. I've lost myself. I lost who I am, I lost the thing I was holding onto. I lost what makes me, me. There's nothing good in my life right now.

I can't even think of my family. I don't even think they know where I am. I don't even know where I am.

"You remember how to get to your cabin, right?" Penelope asks me. She's been a real help to me, all of the girls have. And... I don't know what choice I have. I have to be like them, I have to be *submissive*.

I have to follow the rules like them.

I don't want to. But what happened back there, it really messed with me. And I know in my gut that that wasn't the worst punishment they could give me. I know that was just a taste of what they could do to me. It was just a tiny bit of pain, but it was so much, and my senses are overwhelmed and now just thinking of the pain makes me want to vomit.

I have to avoid the pain at all costs. I can do this. I can be submissive for a couple of months and then go back home. I can make sure that they don't change who I am.

I am strong, and I won't let them "cure" me or whatever.

I nod. Unfortunately, none of my new... what are they? . . . friends, I suppose... none of them are in my cabin.

So, I walk alone, a shattered mess, covered in torn clothes, carrying a broken heart.

The love of my life is dead.

The people in charge think I'm diseased.

The person who I am, the person I figured out for myself, is gone. I spent so much time and energy trying to figure out what my identity is. And finally, I found it, and I felt comfortable in my own skin, and I felt accepted by society... and now...

Society hates who I am.

This world was just turning around for the better.

I know the history of the LGBT rights movement, ever since the term "gay" was invented. Before that, people's rights were stolen from them, people were killed and tortured because "normal" people thought they were possessed by the devil... but then the Stonewall Riots happened, and a movement formed and gathered strength, and same-sex marriage was legalized in 2015...

I don't understand how things can just be on the right track, and then completely go on the opposite direction. We were just starting to rebuild a world where people can live equally and fairly...

What happened to the America that we knew?

# 7

Everyone is settled in the cabin. There are bathrooms and showers a short distance away that we share with a couple of other cabins nearby.

Some fresh clothes are on my bed, the same ones they gave me in the big tent when I first arrived, it seems such a long time ago. I take these, along with my toothbrush, and put on those old-people's moccasins they gave me, which I find under the bed, and I follow one of the guys to the bathroom and shower area.

There is a long line, but what else do I have to do on this fine evening?

There is a bit of mist that curls through the trees and masks my face with little droplets of water that are so refreshing.

I breathe through my nose, and my nostrils get cleaned up. I smell the fair hint of pine and the fresh soil under my shoes.

I see the soldiers lingering by the trees or sitting on lawn chairs in the distance.

Will they ever leave us alone?

Or are they just going to watch us till we are completely brain-washed? I don't know.

The guy in front of me, whom I followed here, turns to face me.

He is white, has wavy, beach-styled, blond hair that cuts right near his ears. "You're Maia? Right?"

I nod.

He holds out his hand and I shake it. He has a firm grip. "I'm Sam."

I let go and feel sweat linger on my palm. I smile, unsure what to say or do.

The people in line and the soldiers are watching. What is allowed and what isn't?

The same-sex rules were plain and simple.

But what about the opposite gender? Do they encourage us to get along? Probably.

"It was really brave what you did back there."

I shake my head and look at the ground. There is a worm slowly moving around my shoe. I let it do so, and it slowly tunnels back into the ground.

"You stood up for us," he says, trying to get my attention. But I don't want to give him my attention. I don't deserve to be honored. I didn't do anything. I just caused more pain, and nothing I do now will stop her from dying. Because she is already dead.

The line moves forward, and I feel bad for just ignoring him, because it is a shitty thing to do. And the government is doing the shitty things that are happening to us. . . I won't become them.

"So, what brings you to this hellhole?" I question.

Sam turns around. "Oh, you can't tell?"

I look at him. He stands straight. I can see his biceps under his slightly tight shirt, and he is actually really good looking. His cheekbones are strong and sturdy, his lips full and beautiful. . . I smile slightly and shake my head.

"I was marching with my boyfriend." He crosses his arms. "What about you?"

"Same," I say without really thinking. I look at him and shake my head, "I mean, I was with my girlfriend marching. . ."

"She was the one who died?"

I nod and look at the ground again. The line moves: people with wet hair and towels come out.

"I'm really sorry about that."

"Don't be. It wasn't your fault."

"I. . ." We move forward. More people add themselves to the line.

"Where's your boyfriend?" I don't want to talk about her. I need to focus on something else.

"He lives in New Jersey, so I'm not even sure he's in this camp. Probably another one."

"That's good." I smile. "When this is all over, you guys can get back together." I look at the soldiers in the distance and I know they can't hear me, so I say: "Fuck 'em."

"Let's hope. I'm not so sure."

I turn to him. "What do you mean? You know they can't change who we are. They might think that, but they are wrong."

"I know they're wrong, but methods still exist to block it from our minds. They are going to brainwash us, make us believe that we are straight and *regular*. One of my friend's cousins went to one of those religion conversion camps in the South, and after a month or two, he really believed he was straight. He got a girlfriend. Last I heard was that that he got married, has two healthy girls, and works as one of the coaches at one of those conversion camps."

"What did they do to him?" I stutter, fear tightening my muscles.

"I don't know. . . He never talked about it, but I know it worked. I could see it in his eyes."

The line moves forward and soon we are in the bath house. It is co-ed. There are three shower stalls on the right and three toilet stalls in front of them, on the left. There are two sinks at the end of the place with mirrors. Under each sink is a wooden cabinet attached to it. I notice there are no cameras in here.

The showers are cheap-looking, with plastic curtains and metal hooks on the outside.

Sam lets me skip ahead of him because I look like I need to be cleaned up the most.

There are some raggedy towels on a shelf, folded roughly, all of different colors and textures. I take a light green one. I enter the shower stall and realize that I am in a public shower without wearing any slippers or anything. I could get athletes' foot or something.

There is a bar of soap in the shower, on the ground, covered in hairs. I put the towel and my new clothes on the hook and close the curtain. It squeaks.

I take off my shoes and clothes and toss them on the other side.

I carefully take off the bandages and toss them on the clothes. The wound is still red and sore, but I don't care anymore. I just want to get clean. I turn on the shower. It's so cold. I try to make it warmer, and it only gets a degree warmer, and I am so cold, but I get used to it.

I scrub myself with the soap, lather it on my body, face, and scalp. I rub it over my hair, and wish for my shampoo, conditioner, and soap. My wonderful mint-scented dandruff shampoo that makes my head feel like it's a popsicle on a dry, summer day. And my lavender and lemon conditioner that unknots my bird's-nest hair. My Dove body soap that makes me smell like a fresh rose in an English garden. Think English, English. Like found somewhere in England, hidden in the countryside.

I don't want to take too much time because of the long line.

I quickly rinse with the cold water and feel under my armpits. My hair is growing straight and edgy. But there's nothing I can do about that. I grab the towel and the clothes, dry myself and dress in the clothes they gave me: a beige long skirt that passes my knees and a boring collared white shirt that I saw the others wearing. I slip on my shoes and wrap the towel around my hair. I find my toothbrush which I left on the floor, stupidly. But whatever real disease may be in this shower, I already have it, because of my bare feet.

I trudge over to the sinks. Sam is there, brushing his hair with his fingers. I see some toothpaste on the sink counter.

I open the cabinet of the sink to see if it has anything useful.

In it are a bunch of cotton pads, all kinds, and sizes. No tampons. I guess a tampon acts too much like a dildo, ha-ha.

I don't have my period now, but I will get it soon.

They've really prepared everything. We are staying here for a long time.

I drop my stuff on the floor, just holding my toothbrush, and begin to brush my teeth. He notices the remains of my old life, the lingering constant reminder that I had an old life. "You're supposed to give those to the soldiers. I'll do it for you."

I spit out the toothpaste and clean my toothbrush.

The towel that covers my hair starts to fall off, and I put my toothbrush down and tighten it more around my hair.

"What are they going to do with them?"

"Burn them, probably."

I look down at my clothes, the ones I wore at the Pride March, and my eyes start to water. I wipe my eyes and hold in the tears. These clothes. . . the shirt I bought with her just last week. The shorts I bought with my mom a couple of days ago. And my lingerie. . . I bought them on my own, but they hold significance. . . These were the lingerie I wore the first time Aimee and I had sex.

*She clipped off my bra and dragged my panties down my bare legs. . .*

I want to remember more of that beautiful memory, to believe that love forever remains in our—no, my mind. Because dead people don't remember. It's only the living who can remember. . . Sad, that all those memories, all those moments, can remain in us only when we are alive.

I nod and leave my stuff on the floor for Sam to deal with.

I will never see those clothes ever again.

Without them, perhaps I will feel less pain? I don't know.

I take out the towel from my hair and toss it in a laundry basket by the door I didn't notice before.

I comb my hair with my fingers and look at my reflection in the mirror over the sink. I don't see myself anymore.

I just see a girl.

A girl who is lost, and forever broken.

* * *

By the time I get back to our cabin, I am exhausted. No. More than exhausted. So exhausted that my eyelids droop downward, my limbs are numb and struggling to keep my body up, my head so cloudy I can't even think. I don't think I've ever been this exhausted in my whole entire life.

A soldier is sitting on a chair with a magazine on his lap. I squint my eyes to see what he's reading, but it's unreadable from my angle.

I am about to flop on my bed, but the soldier stands up and everyone stands in front of their bunks, with their backs straight and their heads down.

Another soldier enters and both of them look around the cabin, under the beds, on the shelves that attach themselves to the wall, and they make a mess of the beds, letting the cheap blankets fall to the dirty floor, and then they inspect us.

It's like we're prisoners—no, we *are* prisoners.

Everyone spreads their legs and raises their arms. I do the same.

A soldier pats me, and I feel so humiliated because he touches areas, private areas, without even caring.

"All clear," the one who entered says, and he leaves, slamming the door closed.

Everyone goes to their beds and falls asleep.

I take off my shoes and flop on top of my bed. Thankfully I don't have to climb; I have the bottom bunk. The person above me is sleeping, snoring slightly. The light in the room is still on, but I don't mind it that much.

I close my eyes, but even though I am so tired and the only thing I want right now is to sleep, I can't seem to drift off into a blissful dream.

My mind is on full alert, despite the signals from my entire body, which is screaming at my mind to fall asleep.

My mind knows it's in a new environment, filled with so much danger and pain. And it won't let me go to sleep because sleep means vulnerability. My mind's stupid paranoia and its "need to survive"won't allow me to sleep.

So, I'm just left with my consciousness, and things just flutter in and out. I hear the others sleep, drifting off to an unknown land in an unknown part of their minds.

People here have gotten used to their new lives, but my life here is just beginning. Will I ever be like the rest and just get used to everything? How can I be submissive to the people who killed my Aimee in cold blood? How can I let *them* pry open my brain and poke about it till I become *normal*?

I hear the crickets of the night, a swing set creaking, and the soft waves of the lake that patter against the pebbly, sandy beach.

I miss the city. I can't believe I'm saying this, but I even miss the noisy part. Where it's so hot inside and your air conditioner is broken, so the only thing you can do is open the window, and it's too noisy; the cars are honking too loudly, the partygoers are shouting and yelling to the moon even though it's a weekday, the ambulances' alarms bounce between the buildings. . . I miss that. I want that noise. I don't want this peace that I hear. Because I know it's not actually peace. It's fake. This is all fake. We are not here because we want peace, we are here because we are *forced* to be here.

I want to go home. I don't want to be here. Maybe my parents will do something, I have always looked up to them, they have always solved all of my problems. They are my lifesavers. I know that they will do something to get me out of this horrible place.

I silently pray, even though I don't really believe in a God, I pray to anything, to Mother Earth, to Zeus, to fate and destiny, *please, please, save me. . . please please guide my parents on the right path to save me. To get me out of here.*

I try to follow the sound to sleep, and I guess it works because I feel my breathing slow, and my body become so heavy on top of the mattress and. . .

I guess my mind gave up.

I am weak.

I guess it won't be hard to break me.

# 8

The sunlight creeps in through the chinks in the boarded window and hits my face. It feels so good.

But that is not the only thing I'm feeling.

I feel my body shaking, and the sounds filter in through my ears, and I open my eyes, feel the crust around my eyelids. My eyes feel watery, and I look around. Sam is shaking me.

I shrug him off and turn on my side, facing away from him. I close my eyes and try to drown out the sounds of the room.

"Maia, you need to get up."

"I just need to sleep. . ." I mutter. I feel like I got five minutes of sleep. I'm groggy, and I can't concentrate.

"Inspection is happening in like six seconds." He shakes me harder, and my eyes open again. "You have to get up and make your bed."

My eyes flutter open. "Or what? They'll shoot me?" My neck aches, so I massage it. My whole body still feels weak from the torture, and I taste metal in my mouth. A headache creeps up and spreads throughout my mind.

"Help me get her up," Sam says to someone.

And I feel several arms pull me up and my head bangs on the

metal from the frame that holds the bottom bunk, and I feel it hot and searing. "Fuck. . ."

My body is being pulled, and I am about to slam my ass on the floor, but I stand up straight, cracking the bones in my legs and probably pulling a muscle or two.

I look around, and everyone is up, making their beds and straightening their clothes like they have OCD.

I'm still here. No one has saved me.

I'm still locked up in this black hole, no way out. Where are my parents? Where are they? They have to have done something. They would go to hell and heaven to find me and to bring me to *safety*.

There was one time in elementary school, where I must have eaten something rotten, and I was feeling so nauseous. I was vomiting in the bathroom. I don't remember the specifics, but both my parents came to pick me up and bring me home. My mom told me later that she had left an important conference at work to pick me up. And my dad had left a lunch with one of his sponsors to make sure that I was okay. Both of them didn't have to come. Actually, neither *had* to come. They could have gotten the babysitter to pick me up or something. But they left, *for me*. That's how dedicated they are to my safety and wellbeing. And here I am, already half destroyed, and where *are they?*

Why haven't I been saved?

"What's going on?"

"Morning inspection," a girl mutters. She has super-blonde hair tied in a bun.

Sam is making my bed, making it completely straight, creating hospital bed corners and folding it ever so perfectly.

"What?"

"We have two inspections every day. Night and morning," Sam grumbles.

I bend down, wanting to help, but he's already made my bed. It's so perfect looking like I didn't even sleep in it.

He looks at my clothes and straightens them and then heads to his bed, which is near the front.

The soldier stands up. He looks a bit different than the one from last night. And then another soldier enters. And we all stand where we stood earlier as they investigate our beds and clothes, making sure everything is neat and perfect. They pat us down, and then we go about our business. We have five minutes till breakfast.

I head to the bathroom. The line is long but goes quickly as people just wash their faces and brush their teeth.

I quickly do it, and then meet Sam and some others as we head back to the cafeteria.

It is crowded with people, talking about nothing, really, and the soldiers watch us intently. We stand on the line. And I see Ozzy sitting with some boys, and they talk to the boys, and they look really sad. Their whole face looks like a mutated grape that got thrown in the garbage. It's blotchy and swollen, but they seem to be eating well. I guess they got a more severe punishment than I.

I still feel the aches and pains, but less than yesterday.

I get my tray and put food on it, and I see the girls from yesterday, and I head toward them. Sam does the same and he goes with me to the girls. I think he genuinely cares for me and wants to make sure I'm settled in. I get some water for everyone and then head back.

I sit with the girls and introduce Sam.

We eat our food: lumpy oatmeal, and a slice of orange.

I long for my parents' cooking. They are both excellent chefs and would always cook together. Dinners every night and breakfasts on the weekends.

Sometimes I would watch them in the kitchen, just the two of them cooking. And you bet, it was like a scene from some commercial; they'd spoon-feed each other, letting the other taste their creations. Playing music that matches the type of cuisine they were making. My kid sister Janice and I would know instantly what type of food we were going to eat depending on what the music was.

Don't get me wrong, sometimes we cooked for the family, or I cooked solo. But I always loved my parents' cooking.

I always loved mornings, when I'd be greeted by classic American pop music and would smell the sizzling of pancakes and bacon on the pan, and I'd wake up Janice, who likes to sleep in whenever possible, I'd flick her back lightly, and she would groan, and I'd tickle her feet, calling "Wake up, Jam, wake up," which would get her moving instantly.

I'd rush to the kitchen, set up the table, place the placemats and utensils, my mom singing horribly to the music, and my dad, who's better at matching the tune, would always out-sing her.

I always looked at their marriage and longed to have that kind of future. To find someone that even in the morning, I could sing along with and cook and laugh about the little things in life.

I did find that someone. . . I feel around my neck for the necklace, but find it empty as always. I should stop looking.

"How did you sleep?" Penelope asks me.

"I. . . I don't know. . ." I just realized I didn't dream. I usually remember my dreams because I like to journal my dreams, but my brain must have completely shut down. I rub my eyes, and the others see that there are black bags under my eyes.

"You'll sleep better, eventually," Penelope says. She grabs a spoonful of oatmeal and stuffs it in her mouth. "You just need to get used to the environment."

"I don't want to," I grumble.

"You *have* to," Sam says, concern in his voice, "unless you want to be tortured all over again."

I sigh and play with my food with the spoon.

"What happens now?"

"You'll get a schedule. They say it changes every couple of months, depending on your progress and how well you are *behaving*."

I rub my head. "I can't. . ."

"Just focus on home," Crystal says, her blue eyes brighter than ever. "They can't keep us *forever*."

"They can only keep us here forever if we're unable to be 'cured,'" I mutter.

Someone is about to reply to that, but a soldier approaches our table with a bright orange folder packed with some papers. "Maia?" she says. I look up and she hands me the folder. She takes out a technology device that looks similar to the scanners earlier and points it at my bracelet. It beeps and blinks green. And she leaves.

I move my tray to the side and open up the folder.

Inside is my schedule, which is tiny for some reason. . . Maybe straining your eyes is part of the torture. There are also some forms with a bunch of phrases I don't understand, even copies of the actual Executive Order Miller signed, and some information about this camp, which I learn the name of. It's called "Camp 17." Wow, a really unique name.

**Project Sunshine: Patient's Records**
**Name:** Maia Anna Robinson
**Camp:** 17 (for teens)
**Diagnosis:** Attracted only to people of the same sex
**Plan of Treatment:** Rigorous Training of the Mind and Body, Childhood Trauma Therapy, Daily Medication, Re-education for Proper Living
**Case priority:** High
**On The Watchlist due to her Offenses**

## Schedule:

|  | Sunday | Monday | Tuesday | Wednesday | Thursday | Friday | Saturday |
|---|---|---|---|---|---|---|---|
| 6:30-7:00 | Meal 1 | Meal 1 | Meal 1 | Meal 1 | Meal 1 | Meal 1 | Meal 1 |
| 7:00-10:00 | Assembly | Rigorous Training | One-on-one | Rigorous Training | One-on-one | Rigorous Training | One-on-one |
| 10:00-13:00 | Church or Rest | Class | Work | Group therapy | Work | Class | Proper Living and Etiquette |
| 13:00-14:00 | Meal 2 | Meal 2 | Meal 2 | Meal 2 | Meal 2 | Meal 2 | Meal 2 |
| 14:00-17:00 | Mandatory Group Session | Special Class | Class | School | Class | Class | Group therapy |
| 17:00-18:30 | Meal 3 | Work | Physical Training | Work | Physical Training | Work | Physical Training |
| 18:30-20:30 | Movie night | Meal 3 | Meal 3 | Meal 3 | Meal 3 | Meal 3 | Meal 3 |
| 21:30 | Lights out | Lights out | Lights out | Lights out | Lights out | Lights out | Lights out |

There are signed papers by official people, documents with words that I don't understand, false statements, numbers, and marks on papers. It's all fake. All of it *is* fake. There's no way. . .

There's a legal paper claiming my parents signed off on this treatment, but there's no way that *my* parents would send me here. It may be my dad's handwriting, but he would never do that to me.

I know in my heart my parents would never send me here. The government is just trying to break us more.

There's no way any of this shitty legal stuff is really legal. It's all taking advantage of loopholes in real laws about pandemics and such. It's garbage. I look at my schedule. It's so fucking complicated and simple at the same time. I don't even know what to think of all of this.

I look at my "Record" and see that it lists "Offenses." And I am on "The Watchlist" because of that.

"What exactly does being on The Watchlist mean?"

"Basically, you are watched more carefully because of your past behavior, and you also have privileges and awards taken away from you," Crystal tells me.

"Like what?" I smirk. "What could possibly be a reward here?"

"Movie night, more free time, apparently if there's tasty food here you get first dibs."

"Movie night?"

"Oh yeah," Penelope perks up. "If you have no offenses on your record, then that is one of the many rewards that you get. I heard this week they are showing *The Notebook*."

I look at Penelope, her words just sinking in. "*The Notebook*?"

"That's like the straightest movie of all time," Yola says, finishing her food.

I shake my head. "I've never seen it."

"Well, good thing you don't get to see it. It is such utter crap."

"Doesn't it have, like, sexual themes? Would they really show *that* here?"

"Well, they are trying to encourage straight sex. . . so I guess it doesn't matter," Crystal says, and sips her water.

"I wouldn't be surprised if they showed us straight porn in class," Yola mutters.

We all burst out laughing and people sitting on the other tables look our way, wondering what there is to laugh about. When the laughter dies down, I look at my schedule.

"Where are all these things supposed to take place? It doesn't say anything."

Penelope looks at my schedule. "It takes some time to orient yourself, but it's pretty straightforward." She looks at the "Thursday" column.

"Today's Thursday?" I exclaim.

"Yep." Penelope chirps and continues, "One-on-one is in the nearest house where the buses were. Head here, and someone will show you to your workstations. Class is where orientation was. . . and Rigorous Training. . . I don't know. . ." She scrunches her eyebrows. "Probably someone will show you. . ." She looks at the rest of my schedule. "Physical Training is out in the meadow, and the Group Therapy, not sure. . . um. . . oh, it should be in the orientation place. I heard it's outside sometimes, too."

She looks up at me and I smile. "Thanks."

"Yeah, no problem. I have Class the same time as you, so we can go from lunch, if you'd like."

"I'd like that."

The conversation moves on, and then it's time to go to our first period or whatever.

But before we can leave the cafeteria and go about our days, everyone lines up next to where the food was.

A tall plastic table is set there with a bunch of mini plastic cups with water and mini paper cups scattered on it. I didn't realize it was set up.

Two women, who look like nurses in their light green scrubs, are standing in front of the table with blue elastic gloves on.

I go with the others, and we join the line. We don't have a choice. And when I'm at the front of the line, I go to the nurses.

"Name?"

"Maia Robinson."

One of them searches the paper cups for a specific one with my name, and hands me one with a bunch of different pills—all different sizes, shape, and colors. She hands me some water and looks at me intently. I eye the other paper cups, and notice that most of them just have one or two pills in them. *Why do I have more than everyone else?*

"What are in these?" I question.

"Swallow them, Maia. We don't have time for your inquiries."

I look at the nurses and my hands start to shake.

They are going to change the chemistry and neurons inside my body, inside my brain. I am not comfortable with that. I don't want to become someone else. I don't want them to change me. But do I have a choice? Everyone is staring at me. The soldiers look at me, ready to close in. Penelope is behind me, breathing on my neck.

I don't have a choice.

I pour the contents in my mouth and drink the water.

The pills surge down my mouth and get stuck in my throat, but I don't care. I move to the side and the other woman demands: "Open up." I open my mouth and stick out my tongue to show that I didn't hide any pills, and then she sends me off to the rest of my day.

A bell chimes from somewhere.

I wonder what "One-on-one" will be like.

# 9

I head to where the buses were. Were. Past tense. They're gone. The only way out is taken from us. We are in the middle of nowhere, miles from the main road probably, and the only way out is by foot—but they'd catch us before we even got the first mile toward home. The tents are also gone.

Soldiers are always watching us.

I haven't felt the effects of the unknown medicines. . . *yet*.

And I might not even realize their effects because I don't know what they are.

All that remains of the buses are their tracks in the gravel.

I arrive at a light brown house with a red roof. It looks so cozy.

The plastic sign says: "One-on-one." Penelope was right. Everything is pretty straightforward here.

I see others hurry into the cozy house.

A guy with jet black hair holds the door for me. I rush in and he slams it shut as we head inside.

There is a nice cozy waiting room with a light blue and white check-patterned sofa on one side, some red armchairs on the other, some green and brown chairs against the back wall. The dark oak floor is mostly covered by a green and blue carpet.

On the far wall is a worn-looking wooden door.

I smell a faint aroma of rotting wood and fresh moss.

People are sitting on the sofas and chairs, looking anxious. One boy is twiddling his thumbs, another is tapping a foot rapidly on the carpet. In the old days, in the normal world, we would all be looking at our phones, checking our messages or playing games—but now there is no such distraction.

I look at the guy who held the door for me. "What are we supposed to do here?"

"Just wait and someone will get you." He smiles and sits on one of the red chairs.

I sit on the green chair, a bit close to him, and there is a silence in the room as people wait for. . . what? It's like they're waiting for some sort of medical test to see if they have like an *actual* life-threatening disease.

I notice something else. Everyone here is around my age or younger. I guess this is really the youth camp.

Every now and then a bell rings and from the worn-out door a camp worker emerges and goes to a specific person, and that person follows them back through the door to some room in this cozy house.

I'm the only one left.

I nervously look around and notice a camera blinking at me from the high corner of the room.

For a couple of minutes, I wait silently, and then I hear a set of footsteps creak on the rickety floor, and a woman with a black pencil skirt, black pumps and a loose beige blouse comes up to me. She is holding a black clipboard in one hand, and she extends the other to me in greeting.

I stand up, shivering.

She has sharp, dark green eyes that just seem to slice their way into my head.

I shake her hand, and I feel the sweat from my palm linger on hers. She lets go and automatically wipes her hand on her blouse. "Maia. I'm Dr. Diamond. Come with me." Her voice is high but not squeaky. And as she turns around I lean forward, almost laughing at her name.

*What kind of last name is* that?

She walks quickly despite those heels, and I run to catch up. She goes through the worn-down door and down the hallway and up some wooden steps. There is another hallway, and she goes to the end of it and opens a light brown door with a black-as-coal knob.

Inside is a cozy rectangular room.

There is a light gray cushioned seat in front of a window, looking out at the camp: the houses, cabins, and the lake that glimmers like pearls.

There is a cream-colored couch next to the door with a coffee table in front that has a glass of water and a box of Kleenex on it.

Dr. Diamond sits on the gray seat and crosses her legs.

I sit on the couch and clasp my hands together on my lap.

"So, Maia. Let's get started, shall we?"

I nod, unsure what to say.

"I want you to know that whatever you say here is confidential." She smiles. "This is a safe place."

I nod and want to roll my eyes, but I don't want to anger her.

She looks down at her clipboard and takes a pen from the clasp. She writes some stuff.

"Let's get right down to business. I'm going to help you figure out the cause of your *disease* and find a way to stop it."

I don't reply. I don't know *how* to reply.

"Let's talk about your family." And she looks at me like I'm supposed to say something. But I'm pretty sure that, whatever there is to say about my family, she must already know because this is the government. Because they know everything.

I don't like this awkward silence, so I just say the basics: "My mom's name is Hana. My dad's name is Carl. And I have a younger sister named Janice."

"How old is your younger sister?"

"Ten."

"Oh, that is young." She frowns. "She'll have to go through serious testing based on your behavior so far here."

I clench my fists. "What are you talking about?!"

"Usually, younger siblings are at risk if their siblings have the disease. But if they don't show any initial signs of it, then they don't need to be sent to the camps. But because of how severe the disease is in you, I'm afraid she'll have—"

"She's not *like* me," I growl, my voice deepening.

"You're very protective of her."

"You can't send her here."

"No, of course not." She shakes her head as if I talked about murdering puppies. "If she does have the disease, she'll be sent to a junior facility, but it's rare for the disease to attack those so young."

"She's totally fine. . ." I struggle with my words. She can't be sent anywhere because of what I did. "She doesn't have the disease, I swear to it," I say, speaking in her terms so she understands it. I can't believe I'm calling my gayness a disease, but what choice do I have? I have to protect my little sister.

I wonder what happens to the adults who identify as LGBTQIA+. . . do they go to a separate camp? One specifically for adults? Is that where my neighbors Jacob and Cason went?

"I believe you," says my therapist, or whatever she is, Dr. Diamond.

I blow out a sigh of relief.

"As long as you *stay* out of trouble," she says firmly, "we won't make her go through the tests, or the curative process."

Oh, now she's threatening me. That's fucked up.

My eyes squint and I clench my fists harder, feeling my nails dig into the skin.

"Understand?"

"Yes, yes."

"What do your parents do?" Her voice is viperous, and I can feel the poison seeping in and under my skin.

They already know all this stuff, yet she asks me anyway. Maybe it's some sort of power thing, like answering questions means that I have already given in to their authority.

She waits patiently.

"My dad is a sculptor. My mom is an engineer at a high-tech company."

"Quite the busy pair, I see."

I don't know how to reply. I don't know what to say.

"They must barely have *any* time to take care of you and your sister," she says pointedly.

"They always make time for us. They did more than I could have asked for."

"Oh, *really*?"

"Yes. Really." I gulp. "They are really good parents. You don't know what you're talking about."

"How many hours did your mother spend away from home when you were young?"

"What does that—"

"A mother's top priority should be to take care of the children, not designing shiny trinkets."

"You have no right to talk about her like that. She is really good at her job, and she loves her job." I shake my head. "If she were a man, you wouldn't say things like that."

"A mother's role is to be a mother. That's all I'm saying."

"Th—" I start to say; she is really getting on my nerves.

"So, you're saying she was a mother to you two, and she somehow spent almost twelve hours every day at her job a couple of miles from home? How can that be possible? Is she superhuman?"

"You—"

"This is where the problem started, Maia."

"What are you talking about?"

"I am here to figure out the source of the disease, and how to cure you of it. It seems pretty straightforward to me, Maia. The source of the disease was the absence of your mother during your childhood, and even now. It has grown and festered inside of you for many years, Maia. I am here to *fix* you."

I roll my eyes. My voice rises, "I don't need fucking fixing. You guys are—"

"Do you want me to call a soldier?" she snaps. "Do you want me to mark your record, add to the offenses you committed when you arrived? Do you want to be punished even further than how you were when you first got here? Because I can make that happen. If you haven't learned your lesson, I have an obligation to report everything you say or do. Do you want me to do that?"

Didn't she just say a moment ago that this session was confidential, that this room was a safe space? I want to remind her of this but I can't, the words stick in my throat. I'm shivering—it's something that I can't control.

"Do you?" she reiterates.

"No. . ."

"No, what?" She smiles.

"No, don't report me."

"Don't report me, what?"

*Like a knock-knock joke.*

"Don't report me, please." I swallow my pride.

She sits back on her chair and smiles even wider. "Now, where were we?" She looks down at the clipboard and doesn't wait for my answer. "Ah, your mother."

I take a deep breath. I have to control myself. What she says about my mom is shit; I won't fucking listen to her—

"The absence of your mother in your childhood life is the reason for your disease. . . her negligence is why you are. . . to use your language, *gay*."

That's a slap on the cheek.

My face turns an angry red; I can feel the heat. "You fucking," I whisper, no, not a whisper—even lower than a whisper. "You can't . . ."

"What?"

What she *says* means nothing.

*What she* says *means nothing to me.*

I shake my head.

"You understand what I'm saying, correct?"

I look at her, my eyes direct and raging. "No, I don't. Could you *please* explain it to me?"

"Because your mother wasn't in your life as *much* as she should have been, you never were fully exposed to a female role model. Because of that lack of a female role model, you began to have a feeling of wanting a female role model at a very young age. That feeling of wanting a female turned into something sexual as you grew older. . . and that turned into a belief that you are indeed attracted to women.

"Maia, this is the disease!" she continues eagerly. "This is the origin of the disease! And because of that, because of what you believe, because of this illusion that is in your mind, you are unable to form true connections with males. The disease is blocking you from attending to your true self—your innate self. It is blocking you from doing the very human thing that all females are born to do—to be attracted to men! You are unable to feel attracted to men because you allow the disease to take over your mind.

"Now, as we go about curing you, we can get rid of the disease, thus getting rid of this false illusion of sexual attraction for females, and then you will realize your true calling! Then you will be free—free, I say!—to fall in love with a man, as nature intends, and produce offspring.

"Oh, Maia," she concludes, smiling broadly, "just think of the happiness that is in store for you, when you finally come to know your true self, and are really, truly cured!"

My mouth opened sometime during her stupid, fucking speech. I understood her, but it wasn't like she was speaking English; it was like she was speaking a foreign language, an alien language not found on Earth. This can't be happening. This fucking shit can't be happening in the twenty-first century.

I close my mouth. I don't know what to do. I don't want to be around people who believe this kind of shit.

And I know I can't react. I know I can't curse at her and do all the things I would do to someone that speaks to me that way. And I want to so badly, but the fear of the soldiers, the fear of that doctor, the fear of the pain coming back, the fear that they could do something worse makes me just not say anything. And. . . Janice, my sister. . . nothing must happen to her. I keep my mouth shut and don't move a muscle.

I am a statue.

I will not move.

I will not breathe.

I will not blink.

"Maia?"

I take a huge gulp of air, coughing as I do so, and blink rapidly.

"Are you okay?"

No, I am not okay.

I nod my head.

"I know it's a lot to take in. I basically just told you that your mother gave birth to this disease inside of you, but you have to understand—I want you to be aware of the disease and how we are going to help you and cure you. We are not the kind of people who keep people in the dark. Because knowledge, *knowing*, is part of the healing process."

Oh my God, oh my fucking God.

I just want to burst out laughing.

They *don't want to keep me in the dark?*

They've already done it—by throwing us onto buses to this shitland without saying or giving us any information, by forcing some unknown medications down our throats.

She smiles. "It's going to be all right, Maia. We'll get through this—together."

I nod slightly, speechless.

"Soon, once you are cured, you are going to thank us. You are going to be grateful that we put you through this tough process. You may not like it now but trust me—you will be a different person—a better person, a person with a good heart and a kind soul, and you can live your future knowing that you are cured, that you are pure, that you are right. That you are fixed."

I squeeze my eyes shut and then open them. "What if I don't want to be *fixed*?" I use *their* language, so she listens and knows that I've been paying attention. "What if I like being who I am right now? What if I'm happy having *the disease*?" I cringe at the thought that I'm using *their* words, but it's the only way they'll hear me.

She leans forward and fidgets with her fingers. "If you are not fixed, you will harm those around you and spread the disease further. Think of your sister, your classmates, your parents, your friends, your future husband, your future children. Refusing the cure would not only harm you deeply, it would harm everyone else. That would be a very selfish act, Maia, and I don't think you're the kind of person to do that. You are a good person. You are not the kind of person who chooses *illusions* and *delusions* and *pleasure* over the welfare of others. You are a good person."

I want to shake my head while holding it in my hands. I want to bite my lip and laugh like a hyena at her nonsense. I want, I want, I want, but what good will it do? It will just cause me more pain. And pain for my sister.

I can't believe they have broken me *already*.

The rest of the three-hour "One-on-one" session is just her telling me different strategies that she will teach me to start the removal of the disease. The process consists of fixing the problems of my past, changing my attitudes in the present life, and hoping for a future, a "good future" in her eyes. It's three hours long, but it feels like ten. Her words just drag on and on and I just nod and blink and answer in a droning voice, giving the answers she wants to hear, trying to keep my eyes open.

It's a skill I'll have to learn.

It'll be tough to master.

But I must learn how to ignore her at the same time that I listen to her.

I must learn how to not let her fake psychoanalysis affect me in any way, but also, at the same time, make her believe that what she is doing is working.

I must act like I'm being brainwashed, so she doesn't try to brainwash me harder, which might actually work—I can't take that risk.

It must appear like she is in control, when really—I am in control.

# 10

After One-on-one, I'm supposed to report to a work station, and I go looking for it. A soldier shows me the way. It's on the opposite side of the camp from where the cafeteria is.

I feel like maybe the medicine is affecting me. I feel drowsy, and heavy, like there's an extra weight on my shoulders. But it could just be the *situation* making me like this.

The work station is in this dank one-floor building where there's only one window to let air in, and it is noisy as hell. It's where the laundry gets done.

There are about a half dozen washing machines on one side, and a half dozen dryers on the other. There is no security camera inside, but we are still being watched. There's a female soldier in the back, scrutinizing our every move.

I'm just putting laundry into the machines, measuring the soap, punching the controls, then moving wet laundry into the drying machines, folding the dry laundry, then onto the next washer, and the next dryer. You get the idea. On and on.

Because of the soldier in the back, watching us, I can't talk to the others.

Two are boys and one is a girl.

One of the boys has brown curls and a face covered in pimples.

The other has very light pink lips and a wave of black hair that surrounds his face.

They are around my age and look as sullen as we all do.

Their faces are tired. They look liked used dolls thrown in the trash. I probably look like that too.

The girl, who has short blond hair, a perked nose, and a smooth chin, looks at the soldier. Her eyes droop downward.

We've been working for over two hours, and the laundry never seems to end. When it finally seems like we are almost done, someone carries in a new load of dirty clothes and towels. They are the same kinds of clothes we are forced to wear, boring, beige, and simple. The towels are the ones we use in the bath house.

The girl slumps forward on one of the machines. One arm clutches her stomach, and the other shakily holds onto the open door.

She coughs; she looks really sick.

The soldier notices and barks, "Get back to work!"

She looks at the soldier, "I'm. . ."

"I said. Get back to work."

The girl stands up straighter, not wanting to get punished, and smiles, holding in the bile that was about to leave her mouth. She continues taking the clothes out of the dryer.

Sweat drops from her forehead. Her head is down, her eyes closed, and she starts to fall again, and I heave from my spot and catch her.

The soldier widens her eyes. "No touching!"

"She is sick!" I shout at her.

"Let her go, this minute," the soldier barks.

"I'm just holding her up!" *Fuck. I'm not doing anything.*

"Don't you fucking touch her, dyke."

I feel like crying, but this girl is in so much more pain than I am. I hold back the tears.

One of the boys goes to me and grabs her arms, and I let go. He slowly lowers her to the cold tiled floor.

I'm shaking my head.

The soldier goes to her, looking her over. "Fuck." She punches a basket of clean, folded clothes and it splatters to the floor, creating a mess of newly washed clothes that are now contaminated and dirty all over again. *Like us. We are dirty laundry now, where we have to be cleaned and fixed.*

"I'm going to have to report this and fill in the paperwork." She groans loudly. "You fucking. . ."

And then in one swoop, the girl snaps her eyes open and stands up quicker than the soldier can react and punches her square in the throat, and the boys glide around her like dancers and tackle her from behind, and she tries to scream, but the girl clasps her hands over her mouth and the boys clamp her arms behind her back and she struggles under their weight. They punch her again and hit her, and the one with pink lips yanks the Taser out of her belt and zaps her with it, holding it sizzling to her throat as she shrieks in pain and shakily falls to the ground like she's having a seizure.

"Way to go, Conor!" the girl shouts.

I am just standing there.

The girl looks at me. "You coming?"

"What are you saying?" I stutter. Everything is happening so fast.

"We are getting OUT," she says and kicks the soldier, who doesn't move. She gestures to the boys and they drag the limp body behind one of the rows of machines, out of sight from the open door.

"What?" I point to the band around my left wrist. "What are you talking about? You can't escape."

Conor steps outside to survey the surroundings. He returns quickly. "All clear."

"What are you guys doing? There are soldiers everywhere, you can't possibly. . ."

"This is our only chance, Maia," the other boy says to me. "Come with us."

"How. . . what are you. . ."

"We don't have a lot of time," the girl says. She sifts through the soldier's belt and pocket and pulls out a pistol, some sort of card, and a set of keys.

"This right, Conor?" She holds up the keys. He takes them and studies them carefully.

"Yep. Let's go."

The other boy looks at me. "Maia, we know what you did during orientation. We know what you faced. Come with us."

"What about the GPS trackers. . . and the soldiers. . . and. . . ?"

"We got a guy on the outside who will help us. We just need to meet him on the other side of the fence. . . ."

"Let's go, guys," Conor says urgently. "We don't have time. They'll be here any minute."

He steps outside. The girl follows. And the boy with the brown curls looks at me, "Come on, Maia. There's nothing you can do here."

The girl shouts, "Jack! Come on. Just *leave* her!"

Jack looks at me with sympathetic eyes. He wants to help, but he knows that he can't force me.

I shake my head, my eyes watering. "My. . . sister. . . they said they'll send her to a junior camp if I try anything." I can't believe I am letting a fucking shrink dictate my actions. "I can't take any chances!"

"Once we're out, we can go to her and make sure she's safe!"

I open my mouth to say something, but he interrupts me.

"Conor has siblings back home; they probably threatened him, too. But he's taking the risk, Maia. Don't let them get in your head!"

And he runs out, following his friends.

Freedom is all I've wanted, but. . . I'm afraid and I'm lost, and my girlfriend. . . the people who killed her are here. Do I leave and risk never getting a chance to avenge her? And risk getting caught and punished and. . . and what about my sister? Who knows what they'll do to her?

But I have to get out. Once we're free, I'll find my sister and hide her somehow.

I run out of the building and look around frantically. I see the others in the distance. They turn a corner and I run after them. I am maybe a hundred yards behind them as they run to the fence that surrounds the whole camp. They are fast. And I am panting and sweat is dripping from my eyebrows. And I don't see any soldiers around, but I know they must be close.

Conor climbs over the fence and immediately an alarm goes off. It's loud and noisy and buzzing and hurts my ears and my hands go over my ears, and then I see Conor on the other side. He is on the ground, whimpering in pain, and his whole body is convulsing in weird patterns, and foam comes out of his mouth. The girl clambers over the fence to help him, and the same thing happens to her. She collapses right next to Conor. And Jack is still on the near side of the fence, staring at the two of them lying on the ground, twitching, dying. What the fuck. What the fuck. It's like something in their bands sent out a lethal shock the instant they passed over the barrier.

So not only is that thing identification, not only does it have GPS, not only does it have a detector in it that sends a signal to alert the soldiers of escape. . . it's an electric shocking device that activates when passing over some metal thing underground, beyond the fence, or when a button is pressed. What the fuck. What the fuck. What the fuck.

They didn't say anything about this. They said there'd be an alarm going over the fence. They didn't mention there'd be pain.

This is cruel.

This is so fucking cruel. They did this purposely, so we'd learn.

Jack turns around and his eyes widen as he sees me. I step a bit closer, but he shakes his head.

We can hear soldiers in the distance. I turn around, turn my back to Jack, and run back to the laundry building. I rush through the doors, and immediately a wave of soldiers passes by the door. They run to where Jack and the others are. I am panting so much, I can't catch my breath.

I sit on the cold floor near the soldier, who is motionless.

I even my breathing, trying to calm myself. I hear shouts in the distance, and some kind of mechanical clicking. I hear Jack scream and a sound of scuffling. I look out the doorway and see soldiers dragging the girl. Her eyes are still and unmoving and her limbs are stiff. They drag her towards one of the cabins. And then Conor. He is in the same state, his tongue hanging out. They pass directly in front of me and I see a tear frozen right under his eye.

Now some more soldiers are coming, pushing Jack, handcuffed and gagged. He looks in my direction, and his eyes are full of sincerity. He isn't going to tell anyone I was part of the escape. So I don't get punished. But what will happen to him? And Conor and the girl . . . are they really dead? They are, I am certain of it, but I feel numb. I never thought in a million years that I would get used to seeing death.

And we have been here less than a week.

What have they turned me into?

# 11

For a few minutes I am alone. Well. . . not really alone. The soldier lies near me, still motionless, behind the washing machines where they dumped her. But other than that, I am alone. And I realize that this is the first time since this shitstorm started that I am really *alone*. No one is watching me, no cameras are spying on me, no one is around me to stare at me with my lost soul.

I sit, my ass on the cold floor, and my breathing slows down even more. I can feel my heart rate losing its rhythm, and I feel the strings of my muscles and the velvet coating of my arteries begin to loosen. Loosen from the tightly woven machine that has kept me alive ever since I was born. All these parts, strings, velvet, it's all coming apart. Everything that I know in my life is falling apart. And I don't know how to stop it.

My eyes feel heavy and dry, and I can feel my eyelashes poke the tip of my eye every time I blink. I just want to pull them out, one by one, so I feel the pain, because maybe the pain can awaken me from this nightmare.

I hear a clatter of footsteps and look up. Two soldiers look down on me, sweat on their foreheads, Tasers in their hands. One holds out a hand to me and I reach to grasp it, and he starts to pull me to my feet, but when I'm halfway up he suddenly snatches his hand from my grip so that I lose my balance and fall back to the ground, hitting the cold floor.

They laugh at me.

I grind my teeth, steady myself, and stand up, looking at them with fire raging in my eyes. I want to challenge them without actually challenging them. It makes me feel better, but I don't even think they notice my glare.

"Come with us," one of the soldier says. And he turns around. But the other stops suddenly, with a sharp intake of breath. "Oh, shit!" he murmurs. "Fuck!" He has noticed the female soldier lying half hidden, unconscious or dead, behind the row of washing machines. He pulls out a walkie-talkie and barks rapidly into it.

The first soldier turns and glares at me with hatred. "What the fuck did your fairy friends do to her?" he spits.

Suddenly there is activity all around. More soldiers surround me, followed by a pair of medics with a stretcher.

I am zoning out. I don't move. I am not paying attention. I am not here, I am somewhere else, in another place and time where none of this is happening.

A nurse appears. She has a needle. The needle is in my arm. I feel a prick and then I feel nothing, see nothing, the world has gone black, I am nowhere, I am gone. . . .

I wake up in an ordinary-looking room with a window overlooking a lake. It is such a pretty view, like something from another planet, the beautiful Planet Earth where I used to live with my family. I am in an armchair. It is very comfortable but my head aches. The nurse is sitting on a stool opposite, staring at me. She has been waiting for me. "Are you ready?" she says. "Someone wants to see you."

I follow her into a hallway, woozily. The nurse holds my arm. "Come this way," she says. I recognize this hallway. We are in Headquarters. The door at the end of the hallway is the door to the General's office.

General Wilson is waiting for me, behind her desk. Her face is still bruised and part of it is bandaged from when I was beating the crap out of her. But she doesn't seem to be in pain. *Too bad.*

There are two rickety old chairs in front of her desk. Jack is there on the chair closest. His gag is removed, but his hands are still cuffed behind his back. He looks at me with calm eyes.

I sit down next to him.

General Wilson doesn't waste a minute. "Didn't think I would see you so soon, Maia."

Still woozy from the drug, I look at her and smirk. "Same here."

She makes a gesture like she's flicking away a fly, and gets straight to business. "Jack tells me that you had no part in their escape plan, is that true?"

I look at him, suddenly wide awake. He nods subtly.

"Yes," I say.

"And he tells me that you didn't even try escaping. That you just stayed with the dead soldier."

Dead. So, she was dead.

I don't look at him again. *He wants me to lie so at least one person doesn't get punished. He cares for me. Even though he never even met me before today.*

"Yes." I look into her inhuman cold eyes. "I didn't want to break the rules, so I stayed where I was."

She smiles, proud that I am so broken. But her smile falters. "Why didn't you stop them?"

I blink rapidly. "I couldn't. It was three against one. I didn't want to get hurt."

"But you didn't even call for help."

"I was scared," I whimper.

Silence.

All I hear is the breathing of Jack and General Wilson.

I hold my breath, waiting for her response.

"That makes sense," she says finally. "You've been through a lot, Maia, and I can understand your reluctance to. . . to get involved."

I breathe out slowly and inhale deeply.

"But you have to understand. Because of your *inaction*, three people are dead."

Jack looks at General Wilson, tears glistening in his eyes. His face becomes wobbly. "Dead? Conor and Alyssa are dead? What do you mean?" He fights with his bonds, struggling with the news.

"I'm so sorry," I tell him. I never knew these two, but I feel bad for him. And they could have been my friends, we could have met in college someday and seen old classics in some artsy movie theater. We could have been partying and teamed up to play beer pong or something. And they were souls, innocent souls who loved differently and expressed themselves differently than other people. And just because of the way they were born, they were sent here, and they had a chance to escape, and now they are dead because they tried to escape.

"That fucking fence killed them!" Jack screams.

A soldier hurries in and stands behind him, at the ready.

"They just wanted to go *home*! What the fuck is wrong with you people?" He tries to stand up, but the soldier slams him down on the chair. "Conor is the eldest of his family! His mom is a druggie, so it was up to him to take care of his siblings. He just wanted to go back home and put food in their stomachs and make sure they were okay. Because they can't survive without him! You can't just kill him for *wanting to go home*. You're fucking insane."

"We told you there would be consequences if you tried to escape. He knew what he was doing."

"You never said anything about *dying*! You never said that these bands could do that!"

"Well, they can, Jack. And we didn't see any use in telling you guys because we assumed you'd be smarter than that. We thought you shits had brains, but I guess you *don't*. But now, everyone will know, everyone will learn their place. That they should be just like Maia and never be like Conor or Alyssa. Obey us and you will not be hurt. Disobey, and you'll be hurt. Right, *Maia*?" She looks at me.

Jack looks at me.

The soldier looks at me.

I nod. I nod and nod and nod and nod. Tears streaming from my eyes. I don't even know why I'm crying.

"You will never get away with this," Jack growls. "You may have the government behind you. You may have the army, but you will never get away with this. The people will know how many died. They WILL know. History will know."

"They will understand the methods that had to be done to remove this disease from America," General Wilson says. "This is war. Against the disease. And the people of America will understand that there are causalities. Because there are always causalities in every war. And like every war, like everything we do for the people, it will be understood, and people will eventually move on. All this will be seen as something that had to be done." She smiles. "You have to accept this, Jack. You have to accept this new life. And soon, you people will thank us for *helping* you.

"But first," she snaps, "you must be *corrected*. For what happened today! A soldier has died, a public servant who was only doing her duty to safeguard the purity of our nation. If you were an adult, and of sound mind, this would be a simple matter indeed. You would be tried for murder, swiftly and fairly, and following conviction you would be executed. But because you are a minor, and *diseased*, we must follow different regulations. Unfortunately! Much as I would love to see you shot, or push you over the fence with my own hands, all I can do now is refer you for *extreme treatment*. And for that lenient policy you can thank your lucky stars!"

"Fuck you," Jack hisses. And he turns to me as if somehow I can help him.

I look at him, at his pleading eyes. He saved me because he thinks I'm worth saving, but am I, really? What have I done, what *did* I do? I just keep surviving while other people get killed or hurt. Because I'm just trying to save myself and those closest to me. I feel selfish; I *am* selfish. All I do is save my ass over others.

I mouth to him that I'm sorry.

Out of the corner of my eye, I see General Wilson look at the soldier. "Send him to the doctor. Say it's for *extreme treatment*. He'll know what to do."

I look at Jack, afraid for him.

Jack widens his eyes, terrified of what's to come.

The soldier heaves him up by the arms and pushes him outside. I don't know what's going to happen to him, but I know it's not good.

He's done worse than what I did. He planned and tried to escape. And the soldier died. So his punishment will be far worse than what I had to face. And I don't know what that could be. What could be worse than pain?

I look at General Wilson. "What happens to me now?"

"Well, I think your punishment is that you have to live with the fact that three people died because *you* didn't do anything. I think that's a good enough punishment, don't you think?"

I know what she says is the truth.

But I blow out a sigh of relief that I don't have to be punished like Jack is.

I can't believe this is who I've become.

And even though I was trying to escape too, and I let him take the fall for everything, I don't feel guilty. I just feel thankful that I don't have to feel the pain again. The pain that I had to feel before still lingers in me, it still shivers me to the core.

The bell rings, indicating lunch. I look to General Wilson for permission. She nods, and I start to go out the door, but she calls to me, so I turn and look at her. "Maia?"

"Yes."

"You should give me more respect," she says, clasping her hands. "I will keep taking privileges away from you until you do."

"Yes, mom," I can't help replying.

She rolls her eyes. "Watch your words, Maia. I can do far worse that you can ever imagine."

I nod and leave. I like challenging her, but what she could do to me scares me so much.

* * *

I head to the cafeteria for lunch, my friends are there. They're friends, right? Like what else should I call them? Fellow prisoners? And according to the rules, everyone can only be friends. Nothing more. Unless you meet someone who could be your future husband or wife! Someone of the opposite sex, that is, and legally husband or wife—now that they have changed the laws back to what they were in the bad old days.

"We heard someone tried to escape," Penelope says. "You okay?"

I nod.

"Is it true you ratted those guys out?" Yola spits.

I shake my head, "No, it wasn't like *that*."

"Then what was it? How come you're still here?"

"It was. . ."

"Did you just freeze there like a deer in headlights?"

"Yola, stop," Penelope says.

"Don't you fucking tell me what to do. If she had a chance to rebel, she should have—"

"They died," I mutter.

"What?" cries Jade.

"The two that jumped over the fence, they died."

"How do you know that?"

"That's what General—"

"Don't believe a crap w—" Yola starts to say.

"I saw them. . . I was scared but decided to go with them, but I was way behind . . . their bodies were so. . . still. . . and their eyes. . ."

Penelope is about to pat me on the back, but she remembers that she's not allowed to touch anyone of the same sex, and she twists her hair with her fingers instead.

So it's Sam who pats me on the back. And it feels nice, but not in a sexual way. Never in a sexual way.

I close my eyes; a couple of tears drop from my eyes.

"So. . ." Yola says. "How did they die?"

Penelope gives her a look and Diana eyes me.

"The wrist bands. Once they pass the fence, once they pass something underground that triggers them, it's like. . . the bands send a shock through your body, and it kills you."

Yola rubs her eyes.

No one has touched their lunch. I look down. Soggy bread and watery soup. I don't even have the appetite for anything.

"Who died?" Jade asks.

"Conor and Alyssa. Good people," Yola says.

"They were in my cabin," Diana says quietly. "They were close. . ."

I look up. "What do you mean?"

"I think they knew each other in school. Founded the LGBTQIA+ club together or something like that," Diana says. She stares at her food.

We talk about them to honor them in some way. But that's the only thing we can do. No one in the outside world knows they are dead. Their bodies. . . what do they do with their bodies? . . . And what about their parents? I shake my head and push my tray forward and lean my head against the table. I feel like sleeping and crying at the same time.

No one asks about the soldier who was guarding us, and I don't tell them. Who the cares about a fucking soldier?

That's how I feel now.

# 12

The amazing thing about time—is that it always moves on.

After lunch, it's class.

Penelope and I walk to where orientation was.

It's gloomy now. The clouds are drifting about, casting a wave of exhaustion over all of us.

"So, what is this class?" I ask Penelope.

We walk side by side, an inch apart of course, our hands close to our legs and our eyes forward.

"Oh, it's just a lot of. . ." She looks around to see if anyone is near us. "Horseshit."

I almost laugh, but I keep it in. "I can't believe this is actually happening."

"I know, right?" I see her smile out of the corner of my eye. She is pretty, like not the pretty everyone would think, but the unique kind of pretty. Where the way her face forms and shifts is unusual yet sexy. I shake my head. I can't believe I am thinking about her like this.

How can I move on so quickly?

I see others gather around the house where orientation was.

I follow Penelope in, and we go through several hallways and through a door. It is set up like a classroom.

There is a chalkboard in front, right next to the window, which overlooks some trees. A tiny bit of sunlight trickles in.

There is a chair in front. A woman I assume is the teacher sits there.

There are two green plastic chairs facing each other in front of the chair she's sitting in.

Her legs are crossed under a long, purple, velvet skirt with vertical bright copper buttons. Her white, ruffled tuxedo shirt is tucked underneath the band of her skirt.

She wears a black necklace made up of a bunch of long black shiny rectangles next to one another. She wears a beautiful diamond wedding ring on her finger. Her long silky hair is tied in a tight bun, with a long metal clip that holds the hair together. She wears grey flats with a bit of heel.

And in front of the two chairs in front is a bunch of chairs with attachable desks. Like the ones you see at school.

Blue and uncomfortable chairs that squeak every time you move with a hard wooden desk like paddles. I don't know where to sit.

Penelope looks at me, about to say something, but the teacher stands up quickly at the sight of me.

"Maia, right?"

I nod.

She struts toward me and holds out her hand. I shake it. It's light and warm.

"I'm Mrs. Blaese. Nice to meet you."

I don't say anything.

People enter the room and sit down, ignoring the two of us.

"It's a bit late to join us, but we can make do." She smiles.

She makes it sound like I had a choice to come here.

I don't answer.

"You're quiet, aren't you. You know, I've heard stories about you.

And you don't seem that way at all." She looks at me as if waiting for me to say something, but I don't.

By now everyone has sat down. And it seems like there are assigned seats because no one is sitting next to one of the same gender. They made it like that on purpose. Like the beds.

I spot an empty seat in front, between a bald guy with light brown skin and a boy with pimples and moles all over his face.

Mrs. Blaese looks at everyone and then looks at me. "This is Maia, everyone. Say hello."

People mutter hi and hellos to me. Penelope, who is in the back, smiles at me.

"How about we continue where we left off last time?" she asks. as if we can say no.

She looks at the bald guy. "Now, you won't have to partner up with me." She smiles. She looks at me, "Maia can be your partner now." She gestures for me to sit. I do so.

She looks at me. "Just to catch you up, we are going to be spending the next couple of weeks focusing on physical attractions toward the opposite sex. All of you are missing it, so here, we will make sure you understand those physical attractions, so the sinful urges don't plague you."

Ah. Now I get it.

"Do the directions make sense to you?"

"What?" I mutter. Everyone is staring at me. Mrs. Blaese is looking at me. She's been talking a lot, and I've dozed off. I haven't listened to anything she has said in the past minute, but I nod along anyway. "Yeah, they do."

"Good." She clasps her hands. "We should just have a demonstration so you can see it in action."

I nod.

She looks at the room filled with bored and pained faces and says two names: "Michiko and Patrick. Come, show Maia what we did last time."

She sits back in her chair.

A tall, lean Japanese girl—with flashy long, dark black hair in a ponytail and beautiful hazelnut eyes—steps up from behind me and sits on the green chair on the left.

Patrick, who I see in the corner of my eye, rolls his eyes, and takes a beat. Then he stands up. He is short and a bit pudgy in the cheeks, his nose perked, and he fidgets with his fingers. He goes to the green chair on the right.

And now they are facing each other.

"Michiko, why don't you begin."

The girl swallows nervously. She stares at Patrick, her eyes wandering around him as if he is a foreign object, trying to find something. "You. . . have beautiful eyes, Patrick."

His eyes are emerald green, and I can see that, in a way, they are beautiful. But this is not what the teacher wants.

"Try again, Michiko. I don't want you to look at him as a human being; I want you to look at him as a potential mate. Find the things in his image that you like romantically and sexually."

Oh my God.

I almost laugh.

Everyone in this room, except the teacher, is gay.

And she is forcing two gay people of opposite genders to compliment each other in a particular way.

*What is this?*

Michiko sighs. "Okay, Patrick. . . your lips are real sexy."

The teacher nods in approval.

"Patrick, your turn. . . and use your *normal* voice, please."

"Michiko," he says, his voice deep, but it's the fake kind of deep voice, one that you'd use to make fun of deep-voiced people.

The teacher doesn't seem to mind.

"Michiko, you have a really cute face."

The teacher nods.

I roll my eyes. This is ridiculous. I can't believe this is happening to us. I can't believe that this is legal, I can't believe... but disbelief doesn't make the reality vanish.

It magnifies it. It makes it bigger and scarier.

They go back and forth like that for several minutes, and then it's my turn.

They leave their seats and I sit where Michiko sat, and my partner, Magnus, sits where Patrick sat.

"Why don't you give it a go, Maia."

I look at Magnus. And I can't find anything pleasing about him. He is scarred by pimples that were not taken care of properly, and he has no hair anywhere except for his unkempt eyebrows.

"Maia?"

I look at the teacher. "I can't do this."

"Do you want to be punished, Maia? If you don't participate in the activities, *there will* be consequences."

I sigh and I look at him again. He looks at me, and I have to say something. I look at his body. I can't see much under his clothes, but I'm going to guess he worked out a bit before all this shit happened. He has broad shoulders, and his arms look tough under his long sleeve shirt.

"Magnus, you work out...," I stammer, "which is, is hot."

Oh my God. Saying this makes me almost vomit, but I swallow it down. I let today's lunch go back down my throat, leaving a trail of sour burning. I'm not going to vomit and make a fool of myself.

The teacher approves, and Magnus compliments me on my hands and then I compliment his ears, and then he compliments something, and it goes back and forth, back, and forth, and I'm getting really confused, because weirdly, I'm finding it easier and easier to find nice stuff about him, but at the same time, it's also getting harder because, one, there is less and less stuff left to compliment and, two, it's making me into someone I'm not.

But I won't let this make me turn myself into a different person.

I am stronger than that.

They are not going to make me straight.

Maybe I'll trick them into thinking I'm straight, and I'll be the one in control for once.

But no matter how much I tell myself that I will stay strong and remain gay, the more I begin to doubt myself.

Because each time I tell myself that, it triggers something inside me, something deep inside, a little voice telling me to give in because not giving in leads to death, and death is the reason why I'll never see my girlfriend ever again.

# 13

I just want this all to stop. I've never wanted *all this to stop* more in my entire life. I never knew things like this were possible. I never knew that all that has happened to me *could* happen to me.

I mean, yes, I was living a sheltered life in the warmth of my home, and it's a shock. But it would still be a shock if I didn't live a sheltered life.

I don't know.

Confusion scrambles my brain.

I am losing touch with *who* I am. I am a dog on a leash. The bracelet is the collar, and the threat of the shockwaves is the leash.

Are these the effects of the medication?

I really don't know.

On top of *that* shit, I still feel the weight of the guilt on every particle of my body. I watched three people die. That soldier *deserved* to die, she was mean, but Conor and Alyssa. . . they are, were just kids. But could I have really prevented their deaths, are the deaths really on my shoulders as the General said? Because, like everyone else—I had no idea that crossing the fence would *kill* them. And how was I supposed to stop, *convince* them to not *try* and escape?

We are gathered in the field in the middle of the camp. Everyone in the entire camp is there. One of the few occasions where we are actually doing something all together. They don't like it when we are together because when we are together, we potentially become an army. And if we could, we'd combine our strengths and beat those fuckers.

It's the first Sunday of our time here and we have a "Mandatory Group Session," which includes everyone in the camp.

Soldiers mass around, in their baggy green uniforms with the red "Morality Guard" arm patches, creeping in between the houses and layering in formation on every side of us.

We are just bunched together, unsure what to do.

General Wilson arrives, with bandages still on her, and behind her are four soldiers carrying. . . carrying a dark, mahogany coffin. It's shiny and glimmers in the early afternoon sunlight. *Did someone . . . die?*

Everyone mutters to themselves and to each other, and all those whispers become a chaos of voices that chirp loudly.

"What the fuck."

"Did someone die?"

"What is going on?" The voices overlap and creates a wave of confusion.

The four soldiers place the coffin in the middle of the field.

General Wilson smiles. "Welcome, everyone." She raises her arms in the air like she is some sort of religious leader. "Welcome to your funeral."

People back away, but the soldiers that were massing around us seem to be closer now.

Some want to flee, but there is no way out. *Are they really going to kill us? After everything that happened?*

"Don't worry." She smiles again. Those words do not reassure us. "You're not going to die, *physically*."

"What are you talking about, lady?" one guy says. His face is scared, and he has a raging inferno in his eyes.

"This technique has been used across America, and it has been proved successful with everyone that participates. It works on your mind and spirit."

A priest dressed in black comes forward. But he does not look like an ordinary priest.

"This priest represents all religions. He will be conducting all of your funerals."

Everyone mutters, unsure what to do, what to say. I look at the ground again, at my boring shoes, and I just. . . I just. . .

"All of you are diseased. All of you are mentally and physically sick. And one way to rid yourself of that *mental* aspect of the disease is to kill it. And in order to kill something, you must kill everything. We are going to have a funeral for your sinful desires and longing. We are going to kill those elements that made you sick. Those horrific voices that cry in your minds every day will be gone once you take the appropriate steps. Once you mentally die, once you go through the process of mentally dying, you will be cleansed." She smiles, but it looks more like a gleeful grin. "For most of you, it will not work completely, and that's why you are staying here for a long time. But it will work bit by bit, and that's what we want. We want to chip away at the disease. Even if it takes a lot of work, we still want to try. Because we care!"

"This is outrageous," a girl yells. Soldiers look at her, and she backs down, her shoulders slumping forward, and her neck bent to the ground.

No one wants to anger the soldiers. Because we know what they can do.

We've seen what they did, and we don't want that to happen to us.

"I want all of you to form a tight circle around the coffin," General Wilson says.

And it takes a while, but we do it, forming a sort of looped oval around the coffin.

We are so close to the coffin that we can smell the fresh wood.

I am standing next to a girl with long brown hair tied in a bun and a man with olive skin and a spiky nose. We are all shaking.

General Wilson opens the coffin, and inside is the soft cushion you would expect to see there.

There is a piece of paper at the top end of the padding, where the head would go. She takes it out and looks it over.

"I will say each of your names one by one, and you will come here and step into the coffin. This is mandatory. If you disobey, you will be punished."

I gasp.

"Frank Babylon."

General Wilson turns her gaze to a kid who looks to be about thirteen, and he starts to tremble. He has freckles over his beige nose.

He steps forward, shaking.

"Come on, Frank. We don't have all day."

He steps closer to the coffin, and he looks like he is going to puke.

He looks at General Wilson, then at the coffin, and then at the guards.

A drizzle of pee goes down the side of his legs, but he doesn't even seem to notice.

People around me mutter. A girl shouts, "You can't do that! He's a kid!" But a soldier steps forward, and she backs away.

"Please. . ." he mutters. "I don't want to die."

"You're not going to die, Frank," General Wilson says.

"I. . ."

"Do you want to get punished?"

He shakes his head.

"So, step in the coffin. Nothing is going to happen to you. We are just going to cleanse you of those devilish sins."

He nods slowly and lifts his leg and then his other leg. And he lies down in the coffin.

General Wilson closes both halves of the lid.

We can hear his muffled cries.

Thankfully there appear to be tiny holes in the top of the coffin, for breathing, but oxygen must be the least of his worries.

He shouts, "Let me out! Let me out! Please!" And we hear his cries, and he thumps against the wood.

The priest steps forward.

"On this day, Frank Babylon's sinful self has died. His sinful self is on its way to hell. When he steps out of this coffin, he will be born again! He will be cleansed of his sins, and he will be a new man!" He says this over the cries and shouts, and his voice becomes louder and louder, and we hear Frank crying out.

Then the priest steps back.

And General Wilson opens the coffin.

I look at Frank lying in the coffin. His eyes are tightly closed, and his body is limp.

"Frank, step out," General Wilson says. He doesn't respond so she says it again, louder, "Frank, step out!"

Frank opens his eyes and looks around. He sits up, tear streaks on his cheek, and he looks so torn up.

He looks like he is about to faint. "What's going on?" he mutters in confusion. "Where am I?"

"Frank," General Wilson says, frustrated, and she gestures to the soldiers. They rush toward him and lift him up by the armpits. "Send him to my office."

They drag away his frail body as his mind doesn't even register what's happening.

Then she says the next name.

"Carla Badia."

Carla vomits.

They repeat the process with her, and then another boy or girl, and another.

Every time they step out of the coffin, they go back to where they were standing in the messed-up circle.

The next and the next and the next.

My legs are tired. I feel the weight on my feet.

The girl next to me almost faints as she walks over.

Luckily they are going in alphabetical order.

So, it takes a while.

One boy refuses, and struggles with the guards. They drag him off to who knows where.

They call Ozzy by their "birthname," and Penelope, and Sam, and all my friends.

And then. . .

"Maia Robinson," General Wilson calls and she searches the circle, looking around with her cold eyes until she finds me. "Maia," she says, her voice as cold as the deepest part of the ocean.

I feel dizzy. I look at the coffin, and it becomes fuzzy in my mind. And I'm unsure where the grass is, and I don't know where the brown shape of the coffin is, it's all swimming in my vision. I don't want to die. I don't want my *mind* to die.

I don't want this. I don't want this, yet I see my feet step forward, going closer to the coffin.

The thought of pain keeps me moving. It keeps me from stopping and running in the opposite direction.

The memory of that pain, the pain all over my body, is a constant presence at the edge of my mind.

And the threat that my sister might end up in a "camp" like this is always at the back of my mind. I can't let anything happen to her.

And there is only one way to avoid the pain. It's to step forward and step forward and then my legs bang against the edges of the coffin. I grip the sides of it, the sharp edges digging into my skin.

I lean on it, in fear for my life.

I look at General Wilson, pleading with my wet eyes.

"Maia," she says again, and the sound echoes in my mind. My name in her voice. My name. Her voice.

I am shivering as if it's negative 100 degrees right now. I breathe in through my mouth and stop. I don't know how to breathe. I've forgotten how to breathe. I try and use my lungs, but I'm frozen.

Soon my survival instincts take over and I take several gulps of air.

I can't hear anything.

I can't see anything.

But I know what General Wilson is saying, or what she is going to say. . .

I lift my leg up and then lift my other leg and sit down. The cushion is soft like clouds; it's warm like a person's belly. It smells of lavender soap, sweat, piss, and the rotten lunch. I feel around the coffin, over the lines of the structure, over the knots of the fabric, and it all feels so cold; it feels so, so, so cold, and I lie my head down on the pillow that is sewed on. Both halves of the coffin lid are slammed shut, and I am greeted by darkness.

At first I breathe slowly, taking in my surroundings.

But then I hear the priest's voice, and I feel the sickening fear of death trickle in.

This is worse than death.

This is torture.

The coffin closes around me, and it suffocates me. I can't breathe. It starts to get hot inside. I scratch at the lid of the coffin, I bang, and bang and bang and tears start forming in my eyes, drowning them in salty tears. I can't move, and my legs and arms feel so heavy.

Heavy with the fear that one day I could die. Perhaps soon. Perhaps now. I could go to sleep and never wake up and never feel anything ever again and never be an "I." I've always known this, but I've never *known* it.

The priest drones on and on, his words slow and unmoving.

And he goes on forever and ever, never stopping. I'm banging against the lid of the coffin. Because I can't breathe. I can't breathe. I can't. Think. I can't. . . I am screaming.

I am dead.

I am dead inside. . .

And.

I.

Can't.

Think.

And then. . . a new thought starts taking form in my mind. I can't help but think of why I'm in this situation. And it horrifies me to start blaming things on myself. It disgusts me that I am placing this horror and this suffocation on the fact that I'm gay.

And this pain, this fear, this longing for love. . .

I blame it.

I center all my anger on that.

And I start to hate myself for being gay.

Did I want love so bad I'd take it from anyone? Did I just want a mommy, like the therapist said? Am I a weakling, a diseased person?

These aren't my thoughts, but I am thinking them.

I start to feel disgusted at everything I did and everything I *was* going to do.

I feel myself losing touch of what it means to be gay. To be gay and beautiful. Gay and proud. Gay and *me*.

I am flying away from the wanting to be loved by another woman, and the wanting to love another woman with all my heart.

I don't understand why I ever loved another woman like that.

Why couldn't I be normal?

Why couldn't I be like everyone else?

Why did I have to be an anomaly?

Why did I have to be different?

Why did I have to want attention from everyone else? Was I greedy?

I feel myself flitting away.

I feel the clouds of the cushion lift me up into the heavenly sky, and time slows, and my body feels like it's flying, no, like it's soaring upward.

It is so calming and peaceful.

Like the sound of the birds chirping at sunset.

Or the waves of a calm ocean.

Or the flutter of leaves on a tree, on a warm, windy, day.

*Am I dead?*

*Maybe I suffocated and am floating to heaven or hell or where the fuck.*

But then this intense light hits my eyes, and sounds start to filter through my ears, and I realize where I am.

I'm in a coffin.

But the lid is open now.

I didn't die.

I am still alive.

My eyes open, and I look around.

I take a breath and climb out of the coffin like a zombie.

I wobble and fall onto the grass, and I smell the grass, the beautiful grass.

I am alive.

I never died.

I stand up on my own two feet, and I feel so tired, yet so energized.

The realization that I am alive and not dead, that I can *at least* survive in this world gives me this energy that I didn't know existed.

I don't know what to think or what to do.

I stretch my legs and find my place in the circle of girls and boys.

I sigh.

The next person is called.

I am okay.

# 14

A couple of days later, I head off to "Physical Training" at the meadow, wearing my sneakers, and I try to hype up my body for the hours of grueling exercise.

Luckily, Yola is in the class with me. Despite her harsh words to me the day of the failed escape, she is my friend now. I admire her spirit, her defiantly sarcastic style. She is great to be around, she makes a lot of jokes and always lightens up the mood. I see her ahead with some other girls who I barely know and walk along with them.

"How are you doing, Maia?" Yola asks and comes to my side, almost touching me, but not.

"I'm fine."

"That's a lie," she says brutally.

I chuckle softly, "I'm so confused. I don't know what this place is doing to me."

"Same here."

"What are they having you do?" I ask. I'm curious to how they are treating her, and how they are changing the story to make it look like she's sick.

"There's this class they are making us take, it's *just* for bisexual girls," Yola says, and nods to the two other girls who are talking amongst themselves but still close to us. "They are in my class."

"What goes on there?"

Yola sighs, "They are trying to convince us that we like girls, because we never found the *right guy*."

I roll my eyes, "This place is such a joke."

"Well, yeah. And you know what's so sick, they assigned us to be *pen pals* with straight guys from our school, who they think we'll get along with. Of course, they read the letters before they are given to us or sent to them. To make sure we are not giving any *confidential information* away." She makes air quotes.

I laugh. We approach the rest of the group for "Physical Training," who are stretching, getting ready. We sit on the ground, and I stretch out the muscles in my legs.

"The crazy thing is, they actually gave me a cute guy."

"What?"

"Like they showed us a picture, you know. And he's not that bad."

"But. . ." I bend my leg, stretching it hard.

"It's not working." She smiles lightly. She looks around and whispers: "I'm still bisexual, if that's what you're worried about."

I smile back.

If she isn't changing, then that means it's possible for me not to change.

But I don't know if I'm strong enough, like her.

\* \* \*

Famished now, Yola and I rush into the cafeteria, head to the line, and wait impatiently for it to move. It moves slowly.

I tap my foot, my forehead still sleek with sweat. I want to take a shower, but there isn't time in between. So I have to smell like this in front of my friends.

I look around for them, I don't see them, they are probably on their way here.

I look at Yola and notice her classmates are not with her. "Where are the other girls?" I pant.

Yola shrugs, "I think they went with their other friends." I frown, I wanted to get to know them, they seem nice. But I know that there are some people who don't want to hang out with me, because I'm known for trouble.

The line finally moves, and we get our tray and utensils, and the food: Mashed potatoes and some sort of fried meat. I'm too hungry to care what it is. We head over to our usual table, and I get water for everyone.

I sit down and look at my food and begin gobbling it all up. I'm not the only slobbery mess. Yola is doing the same.

"What did they make you do?" Penelope questions and scrunches her nose. "You guys stink."

Between swallowing, I mutter, "Suicide drills. . . And more running. . . and more suicides."

"Yikes." Penelope says.

We eat in silence for a moment, and I drink some water, and it goes down the wrong way and I begin coughing. Everyone looks at me, worried, but I put a hand out to reassure them and cough a bit more. For a second there I couldn't breathe. But I'm okay now. I'm okay.

I begin to laugh, because for a second, there, as I was just choking on water, and all my friends surrounded me, worried for my health—it felt like I was back at school. At a school cafeteria. On a normal school day, just munching on some crappy lunch food, gossiping about the jocks, snickering over how the teacher's fly was down, complaining of the next test on Monday. And I'm laughing because I'm here. I'm not at school, where *I* should be, I'm at a camp bent on trying to "convert" us to normalcy. I'm laughing because these circumstances are so unusual, they don't *feel* real, even though they are *happening* to us.

And the others join me in my hysteric laughing, they know why I'm laughing, they know what's it all about, and I look into each of their eyes, their faces, as they look back at me.

Penelope's face, glowing with energy. Yola's determination set in the stone of her eyes. Sam's nose, how it crinkles hard with his beautiful smile. Diana's soft chin, the way her eyes drift all over the features of my face. Jade's eyebrows, long and furry, black, and beautiful. Crystal's soft face, innocence radiating from her.

# 15

I miss home.

My loving parents. . . who I still pray every day are doing everything in their power to get me out of this evil place. I know they are not superheroes, they are not powerful politicians, but they have friends, who have friends of friends, who have some power in this messed up world. They have money saved up, and I know for sure they'd use it to save me. Because they love me unconditionally.

I am certain they haven't given up on me.

Or maybe I'm giving myself false hope, I'm just creating delusions for myself, and it'll only hurt me in the future when *nothing* actually happens.

But I need some false hope. I need to believe that the future is better in order to survive the present. And when the news comes that I will never be saved, that they have failed as parents, I will be devastated, but I'll just deal with those feelings later. Right now, I have to survive, and this is how I survive. To look forward to a future where I see their light blue car come rolling down the driveway, and me jumping in their warm hugs, and climbing in the backseat, leaving this place behind, forever. I need that thought to stay alive, to stay sane.

If I am even sane as of right now, I really have no idea, they have been doing stuff, just. . . they've turned me into something that I have no clue *what* it is.

Sometimes, they show us Fox News clips.

Since it's Fox News, I know it's all bullshit, but apparently we have to be kept informed by the "most watched news source in America." It's mostly propaganda and lies disguised as truth. Gross misunderstandings of small incidents that members of the LGBTQIA+ community did, with no intention of harming anyone, but portrayed as if they were evil, sinister psychopaths.

They are showing us a clip about a gay couple who tried to get their marriage license at the beginning of May, *when gay marriage was legal.* They had all the requirements and were entering the town hall but were blocked by a bunch of bible-thumpers who had nothing better to do. I remember when this happened, it was all over social media. It was in one of those really super conservative states, but eventually the couple did get their license and it all turned out happily.

At least for a while. Now they are probably in a camp somewhere too.

And we are watching this *news report.*

About twenty of us are in the auditorium where orientation was, sitting in front of the television screen, forced to open our eyes and listen intently to what the plastic lady with puffed blonde hair has to say. "Instead of behaving like reasonable human beings, the diseased men chose to attack a group of citizens who were kindly offering to help them see the error of their ways. They resorted to violence against peaceful citizens who were practicing their freedom of speech." There's a clip of when the couple lightly pushed one of the protestors back. And then they are replaying the footage in slow motion over and over.

I'm shaking my head inwardly. This is not what really happened. Yes, there was a small fight. The guy did push one of those nutcases.

But that's because the guy punched his fiancé out of the blue. And so in defense he pushed back.

These fucked up news reporters are taking the whole thing out of context, to feed into the lies that gay people, that people who are part of the LGBTQIA+ community, are violent, erratic, not thinking straight.

I want to scream at the television screen, I want to stand up and smash my chair against it. I don't want to see this crap.

But the soldiers are leaning against the walls, watching us. So I keep my ass on the seat, fold my hands neatly on my lap like a good little girl, and continue watching the footage. I don't want them to hurt me again.

I don't want the pain.

The clip changes.

Now a male reporter is in front of a movie theater. The gel in his hair glistens and his teeth are too white. "We just got reports of a pedophile in a women's bathroom. A pedophile, can you believe that? In the year 2026, when Doug Miller is our President, we still encounter these perverts?" He shakes his head, over and over, and then looks intently at the camera, "This pedophile was one of the *diseased*. He claimed he was a *female* because he grew out his hair and applied makeup on his face. But he was born as a male. He was born with genitals. God created him as a man, and instead he became *diseased* and sneaked into a bathroom full of little girls. What a way to traumatize their childhood."

It horrifies me that this is what the news is now.

The person in that bathroom, the woman, was probably just having a normal day, and did nothing wrong. Someone might have noticed and told the manager or something. But she had every right to be there. It's a bathroom for God's sake. You can't expect someone who identifies as one gender to be forced into a bathroom that is dedicated to the opposite gender. I would be horrified if I had to enter a men's room with its smelly urinals where guys are aiming their things at the bullseye.

I tune out what the yikkety-yak panel has to say about this issue.

# 16

During work, for a while it was just me doing the laundry.

But then Jack came back, looking broken, bruises along his arms and his face empty, with a lip that can't seem to stop bleeding. He ignores me as much as possible. Even though he helped me get out of a bad situation, I guess he is still mad at me for my cowardice—even if I would have died if I had tried to escape and crossed the fence with them. In fact, I probably saved his life by delaying him. But he expected more from me. I'm not sure what to say.

My record got cleaned after I "didn't escape" with the other Laundry Rebels; that's what they are called now.

Since my record is clean, I get to sit during Movie Night but it's more like a punishment than a reward. Romantic comedies are so boring.

Some other girl joined us in the laundry crew. And then Crystal turned up with her small smiles and quiet demeanor.

Two soldiers stand by and watch us. One inside and one by the door, but I don't really care about them anymore.

I smile at Crystal, she smiles back. It's nice to have a familiar face around here.

They added a video camera after the escape attempt, so we are watched constantly, but Crystal and I help each other out. She irons the hot laundry and I fold it.

We walk to dinner together. The air is hot, and I find myself sweating all over my back. I look at Crystal, she looks back at me.

I know I'm not attracted to her, and she's not attracted to me. What we have is a sort of friendship I suppose, she's someone I want to look after.

"How old are you?" I ask suddenly. Eyeing the soldiers, seeing if they will hear us, but they are just watching from afar.

"Fifteen," she says softly.

I take a deep breath. That's young. Just five years older than my sister.

"What school do—did you go to?"

"The Mary Louis Academy."

"Oh, is that—"

"Yeah, it's a Catholic school."

"That's cool." I don't know a lot about religious schools, just that they wear uniforms and usually don't have members of the opposite gender there.

"It was. . . okay."

"What is—was your favorite subject?"

"I liked science. . . and visual arts was fun." I hate to hear her use past tense with everything. But that's what I've been doing, too. We are talking about the past, something that *happened*. And we have no idea if we will ever get *that* life again. They say we'll be able to get back to society once they've "cured" us, but how can we live our ordinary lives after going through this kind of hellish experience?

"My sister likes to draw," I tell her.

"Yeah?"

"She loves watercolor, blending the colors together always creates a mesmerizing image, is what she always says." I smile at the memory.

"There's this cool technique with water coloring," Crystal says, her face animated. "You wet the paper first and then you put the paint on it after, it creates a really beautiful reality to it." She smiles, I've never seen her smile that big before.

"You should teach her," I say, "I mean. . . after all this. . . when it's over you should come over and teach her tricks."

"If, Maia, if."

"No." I look at her deeply, almost getting lost in the ocean of her eyes. "When we get out. They can't keep us here forever."

"Is that so?" Crystal says.

I shiver.

Could she be right?

Will we ever leave this place?

# 17

My therapist has been telling me things. Things that I know in my heart don't make any sense at all, but somehow, she is able to slime her way into my mind and turn things upside down. Make me re-think the past, make me put things together in a way that I have never thought of before, making connections that I never want to think of.

We are in session, on some day, I have lost track of everything. I just follow the schedule blindly day after day after day.

I am sitting on the same spot, my hands squeezing on my knees, trying to contain my anger, but it's really hard when she is ripping those I love apart.

"Do you think your mom ever wanted a family?"

I look up at her, look at her blank stupid face, hear a bird chirping outside the window, singing their heart out, I squeeze my knees tight.

She wears another pretentious outfit, clearly showing off how much she's getting paid to demonize innocent young people. A long black dress with what I presume to be velvet white powdered roses in even patterns on the dress and open-toed high heel boots with bright red polish perfectly painted on her toenails.

"What?" I almost choke on my words.

"Some women don't want a family. Which is understandable, that they choose their careers over having children."

"Of course, she wanted a family," I bark.

"Now, now, Maia, no need to be aggressive." I sit back against the couch and start to fidget with my fingers. "You have to control your anger."

I am a teapot filled with water, boiling and fuming, about to burst.

"You understand what I'm saying, correct?"

"Yes." I mumble.

"Okay, let's get back to business." She picks up a fat folder that I hadn't noticed before, which was on the floor by her feet. She opens it and begins scanning quickly. "So, I have records from your schools, specifically PTA meetings and parent involvement."

I gulp.

"Your mother never had the time to join any of the PTA meetings. How unfortunate."

"She was busy with work, as you know. It's understandable."

"But your friends' moms always participated, and it seems like they had respectable jobs, too."

I see where she's going, and I know she's wrong, I know she's just saying this to make me feel like my mom did the *wrong* thing.

"My mom is an engineer. She is at the cutting edge of advanced technology, that's a huge responsibility. Technology that gives sight to the blind, devices that saves people lives, she is a trailblazer."

"You just sounded like an advertisement."

I look her dead in the eyes, how am I dealing with all of this? How come I haven't punched her in the face? I don't understand myself. I don't get it.

"She. . . she's an amazing woman. I'm grateful she's my mom, proud to be her daughter," I ramble on, because I don't know how else to defend her. "I'm fine that she wasn't always there for me when

I needed her, I'm okay with the fact that her absence sometimes embarrassed me in front of my class. Because she did great things. I'm only one person, she did the right thing to save hundreds of lives instead of making *me* feel better."

Dr. Diamond's eyes widen. I've said too much. Fuck. I've said things I shouldn't have. How did she do that? "But you're her daughter, it's her job to make *you* feel better."

"I'm not bothered by it, never have been." I want to laugh. "I. . ." But was I *bothered* by it? I'm thinking back to those times, when she should have been there, even times where she *promised* she would be there, and she wasn't. Was I devastated? "I. . ." I don't know. I'm so confused. "My dad was there when she wasn't."

"Tell me about it."

I look down at my palms, feel them out. They are covered in sweat. "I. . ." I feel like crumbling into dust.

"Tell me, Maia, don't withhold any information."

I don't want to tell her anything anymore. I've told her enough.

"Do you want to be punished? Do you want your sister to—"

"There was a bake sale one time in middle school. The money would go to Greenpeace to help combat climate change," I quickly say, and I don't have time to come up with a lie, so I just tell her the truth. "Me and my mom had spent the previous night making cupcakes, vanilla with pink frosting." I remember she'd playfully place some frosting on my cheek, and I'd do the same to her, and we'd doubled over and laugh.

"Go on."

"She was supposed to show up at the school with the cupcakes, but she never did. . . Instead, my dad had to come over from his studio, and there wasn't enough time to go back home and to my school, so instead he stopped at the deli near my school and bought in some cupcakes from the store." I sigh. "It was clear to everyone that they were store bought because they tasted like plastic trash."

"How did you feel?"

"I don't know."

"Yes, Maia, you do know. Tell me."

"It. . . I was a bit angry because we had made those cupcakes together, and she promised she would bring them, and she didn't. She broke our promise together."

"It must have been embarrassing. In front of all your friends."

"Well. . ." I think back to that memory, which was just something that happened, and something I've moved on from, but now, it's open and dissected, and she's making it into something *it's not*. It's like she's pissing all over my memory, her yellow disgusting liquid and I don't know what to think anymore. I don't know what's real or what's not real.

Was I embarrassed?

"Maybe a bit?"

"Think about it, *realllyy* think about it."

I think back to the memory. I remember seeing my friends, with their moms, holding hands, proud smiles on their faces, showing everyone how they are a team, that they really get along together. And I was mad because me and my mom get along really well together, but because *she* didn't show up, it made it look like to everyone else that we *didn't* get along. "I was mad at her, because everyone else had this perfect parent with them. . . and I was mad at my dad, because he just got the most basic thing ever from the deli, and. . ." I shake my head.

"You bring up another point," my therapist says and crosses her legs. "Your relationship with your dad."

I scrunch my eyebrows together. "We have a really good relationship."

"Really?"

I nod hurriedly. She's already confusing my memories with my mom. She can't do it to my dad.

"You know, there's this theory that I see playing out in a lot in girls like you. That because they had a difficult relationship with their father, they come to believe that all guys are like that. And because of that, because they fear that any guy they meet will turn out to be as unreliable as their dad, it makes it hard for them to have real relationships. I mean natural relationships with guys. No wonder you feel you are attracted only to women, it's your last effort at finding love. You believe that all relationships with men will be bad, so you go to women to find love. But really, you're just falling prey to the games your mind plays on you when you're at a loss."

No. No. No. She can't undermine my parents like that, she can't blame them for everything.

But I can't help but think of the arguments I sometimes had with my dad, how he'd get mad at something so tiny, at something that was a simple accident, and we'd butt heads, it would become this whole tornado of rage and anger, and. . .

I see my therapist's smile smirk at me.

She's twined her way into me, she is a virus that I am unable to fight off.

And I can't help but admit that it's working. That whatever she's doing to me is working. No matter how much I try and avoid what she says. I try and deny everything, but. . .

I can't seem to find a reason or a fact or something to prove that she is wrong.

I don't know how, but. . . she might be right to some degree. And I hate that. I hate it I hate it I hate it that she has turned me into. . . that she unwound me.

So many years I was lost, trying to figure out my identity, who I am to the world, and finally, after realizing my sexuality, I was able to accept who I was and live life to the fullest. I found myself in my sexuality.

But now this *therapist* has completely pulled out the roots of my identity and made me confused all over again.

"Let's talk about your dead girlfriend," she says in a matter-of-fact tone. And I shiver. I don't want her to ruin more of my past.

I cringe in my seat. I don't want to talk to her about Aimee. I don't know what she's going to do with the untouchable memories of her.

"Talk to me about her."

I shake my head.

"Maia, did you not understand my question?"

I open my mouth, I want to fucking spit rage at her, but I close it and shake my head. I have to think of Janice. I have to protect her.

"Like what?"

"A memory, any memory."

I think back to the many memories with Aimee. The way her beautiful eyes crinkled in the sunlight, that one time I had to hold her steady on the sidewalk, when we were both wasted. She was more drunk than I because she, being her wonderous, adventurous self, wanted to try everything and drank much more than she should have.

Aimee. . . I just long for her. I want her in my arms. Aimee. . .

I chuckle softly at a memory that drifts in my mind.

"Have you found something?"

"Yeah." I know this woman is going to ruin the memory, but I need to say it, I have to give voice to it, because it gives life to her; even if she is dead, it gives a bit of brightness to her dull eyes.

"Go on."

"One time we were just eating lunch together and we were talking about our names." I smile. "Our names are similar, you see. Each could be spelled differently. Maia can be spelled M-A-Y-A and Aimee can be spelled A-M-Y." I look at my fingers, they are raw and uneven.

"It was meant to be, you know. Out of all the names, out of all the people we could have gotten together with, we chose each other. And—"

"Seems like just a coincidence!" my therapist almost spits at me.

I dart my eyes at her, "It's. . ." But I hold my tongue.

"Boring," she says simply.

*It was not boring. It was a cool rain on a humid day. Something beautiful. A feather drifting in the sky.*

My eyes dart at her eyes. She doesn't have a soul. I know she doesn't.

"Tell me another memory. . . something more. . . significant. Tell me how you guys became *official*. Well, in your notion of what *official* is."

I gulp.

I think back to that time. That time with Aimee, when we were talking about if we should be in a relationship together. . . and. . . I can't seem to remember it. It's such a tiny, yet important memory, and. . .

"I don't know, we were at dinner and. . ."

"Were you guys ever *official*?"

"Yes," I automatically reply, "she's my—was my girlfriend. . . and I was her girlfriend."

"If you guys never said you were in a relationship, then it seems like there was never a relationship at all."

No. The dinner. The baguette sticks and spaghetti sauce on her chin. I grasp at the memory, but it's been so long, and sometimes memories are under twines and spiky vines.

"No. We said so. She. . ."

"Maybe you thought it was a relationship and she simply saw you as a *friend with benefits*." She crosses her arms. "Communication is always important, you see."

I shake my head over and over again. No. No. No. No. That can't be true.

I don't believe her. I don't.

But. . . maybe I do?

No, I feel a tug in my heart. She was my girlfriend. We were in a relationship.

This place is making me doubt everything.

Am I strong enough to not believe their false claims?

Can I make it out of here intact—and alive?

# 18

On a beautiful Monday afternoon, when the weather is absolutely perfect, the sun giving just the right amount of warmth and the sweet summer breeze swaying through the hills and trees, I am stuck inside, watching some bullshit "health" video.

We are in another house, which looks like it used to be an arts and crafts area, where streaks of colorful paint and glitter litter the floor, and tape is stuck to the walls; probably it once held a drawing on construction paper that a kid made.

The chairs and desks are facing the front of the room, where there is a blackboard and another simple TV screen.

This is "Special Class" which consists of reading texts from books such as "The Complete Kāma Sūtra."

It's a rather strange book, teaching the reader certain techniques on how a man can please a woman.

And now we are forced to watch a video educating us on a healthy sex life, specifically a "straight" healthy sex life.

"It's all very simple, really," the old woman with the curly grey hair and a Polish accent on the TV screen says as she crosses her legs, sitting on a large velvet red chair in the midst of a small little room containing white ruffled curtains, pink flower wallpaper, and a dark green carpet. "God, the heavens, whoever you believe in, all made it really simple." She smiles. She makes a fist with her left hand and with her right hand makes a pointing gesture, and jabs the pointed finger into the fist. "The man delivers the sperm to the vagina, and the vagina receives the sperm." Then she takes the finger out, and repeats the process. "It's a rather lovely process. . ." She smiles, "Our bodies were designed this particular way so we can live fully, pleasurably, and productively. They were designed to bind man to woman, and woman to man, and bring life into the world."

I am holding my breath, trying to contain the burst of snorting laughter inside of me. This is absolutely insane. This whole situation is insane.

Finally the video ends and the lights around the room turn on. The teacher, a forty something year old man, a married man, judging by his wedding ring, looks at all of us. His excessively large eyebrows furrow, trying to figure out what our reaction is. I look at the others, they seem to have the same reaction as I do, trying to contain their mirth, but it's really hard to do that, I mean—our bodies *are* designed to make noises and blow out puffs of air when we see and hear something *so* stupid.

A hoot of laughter pops out of me.

The teacher, Mr. Adams, crosses his arms and looks at me. "Is there a problem, Maia?"

I shake my head. Can't get in trouble. *I can't.* Not with so much at stake.

"No, really, Maia, tell me what's on your mind."

*I have to think of something. Anything!* "It's just funny, that's all."

"Really? How so?"

"Umm. . . Well, I just *didn't* know any of this, so I'm finding it a bit funny. Sorry to disturb you." I feel like I'm back at school. *Technically, I am.*

"Ah I see."

I blush deeply, and look at the desk in front of me. This is very embarrassing.

"Let me ask you this, Maia."

I look up at him, a bit scared of what he's going to ask.

"You claim you were born gay, right?"

I nod. . . where is he getting with this.

"To love women and live happily ever after with them, correct?"

"Yeah. . ."

"Well, if that's true, then why were you born with a body that was designed to have a penis inserted inside you and give you sperm, which will then make you pregnant? Your body was designed for a heterosexual lifestyle. Isn't that clear as day?"

I swallow. I look at the others, who are paying close attention, waiting for me to have some smart comeback. I don't. . . know. But I have to think of something, they look up to me, whether I like it or not. I think hard. "Just. . . just because we were designed a certain way, doesn't mean we actually have to use it that particular way, or have any use for it.

"You have nipples, but you don't breastfeed," I tell him. He lowers his head, shocked. "You were *designed* with them, but you have no use for them." I'm not sure if I'm scientifically right, but it's not like I have Google to fact check myself. "We have appendixes, but people remove theirs all the time. They are a useless organ. We can't just look at our bodies, and assume that there's a right and wrong way. There's always an in between, there's always something else. The world is not black and white."

*It's rainbow*, I want to shout from the rooftops.

"That's very true, Maia." Mr. Adams says. He looks impressed. "Our bodies may have multiple purposes, and many different aspects. But I want you to think back to your relationships with other girls. Especially the attraction and physical parts. What made them attractive to you? What was so great about the lesbo sex that can't be replicated with a man?"

I am very. . . I can't believe he is talking to me like this. Like I'm some. . . sick person who needs to be cured? I don't want to be here. *But I don't have a choice.*

"The kissing. . . Women have lips, men have lips. Why do *you* need a woman to kiss you and not a man? Women aren't special."

I want to spit at him.

"The things girls do to you, Maia, especially sexually, a man could do, he probably could do it better, because he was born with the urge to please a woman, because pleasing a woman is part of his circuitry. Pleasing a woman means that he will be able to impregnate her and reproduce, which is his life goal. . . Why were you different? Why did you choose to be that particular way? Was it to get attention? Or was it because you were dissatisfied with yourself and thought that doing something different than the rest of us would give you *some purpose* in your miserable life?"

I don't know what to say.

I don't have any more comebacks.

He is the elder, he is the one with knowledge in the room, he is the one in charge of this class, and. . . I don't know. I know what he's saying is shit that shitted itself, but his words still ring in my mind. I still registered every syllable he said.

And even though I don't want to let what he said affect me, I think it does. Maybe it's being here for a while, the pills they are giving me, or something else for fuck's sake.

But I'm forced to think.

Why Aimee?

Why did I pick her?

Why didn't I pick my lab partner in Chemistry? The guy with the short black hair and sincere brown eyes?

Why?

# 19

I am numb inside.

I no longer want to think or speak or wake up.

I can't believe I am letting this happen to me. I can't believe it. I wish I could be strong like Aimee was. . .

But I have to think of my sister. It's either I face this alone, or she has to face this with me. And I would never let anything bad happen to her.

Even if I am physically dying inside, I just can't let anyone touch her. She's innocent in all of this. I am the one that's different, I am the one that is "diseased." She plays no part in this hell I've made for myself.

I will do whatever it takes to make sure she is safe. Just like that time when we almost got lost in a foreign country a couple of years ago.

Every couple of years, during the summer, my family would take a trip to visit my mom's family in Seoul, South Korea. She had been the only one of her family members to immigrate to the U.S., so it was always a big family reunion at her birthplace.

She had gotten an engineer's degree and met my dad at a coffeeshop.

She was working part time as a barista, and he was getting his BA at a small liberal arts college. He was working on an essay, and she had refilled his coffee cup for free, and then she approached him and told him she wouldn't charge him for his coffee if he gave her his number.

A bit aggressive of her. . . but it worked out somehow. . . a love story blossomed.

I remember the humidity in Seoul, the sharp scent of food at every corner, the mix of beautiful traditional houses with the sloping dark tiled rooftops and modern buildings. I remember bright, surprising colors, and rooftops with laundry drying in the wind. . .

My mom, being my mom, had the both of us take Korean lessons early in our childhood, so it'd stick in our minds. Janice was still young, she could get by with a couple of simple conversational words. And me, even though I was already in my teen years, I always found it hard to speak. Languages were always hard for me. Even learning Spanish in school, I'd always just barely "passed" because no matter how hard I tried, I could never learn new languages.

I know, I know, it's my culture, it's a part of me. I should definitely learn it. But I guess I never had enough motivation to speak Korean. Anyway, I should have tried harder to learn.

One time, my parents wanted the day to themselves, to just enjoy being with just each other for a change. So my cousin took Janice and me to Lotte World. It's an epic indoor and outdoor amusement park filled to the brim with haunted houses, roller coaster rides, artificial boat rides, carrousels, bungee drops, and so much more. I loved that place.

We had an amazing day filled with laughter, almost vomiting on the violent rides, eating all sorts of sweets like cotton candy, salty treats like chips twirled on a long stick, and bite-sized chicken nuggets.

At the end of the day, our cousin, who had been the official tour guide and translator, had to head to a hospital to visit a friend. He had no choice but to bring us along there, and we stayed by the reception desk as he checked on his friend. Janice was getting super hungry, and I thought, why not, let's just get some more snacks. Throughout the city, there are always little carts filled with dukboki (rice cake in hot pepper sauce) and fish cakes. So, I took hold of Janice's hand, told her, "Come'on Jam, let's go get some food," and led her outside into the evening air, where the humidity was falling to a nice cool breeze. Onlookers gave us worried looks, but I *thought* I knew my way around.

Stupidly, I didn't have any cash on me, but I had an ATM card, so I started looking for a bank to get some cash. I was looking at Google Maps, following the directions, when my battery went out.

Janice didn't have a phone then, because my parents were very strict about introducing technology at the right time and age.

So, we were lost in a foreign country, barely speaking the language, no cash on either of us, phones dead. No way of communicating with our parents or our cousin and calling for help. We were just wandering around, stupid me with the broken compass I call my head, and Janice hungry and whining, and I wanted to just tell her to shut up. Eventually I snapped at her, telling her that I needed to concentrate. I felt bad about that and apologized to her later. By that time she had already forgotten all about the incident.

I was trying to remember which direction we had come from and trace back our steps, following the signs which luckily were in English as well as in Korean, and I wanted to ask someone for help; maybe ask for their phone and. . . but I'm just stupid. I didn't have any phone numbers memorized in my mind. Like why would I, when my phone did everything for me?

I really hated ending the beautiful fun, day with this mess. I can't believe that I was the older one, and I had fucked this up. Who knows how much longer we would be wandering around the streets?

Janice was getting slower by the minute, tugging on my arm. I had to put food in her quick. Eventually I spotted a police officer and tried my best to speak in broken Korean: "Ahjusshi. . ." He looked at me, trying to figure me out. "Um. . ." I had blanked out. But then my sister blurted in English, "We are lost, do you know where the nearest hospital is?"

He smiled broadly and answered in almost perfect English. He walked us to the hospital, where our cousin was anxiously waiting.

I'm the older sister, and I'm supposed to do everything, and take care of things, but here, lost in another country, Janice was the one who saved us. Even though I could have thought to speak English, she was bold enough to ask the police officer right away, instead of me blundering in my chopped up, heavily accented Korean.

Even though I know she's strong and capable of facing anything in life, I still can't let anything bad happen to her. I just can't.

\* \* \*

The days go on and on. I just go through the days, sleep, wake up, and repeat.

But today's a special day. Well, let's not say special actually. It's just an ordinary thing, but there is one thing that is going to happen differently, and it's never happened here before. At lunch they are going to give us letters from our families!

We are allowed to read them, of course, but we are not allowed to send anything back.

They have given us this much decency, and we should all be grateful for it.

Because they are nice and caring for us.

At lunch, we all eat anxiously.

I am just sitting there, waiting, hoping for my letter, because I do miss my family, I do miss them so much, and I'll do anything to read their words and know that they are doing okay without me.

Of course, they are doing okay without me.

There were plenty of times when I was gone, and when I came back, it was as if I'd never left. Everything was so normal.

Our family is a well-run clock, always ticking no matter what, and everyone always plays their parts and does the necessary thing to live and thrive.

But I just want something from them.

Anything.

I didn't get to take anything with me except for the clothes on my back, which are gone forever.

All I have left are the memories.

Several soldiers come in, with plastic crates in their hands that are filled with envelopes.

By now, they know who we are and what our names are.

A soldier comes to our table and places a pile on it.

Penelope grabs the pile and begins handing out the letters.

The envelopes are already opened, of course. What did we expect, for them to *value our privacy*? Ha!

My envelope is a long rectangle with butterflies around the edges.

I can tell there was a sticker holding it together, because bits of it remain, but I'm unsure what the image was.

I carefully take out three nice letter papers that they probably bought at Paper Source or something fancy like that.

And it's kinda folded weirdly many times over.

There are only three letters, one for each family member.

I see three types of handwriting.

Dear Maia,

Your mother, your sister, and I were so joyful when they let us write a letter to you.

Of course, they didn't give us an address, we had to give these letters to an Officer who would send this to the right place. I hope this got to you safely.

I hope you are taking good care of yourself; I know ███████████████████████████████████████████ t ████████████████████████████████████████ ████████████████████████████████████████ can ████████████████████████████████ I hope you are making friends; ████████████ hard, ███████████████████████████████████████

Love,
    Dad

Hi Maia,

I miss you a lot.

I wish I could see you, I miss when you played with me.

Mom and dad got a dog! I named her █████

She is so cute all the time, and I love taking long walks with her in the park with Dad.

I hope to see you soon,

Love,

Jam

*Dearest Maia,*

*Mom*

My eyes are wet, and I feel like my tears will drip onto the paper, so I wipe my eyes before anything can happen to it. I fold it again neatly and put it back in the envelope. I cherish it with all my heart.

So many things got crossed out, but I know what they said, or I think I know.

Like in Jam's letter, why in the world would the censor block out the name of her dog? Could it be that she named the dog. . . Aimee?

I am just going to follow my own hopes and believe what I think they wanted to say, even if I'm wrong.

They seem fine. Like, I really don't know what's behind those words, but I have to believe that they are okay. Because I need that belief to keep my sanity.

I think back to Janice, her nickname is Jam.

It goes back to the time when she was around five, and she would always ask me to make her a snack every day. And she always wanted the same thing every day at exactly three o'clock when I came back from school. "Maia, Maia, can you make me the peanut butter and jam sandwich without the peanut butter?"

"You mean toast with jam?" I would reply.

"Nooo the peanut butter and jam sandwich without the peanut butter!"

I would laugh and ruffle her hair. So, from then on, she was always "Jam" to me. My lungs shiver at the memory.

"Hey, you okay?" Penelope questions. She looks teary-eyed, but she is toughing it out.

She clutches her letter in her fist.

"I'm okay. You?"

She nods, and then looks off into the distance.

"I want to go home," she mutters.

# 20

The next morning, I wake up to someone shoving me. My eyes blink open, and I see that everyone is being shoved awake by soldiers. I hurriedly look at Sam, and worry streaks his eyes.

Is this when they kill us?

I shiver, no that can't be it. They have to make it look like they are "curing" us. They wouldn't kill us, that's genocide.

Soldiers bark at us to change into our exercise clothes and I shove my socks on the wrong way and quickly tie my shoelaces together. *What is going on?*

I'm still groggy from my sleep, I barely got any sleep because all my mind was doing was raking itself into smithereens. I was going in circles, trying to figure out my life, make sense of everything that has happened to me so far, and I realized that. . . that I. . . I forgot what makes me truly happy. Like what are my pleasures, what do I like? It's insane, because it hasn't been that long, right?

They herd us outside, and I see other people with sleepy eyes lingering by their cabins, wondering what the hell is going on.

The soldiers then bark at us and hurry all of us to the field in the middle of the camp. General Wilson is there, surveying us all.

She looks healthy, no longer covered in bandages.

I shiver. *Are we attending another one of our funerals?*

Once everyone has gathered, General Wilson clasps her hands. "Everyone sit," she demands. So we all sit down on the cool grass, shivering in our short sleeve shirts, about to fall back asleep, but unable to. No one complains.

I guess we're sort of at that point in this fucked up journey (hopefully it's a journey where there's an *end*), where we are all broken down, unable to argue, even *choosing* not to fight back.

"Who likes hiking?" General Wilson asks us all.

People grumble some yes's and no's.

"Who likes overnight camping?" My eyebrows go up. *What?*

I hear some cheers.

"Now, today, we are going on a hike. . . To get in touch with our inner selves and really dive deep in why we are the way we are and what can be done in the future to be better versions of ourselves. Two of you will get a week-long vacation." She smiles. "You'll see the beautiful sights of the Adirondacks, such as the Shelving Rock Walls and the Ausable Chasm. You'll spend the nights in a very comfortable tent by yourselves and have delicious food such as burgers and s'mores at your disposal. Of course, there will be a couple of chaperons, but it will be an adventurous week and if you want, it can be romantic!" She winks. I cringe. "Of course, it will be one boy and one girl." She smiles brightly. "Because that's the *right* way of things."

Ugh.

They woke me up early for this shit?

"The rest of you won't get anything. You'll just have to go on with the rest of your life, here."

What is she up to?

"Who will be the two lucky people? You must be wondering!" She gestures for several soldiers to step forward. They hold stacks of index cards and tape with them. "You are all going to be playing a competitive game. And the winner gets to choose the person he or she gets to enjoy the week with. The game is simple. You will be separated into several groups, and each of you will be given an index card. Each card specifies the type of *disease* you have. You will tape that card to your forehead, and the goal of the game is to basically *roast* everyone else, specially targeting their disease. No cursing of course. Not too harsh, of course. Just harsh *enough* to make the other person feel bad and ashamed of their specific type of disease. I have designed this game to make everyone realize what their type of disease truly is in the real world. The point is to make you realize *really* how disgusting you all are!"

I absorb her words.

This is illegal. She is inciting us to hate speech.

But of course, there is no such thing as legal anymore. Not here, anyway. It's just the person in charge gets to do whatever they want to everyone else. I should stop being shocked at everything. I should just get used to this.

"Each soldier will be the judge of who is the harshest of each group. And those that are deemed most harsh will continue playing, while the rest will be eliminated. Then those remaining will be split into smaller groups and compete, and the same thing will be happening. We will repeat the process until there is one left standing. Each round will be ten minutes long." Like a soccer tournament.

Sounds like she's trying to break our morale. Having us attack each other, dividing us up so we are easier to control. I'll just not participate. I don't care about some stupid waterfall. Or some tent.

"Of course, in order to ensure that everyone participates, you will each have to say *at least* one insult to someone else. If you don't by the end of the round, then you will be punished accordingly."

A cold, wet hand slimes my way down my spine. It's like she read my mind.

"And it has to be an insult. It has to be real and harsh. Not weak and wimpy."

I fist some grass and pull out the blades, tearing them apart, and I drop them to the ground.

Why can't I just go home?

She calls our names, and we are split into groups. I follow a small group of about ten people led by a woman soldier with dark black hair in a ponytail. She looks like she is constipated.

She seems to know each of our "diseases" and gives me an index card that says "lesbian" written in thick, black, sharpie, along with a piece of tape. I notice Crystal, with the same card, is in my group and we stand side by side, terrified of what we have to do next.

"Place them on your foreheads."

I shiver as I tape the index card to my forehead.

I look around. The group has almost every "type": three gay guys, one trans man, one trans woman, one intersex person, and two asexual people. *Oh God.* Who am I going to pick? I don't want to do this.

I can't pick.

The soldier takes out a notepad and pen and makes all of us go in a sort of circle, with her in the middle, watching us all closely. She tells us that if you have an insult, you enter the middle of the circle, turn toward the person you are insulting, point, and say the insult. This reminds me of a play my parents once took me to, "The Crucible," where these crazy mean girls accuse their friends of being witches. It also reminds me of an old TV comedy my parents used to watch, which made them fall over laughing. What was it called, "Office"? There was an episode where the boss made all the workers wear cards on their heads, labeled with racial stereotypes. . . .

I look around, other groups are in circles, backs bent and scared. General Wilson is not far from where I am, and she looks at all of us, satisfied. She checks her watch and yells: "Round One. . . BEGIN!"

I look at my circle. No one says anything at first.

No one wants to start.

We are all brothers and sisters in this unlawful, weaponless war.

We aren't the kind of people that insult others just because of how they express themselves or who they love. There are people like that, the ones who wore the red Trump hats and were full of rage toward at anyone who was different from themselves—all to cover up for the fact that deep down they were really angry at themselves, and ashamed, for being such losers.

Someone starts, I don't even see a face, all I hear is their insult, directed at one of the gay guys. "You faggots, all you do is rape innocent church boys!"

And then it goes quickly. Most people just say one insult, they don't care about the prize. They just want to do the minimum that's required, and be done with all of this.

One or two, I'm not sure of their names, say more than one insult.

The soldier nods approvingly. She writes in her notepad from time to time.

One or two insults are directed at me.

No one insults Crystal. She is too innocent. Young. Someone who has never harmed a soul in her life.

People point and shout.

General Wilson yells. Five minutes.

It's my turn. I have to go. I don't want to be punished.

Crystal hasn't said anything either.

There is silence, I hear the other groups shouting insults at each other.

An attack on a trans woman leaves her falling on her knees crying. "Perverts. All of you. You're sick! Just wanna watch little girls piss." She is pulled up by a soldier and forced to remain standing.

I see people all around me, faces of pain, tears streaming from their eyes.

"Three minutes!"

I have to go.

I don't want to be punished.

I go to the center of the circle.

I turn and look at one of the asexual guys, he has sharp, dark eyelashes. I point at him. "You. . . people. . . don't even have sex. . . which is gross!"

The woman soldier looks at me, "No, Maia, not good enough! Doesn't count."

Ugh. I don't know how to insult people.

To hurt people who are innocent, where there is nothing wrong with them. How do I say something when I don't believe it? But I realize. I've been doing that my whole time here. Being someone I'm not. Or being someone I am, or being someone, they want me to be?

I don't know. I now have a huge identity crisis.

I turn and look at the one of the gay guys who got the least number of insults. I point at him. "You are so. . . retarded. . . having anal sex all the time in bar bathrooms!" I mouth: "I'm sorry" at him, and he nods, he knows it's not my fault.

I look at the soldier, hoping that was harsh enough. Who have I become? Hoping what I said to another human being is *harsh enough*?!

She nods and I blow out a sigh of relief. I am disgusted with myself. I go back to my place.

"Sixty seconds!"

I turn and look at the last person who hasn't said anything. Crystal.

We all look at her. The seconds are ticking away quickly.

"Crystal, just say something at me, it's okay," I tell her quickly in a whisper. I can't let her be punished. I just can't.

She doesn't budge.

"Crystal!" I almost yell.

The soldier looks at me cautiously.

"I can't. . ." she whispers. "I can't be. . ."

"I know you don't mean it," I gulp, and I gently shove her toward the center of the circle. She widens her eyes and almost trips. She turns directly at me, almost mad, but then her face softens. She shakes her head.

"Ten. . .Nine. . ." General Wilson.

I nod at her.

She is frozen.

"Come on!" I grit my teeth.

"Five. . .Four. . .Three. . ."

Go. Go. Go! I squeeze my eyes and give her a death look. She *has* to say something, anything.

"Dyke!" Crystal shouts at me, pointing. "Eat my shit!"

"Zero! Okay, times up, everyone!"

I blow out a sigh of relief. Crystal goes back to my side, and I look at her, my eyes warm up at her. I want to hug her, but people are watching. "I'm so sorry," she whispers.

"Don't worry about it." I smile back.

I see the soldiers heading to General Wilson and talking amongst each other. Two kids get dragged away; they probably didn't say anything. They are good people. But they will now be punished.

I feel bad that I wasn't one of those people, who chose their own pride and goodwill over everything. But I can't take the pain anymore. It's too much.

I'm glad Crystal said something.

She wouldn't survive with all that pain.

Those of us that were eliminated are gathered together and are forced to sit down and watch the rest of the "semi-winners" battle it out, spewing insults at each other.

I take more fistfuls of grass and pull them out. I hear a girl yell at a bisexual girl: "You're just greedy and slutty, wanting to sleep with *everyone.*"

I don't want to hear them, but it's impossible to tune out something so ugly and loud.

"Dumbo."

"Tranny."

"Butch."

"Whore."

I don't want to hear any of this.

But soldiers are watching us as well, making sure we are watching the contestants, listening to them, hearing all these harsh, evil things spew from people we see as friends. From people who are in the same community as us. And it makes. . . it makes our whole community, the queer community, dismantle itself into tiny pieces, into shards of glass, into powerless beings, into nothingness.

Atomized, that's the word I'm looking for. They want our community to be atomized.

\* \* \*

I rip off my index card as they announce the winner: Peter. A medium height guy with round glasses.

As a winner, he should be smiling and waving at us all like he's royalty. But instead he looks guilty, like smog is pressed against his face. His eyes are droopy. He regrets what he did. But he wanted some pleasure in this sullen, grey, life.

I understand him in some sort of weird-ass way.

He calls over a tall, pretty girl with long silky hair whom I haven't noticed before. General Wilson shakes their hands, beaming. And the three off them walk off together, looking proud. She taught Peter well!

I'm glad I'm not him. I'm glad I didn't win.

But now I'm starting to regret it maybe just a tiny bit.

A vacation does sound nice.

But at what cost?

# 21

You know, like sometimes when you wake up early in the morning because you have to be somewhere at like three am? And you are so tired, but you know you have to go through your morning routine because you have to be at this place at three am?

And even though your mind is muggy, and you can't think, and the night still lingers on the fingers of your soul, you know you have to do this stuff, so your body just does it for you. Your body puts clothes on it, and you go to the bathroom. Your hands splash water on your face. You brush your teeth half asleep, probably not even doing a good job, but needing to feel like you are doing something right, and then you force yourself to go to the kitchen to eat some trail mix or a banana, and then you are out the door, and now you are at last fully awake and you're like: "Whoa. Did I just do all that while I was half asleep?"

Well, that's me, that's us, without the actually going out the door part. Like for us, we get ready, our bodies just going through the motions, and we repeat the day, wake up, get ready, do the motions of the whole day, and maybe from time to time, in a calm moment, we realize how long we've been here by looking at how long our hair has grown. You realize that it's been so long, and yet your body has just been doing everything for you, and you've become this robot, this null robot, just wandering around without a soul.

I am in the shower, washing the day away.

Today was "Physical Training," and it was very tough.

I sweated so much that I didn't need to pee all day today. All the liquid just escaped through my skin.

They made us do like a million push-ups and then a billion sit-ups and then burpees and then squats, and they made us run with wet backpacks filled with rocks, and it's kinda stupid in a way because they are only making us stronger.

But strength alone will not free us. They have forces that are far beyond our control. They are smart and have been planning how to keep us in their cages for a very, very long time. They are much older and better trained than we are.

My skin feels sore against the cold water, and I want to sit on the shower floor because my legs are sore and shaking from all the work.

I was never really that fit; that was more of Aimee's thing.

She was the one who went to the gym daily; she was the one who would always focus on keeping a fit and healthy body.

It was always so hard to keep up with her. But I enjoyed it.

I enjoyed my lungs burning and my loud panting and the spit flying from my mouth, I liked trying things with her. I liked pushing my limits for her.

It was fun to catch up with her.

I remember running with her on the Brooklyn Bridge. It was a hot day for spring, and all my clothes got drenched in my own sweat, but I got to spend it with her.

*The clouds are white and beautiful, the sky so blue and clear, the air with a tinge of pollution, but still breathable.*

*We decide to start on the Manhattan side of the Brooklyn Bridge, and it's pretty crowded, because today is Saturday.*

*The skyscrapers soar next to each other, each one glittering in the sun, each with its own unique wavy reflection of the East River below.*

*People cluster, blocking the walkway—mostly tourists with their fancy cameras and straps and their newest, latest edition phones—but we pass them as our slow walk turns into a jog.*

*It's easy, and I'm jogging right next to her, my hair whipping against the back of my neck. Strands of her beautiful long, wavy brown and purple hair fly from her almost tight braids. She has two braids, one on each side of her face, and it makes her look beautiful and adorable at the same time. She recently dyed her hair purple, but not all the way purple, as per my request. Because I love her black hair.*

*And we are listening to the same music, with two pairs of ear buds synched with one phone. Thank God for Bluetooth.*

*We are listening to "The Fame" by Lady Gaga. An old song, but it still resonates with the present world.*

*Our jog turns to a run, and my fists beat the air in front of me faster, and I feel acid soar through my lungs and explode in the pit of my stomach.*

*But I have to keep up with her so we can still listen to the same music.*

*She looks at me, "Ok?" she mouths. I give her a thumbs up.*

*She looks so sexy. Sweat has beaded on the top of her forehead, and her elastic bright green and pink top curves tightly against her breasts and smooths against her flat stomach.*

*And her leggings—light blue with dark blue spots scattered all over them in random places—are tight against her skinny legs, and oh, her butt, those leggings were made to show her perfect butt to the world. I just want to kiss her right now, but I can't.*

*We keep running and running. I bump into a couple. They look at me with anger in their eyes, but I keep running until they are just dots in the distance.*

*I am breathing through my mouth, which is wide open for flies to go in (except they don't), and my eyes are watery, and I feel the impact of the* ground on my feet, and I want to just sit down. But I don't because she keeps on running. She is like a machine.

A new song comes on that came out last month, called "Time Forever." It's by a new artist, Renee R'Noir. It's pop and fun to listen to.

We take a break, and she looks over at me, grinning. "You okay?"

"I. . . am. . . so. . . fine," I say through pants and huffs.

"We're halfway there, Seven!"

My eyes widen. "Halfway?"

She pokes my stomach, "Yes, halfway."

"Maybe we should just Uber the rest of the way," I smile.

"Come on, Seven, you got this. You just gotta push your body. Because you are capable of so much more than you realize."

"I feel like I might fall through the ground into the river," I say. My breath is even now, and I feel the dizziness slowly fade.

"That just means that you're running right."

"There's a right way for running?"

"Of course, there is. There is always a right thing for everything."

"There is always a *right* thing for everything," she once said.

During that beautiful day, she used her beautiful high-pitched voice to say that. And it lingered in the air for a couple of seconds, and. . . I took her for granted. . . I didn't know that'd be one of the last things she'd ever say to me.

I thought we had eternity.

I was stupid to think that it'd last forever.

I just didn't think she would die in a couple of seconds, and. . .

"There is always a *right* thing for everything."

Right vs. wrong.

There are always right and wrong people.

There are always the right and wrong choices.

She would hate me.

I am choosing the wrong path when I should be choosing the right path.

I am obeying these soldiers, these *people*, who are so sure they are right.

I am submissive to the people that killed her.

She would absolutely hate me for that.

But I can't risk Janice going to a *place* like this, a place that will tear her apart. She is strong, don't get me wrong. But she's ten. Her brain is still growing and developing. I am not an expert in neuroscience, but I know that if there's loads of trauma feeding into the cortex or whatever, the brain will be damaged. For the rest of her life, she will be traumatized, and she won't be able to *live* a normal life. I can't be the reason that she doesn't live a normal life. I don't know if she's like me; there was no evidence that I could see, but these people, *these* people—they will swallow her whole, no matter what. I can't let that happen. I won't.

# 22

It's another day. . . or week, I've so completely lost track of time that it doesn't even exist for me anymore.

I trudge to "Special Class." I don't want to go there. It's. . . it's making me believe things that I don't want to believe.

I don't have a choice.

I head to the back of the room, wanting to get these three long hours over with.

Mr. Adams is there, standing in front of the blackboard, in a crisp blue button-down and black pants. He must be hot. The weather has been getting humid and stuffy. I assume it's August, but because there's no way to tell for sure, I could be way off.

Written on the chalkboard in fine print is the word "Addiction."

Um, okay.

The past couple of classes have been about applying the attraction we learned in the other class to physical and sexual chemistry. It's been going in one ear and out the other, but I can't help it if some stuff sticks to my brain. I hope it's not affecting me, but I have no way of testing if their techniques really work. They don't allow any kind of same-sex relationship.

As the rest of the class files in, people in their usual attire, gloomy faces, I tend to my hair, which has been bothering me. It's been growing longer than I would have liked, and strands have been blocking my view. I twine the strands together and put them behind my ear. My hair has a mind of its own and goes back to where it wants to be. I wish they would allow haircuts here, but they don't for girls. Girls should have long hair and boys should have short hair is their motto, so yeah, I'm stuck.

I'm stuck like that piece of chip behind my wisdom teeth that I can't ever seem to get out.

Diana sits next to me, as usual, and a kid with a curved nose sits on the other side. I don't remember his name, but I know he's nice.

When the class is full, Mr. Adams clears his throat and looks around the room. "What is addiction?" he asks everyone.

A few people raise their hands, trained to be obedient.

He picks a girl with dark blonde hair and long bangs. "It's something that you always need but is not necessary for your survival. And the more you use it, the more you depend on it. And when you don't have it, you get irritable and can't control yourself."

"Good."

He picks a boy with light green eyes. "It's something that you can't stop having, something that you are always longing for. It's a severe mental disorder."

"Yes." He smiles. "What can you get addicted to?"

He calls on another girl.

"Alcohol, drugs."

"What more?"

He calls on the first girl again, the one with dark blonde hair.

"Online games, certain types of food."

He sighs. "None of you mentioned sex," he says. He sounds disappointed, like he taught us better!

I close my eyes for a second. I am so sick of this.

"Sex, masturbation, and porn. All forms of addiction, you see."

Ughhhhhhhhhhhhhhhhhhhhhhhh.

I keep my mask on, I don't want him to call on me. I just want to blend into the background and disappear.

"Today, we have a special guest," he says, and just as he says "guest," a man comes in. Maybe sixty years old or more, with a white mustache, a beige suit, and a brown briefcase, the man is standing tall and proud, like he's going to get a trophy or something. "This is Dr. Lawrence. He is a doctor specializing in addiction therapy and he helps people from all around the world live better, fuller lives without any need for whatever it was they were addicted to."

Dr. Lawrence nods at all of us.

Shivers come down my spine. Something about this does not look good.

"Now we only have three hours of his time today. So we can't use his full technique, but he does have a quick fix that might help some of you."

Mr. Adams nods at the doctor, who looks around at the front of the class and, after pausing for a moment of what looks like deep thought, says to a girl with pigtails, "Please, may I borrow your desk? Would you be so kind as to stand to one side for a moment?"

She nods quickly, confused at his politeness, and stands.

He pulls the desk to the front of the room, along with the seat it's attached to, and places his briefcase on it. He slowly unzips the briefcase, and inside, I can't really tell what's there because I'm so far in the back, but the girl with the pigtails gasps.

This is not good. I want to leave.

"What is your name, sweetie?" he asks pigtails. She is probably thirteen or fourteen years old. She reminds me of my sister. She doesn't deserve this. No one deserves this.

"My name?" Her voice is high and shaking. "A. . . Aiden."

"Aiden, what a beautiful name," the doctor smiles. "We have to get you fixed so you can live up to that name. Please resume your seat." From the briefcase he takes out a glass vial filled with little round bright pink pills, and he puts it on the desk in front of Aiden.

Back in the seat of her school desk, the girl is shaking. I can hear her teeth chattering.

"Don't be scared, Aiden. Everyone is going through with this process."

She doesn't stop shaking. His words don't help her.

I'm suddenly as scared for her as I am for myself.

She's too young for this, she didn't do anything wrong.

*I* didn't do anything wrong.

He takes out another glass vial, the same size as the first one, but the pills in this one are dark blue.

The girl looks like she is about to faint. Her face is pale, her forehead is dripping with sweat. I'm reminded of that time I went with Janice to get her ears pierced. Mom was working, of course, and I had to go with Janice. Usually they use piercing guns for this, but this time, I don't know why, they didn't. They used a needle. Janice gripped my hand hard, her eyes brimmed with terror, as the lady with the latex gloves pulled her ear with one hand, and pointed the needle inward, into the flesh. It was quick, in and out, but the pain was so intense and so sudden that Janice fainted. Her whole body was sweating and shaking, and she couldn't take it anymore. I quickly ran to buy soda because the lady told me she needed sugar, and when I came back, Janice was up already, and the needle was being stuck in her other ear. I almost fainted from the sight. She was only eight. . .

The girl, Aiden, is about to faint, but she sits up straight, rolls back her shoulders. She has determination, because she knows, if she does faint, pain will be the only thing that greets her when she wakes up.

Dr. Lawrence now takes an iPad from his briefcase and opens the cover. The screen glows. My eyes widen. Technology. I haven't seen that in. . . how long has it been?

I haven't had access to my phone, tablet, computer. . . I've forgotten that they existed. *How is that possible?*

He taps on the screen for a few seconds, and then from the briefcase he takes two small oval gadgets that look like they're made of rubber and wire. He approaches Aiden with these things in one hand and the iPad in the other.

"Stay still," he commands. She holds her breath and stays still as a statue. He places the weird oval things on both sides of her forehead, and they stick there. He taps on the tablet a couple more times, and the oval things buzz and flash green. "Okay, feel free to move."

She doesn't. She stays still, like if she moves, she'll die. It's a horror movie for her. It's a horror movie for all of us.

He goes to the person next to her, and says the same things, does the same thing he did with her, with another pair of oval gadgets. Meanwhile Aiden hasn't moved an inch. The doctor—is he even a doctor? He may have gotten some fancy degree at an Ivy League college, but he terrifies young girls. People who do that don't deserve that kind of title—Dr. Lawrence looks back at the girl. "You can move, sweetie, don't stay still like that, it's bad for your posture."

She unclenches her jaw and starts to loosen up but is still leery of the things attached to her forehead.

Row after row, with slow steps he goes, and I'm anxiously hoping he somehow ignores me, maybe, like maybe I'm invisible, or maybe I'm a ghost just watching this, maybe he'll give me special treatment? I gulp. Do I want special treatment? He's going to ask for something in return, that's always how it goes. I shiver.

It's Diana's turn and she says her name shakingly.

"Your *real* name, sir."

Diana swallows her pride; she doesn't have a choice. "Santiago," she says quietly. He nods in satisfaction and places the things on her forehead.

Then he's right there, in front of me, looking at me with those deadly eyes. I shake, I really shake. . . This. . . this can't be happening to me.

He takes out those mysterious oval things, and close up, I see the red and black wires vividly—almost suspended in the rubber, somehow, where the rubber is transparent and light blue at the same time. I've never seen this kind of technology before. What more has the government been developing in secret?

He is about to place one on the right side of my forehead, right on the temple, but I flinch back. "Maia, you have to stay still." Did I tell him my name? I don't think so. He *knows* about me. I think I've made a name for myself.

"What is that?" I ask him.

He doesn't seem shocked that I talked back to him. He almost seems pleased.

"It's just going to monitor your brain waves," he says simply. "*This* won't cause you permanent damage."

Before I can say anything else, he clasps the things on both sides of my forehead.

They feel sticky and cool against my skin, and he taps on his iPad, and I feel them warm a bit, and that's it. Nothing else happens. He goes to the next person, and the next.

He heads to the TV that's always at the front of the class, with a disk player on the top, and he turns it on. There is a picture of a simple bedroom, with white linen sheets on the bed, and a purple pattered carpet. There's a wooden door in the back, painted orange, and through a couple of windows on one side you can just barely see that we are in a city with small, old fashioned looking buildings.

"This type of immersion therapy has been proven successful all around the world," he says proudly. "I've been using it for the past couple of years—so do not worry, it won't change things that we do not want changed. It will only cure you or continue the curing process. *Or it may begin to start the process of curing if that has not happened to you yet.*"

What is this? *What is he going to do to us?*

"I want you to watch these two videos, fully, each one is *only* five minutes. And *you have* to watch them, or. . ." He looks at Mr. Adams. "Or we will take the necessary corrective steps! Got it?"

We all nod, scared of the unknown.

"Let all your emotions flow, that's all right. I don't want you to suppress *anything*. Got it? This is the one time that we let all your sinful desires play out like this. Understood?"

We nod and nod and I don't. . . and I nod and nod.

The lights dim and he presses play and then he leaves the room, still carrying his iPad, followed by Mr. Adams. The doors close. Dr. Lawrence has left his briefcase behind. I could run forward and grab it, I think, maybe there's a gun inside, surely this man would have a gun. But of course I don't dare move. Like everywhere else, there are cameras in the corners, watching us, even in the dark like this with their infrared high-definition cameras.

The video playing on the screen is vivid, shot in high-definition, with a light playful tune playing in the background.

Two men in just their boxers enter, with their abs glistening, their hair combed and gelled back. And then two women in fancy, almost see-through flamingo pink and dark red lingerie come in.

And. . . I'm forced to watch. . .

Porn. Specifically gay porn. Girl on girl. Guy on guy.

Both couples are on the bed, on different sides.

Performing at the same time, next to each other, panting and moaning. Out of the corner of my eye, I notice the others shifting uncomfortably as they try to control their reactions, it's been such a long time since. . . I try to create a blank canvas in my mind, now that I maybe have a clearer understanding of what this is, this *experiment*. He's seeing how our brains react or something. . .

I try to distract my mind with other images. Have my eyes stare at the screen but think of something entirely different in my mind. I think of my grandma. I think of puppies in a basket. I think of the NYC subway— inside the cars, the bright yellow and orange on the 1 train. Anything but people fucking. Anything but the moans. Anything but the fake pleasure screaming out of their lungs. . . but. . .

I fail. Like I always do with everything.

The screen changes to a different scene. A different bedroom, but simple like the last one. The bed on the opposite side, a quilt with yellow daises draped over the end of the bed.

This time a different man and a different woman come in, they looks slightly different from the first ones, but of similar age, and they are skinny, super model types, the lady with a big butt and big boobs, the man with tough, glistening abs. . .

They begin to have sex, and it's brutal, and I don't want to watch anymore. . . it's like watching a hippo taking a shit or something. I don't want to watch; I really don't want to watch. But I know if I look away, if I just glance one way, *they* will know. And I will be punished. And I can't afford to be punished.

Soon the ten minutes are up, the video stops, and the lights go on. Dr. Lawrence comes strutting in, looking down on his iPad, nodding along to something. Mr. Adams follows and closes the door behind him.

The "doctor" looks around at all of us. His eyes dart to mine, as if I did something wrong. But, I didn't. . . *right*? I don't know what I'm capable of anymore.

"Okay. If your names are called, please stand up," he says, his tone even.

"Marissa."

A girl with really long brown hair stands quickly up.

"Cameron."

A girl with a scar next to her mouth stands up.

"Rebecca, Jeffrey." And he continues rattling a bunch of names, and people are standing, worried.

I'm relieved that my name wasn't called, but I look at Diana, whose name wasn't called either, and she looks really scared. This isn't good. The people standing up did something that we didn't. And they aren't being punished, or what?

"You may go," Lawrence says. "Please return my devices to me as you leave. You may drop them in the briefcase here, if you would be so kind."

Relief washes over their faces, and some glance sympathetically at those of us who are still sitting, but most just quickly leave, peeling the oval things from their foreheads and dropping them in the briefcase that sits open on a table by the door. As they rush out, Mr. Adams calls after them, telling them they can take a nap in their cabins, like they are little kids.

Once the last of them has skittered out, I am desperate to stand and quickly follow, maybe I can get away with running away, maybe. . . but I know I can't. Especially now, when Lawrence is staring at me. He looks at me, pity streaking the folds of his face. No, I don't want him to pity me! Like what the fuck, there's no need to pity me. Stop giving me those watery eyes, stop looking at me like that. *Stop it.*

Lawrence looks at Mr. Adams. "Can we get some water please?"

Mr. Adams nods and quickly leaves the room.

I look around. There are about ten of us.

Diana is there, and I know she's just as scared as I am.

Mr. Adams comes back with a package of small plastic water bottles.

"Thank you so much." Lawrence takes the bundle from Mr. Adams and places it next to his briefcase. He pokes a finger in the plastic wrapping and peels it quickly off. He rolls up the plastic and tosses it into a wastebasket in the corner of the room. He peers at his iPad, which is laid now beside the bottles of those colorful pills.

"Maia," he calls out and looks at me. "Come over here, please."

I look at him, my eyeballs feel like they will fall out of my head. My legs start shaking up and down, rattling the desk above them.

"Don't worry, I don't bite."

I don't want more pills *in my body*, pills that I have no idea what is in them. I don't want my chemistry or my brain or the whatever in my body changing. They already make us take pills in the morning, and I'm not really sure what those are doing. Probably changing my mindset about this place quietly, making me *like* it more or something. Or have they been altering my hormones? Like some sort of birth control? Are these things some kind of drug that's supposed to make me happier, even though I don't actually feel happy? It's too hard to figure out what they really do, because I'm just living life, experiencing as it is, and I have no idea, I don't even remember what I was like before this. Has my *consciousness* changed?

"Would you like me to invite the soldiers in, to escort you here?"

I shiver and quickly stand up. I don't want them to touch me.

I walk to Dr. Lawrence, one foot in front of the other, almost tripping over myself. He looks at me and smiles. "You, Maia, really, *really* need help," he says simply. handing me a water bottle. Then he opens up the glass vial with the dark blue pills and takes out five of them and places them on my shaking palm. I'm afraid they're going to roll off and drop to the ground.

"Please take them, now," he commands.

"What is in them?"

"Just something that'll help you."

"What do they do?"

"You'll see, Maia." I look at him, I want to challenge him more. I can't be compliant. I can't do this anymore. I can't. . . But I know I have to follow his instructions. For myself, for Janice. . .

Aimee would be ashamed.

I put them all in my mouth, unscrew the bottle, and drink the water with the pills, washing them down whole. Letting the unknown substance swirl down my throat and into my stomach.

He asks me to open my mouth and I do so, sticking my tongue out. He checks to see that I really swallowed them and then satisfied says, "You may sit."

So, I walk back, water bottle in my hand, to my desk. . . and I feel the same. Nothing has changed, but of course, pills don't work that quickly. Right?

I sit down and he calls another person, and another, and they do as he says. Are they following his instructions obediently because I did? Do I really have that much influence around here? I don't know.

I notice that he gives them three dark blue pills or less. Why did I receive five of them? He must have been watching our reactions somehow on the iPad, and depending on the reactions, that's how many pills we get. But do more pills mean that I had the biggest reaction or the smallest reaction to the clips? What does this mean?

And soon, everyone is sitting down again, still wearing the oval devices on our foreheads, and he looks at us. "Okay, now you will be watching a longer clip. Whatever you do, watch it. And do not do anything else. You may want to look away, or do *something other* than watching, but. . . these are my instructions, and if you don't follow my instructions with 100% dedication, then. . . we will have no choice but to *chastise* you. And remember." He smiles. "This is for your own good. We are curing you. We are cleansing you of your sins." He turns on the TV screen, tapping away at it, and he turns off the light and leaves again with Mr. Adam, who closes the door behind them.

Three beautiful women are sunbathing next to a glittering blue pool with some plastic colorful floaties drifting about. A large fancy Hamptons type house stands behind them, white and glowing with prosperity. A large white fence encompasses the pool and sunbathing area. And next to the pool, on the grass lawn are two men tossing a football back and forth to each other. Some pop music plays quietly in the background.

"Heyyy I have an idea," one of the women, glowing with almost golden skin and silkily black hair perfectly combed says, "let's fuck."

Oh, great, another porn movie.

The men drop their football and head to where the women are. And they all start kissing each other aggressively.

A blonde woman, with a bright pink bikini and a stomach that is paper thin, goes to the golden-skin woman and starts kissing her. And the other woman watches the two women kissing and begins touching herself.

It's hot. But. . . I feel something bubble in my stomach, like an acid volcano is erupting in the pit of my stomach. I feel uncomfortable in my body, the skin feels saggy and cold. My bones are sore, a banging shatters my brain.

The porn movie continues. And I don't want to watch it anymore.

I feel like vomiting, but nothing comes out.

I feel like falling asleep, but I am not allowed to sleep. I want to leave, but I'm not allowed to leave this room. I have to watch.

They continue kissing hard and touching each other and moaning and panting.

The acidic volcano grows larger and larger, exploding and erupting. My stomach feels inside out, I feel weak in my limbs.

His gross. . . thing. . .

Her boobs bobbing up and down.

And. . . now I know what this therapy is. Somehow. . . he's trying to condition my mind, my body, to believe that this discomfort and pain is the result of watching gay porn.

It's trying to suppress my libido, making me feel that my sexual attraction to same-sex sex creates discomfort and pain. And also vice versa. That this discomfort and pain creates the sexual attraction I have toward women.

And is it working?

I don't know. I don't feel hot or turned on by the women anymore. I just don't want to watch them anymore. I try switching my eyes to the men fucking, but I still feel that disgusting rage inside me, threatening to destroy me from the inside.

I feel like fainting. . . and yet this goes on and on and on and on.

Nothing is possible, everything is possible, the pain and discomfort grows and grows and grows. I feel like my body is attacking my body, I feel like the muscles inside my throat are strangling my windpipes. And then I feel a hot, searing pain all over my skin. Hot and itchy and it feels like my skin is peeling. I look down at my hands for a second. They are fine, the usual dirty skin of my hands, the broken chipped fingernails.

My lungs are shrinking and shrinking and shrinking and I can't breathe. I can't breathe. My heart burns, and burns, and I can't. . . I want to faint, I want to fall asleep and never wake up. But I can't. I can't leave. I can't close my eyes.

All I can do is hear the fake moans, see the sweat on the inside of their thighs, watch as their faces reach that tipping point. . . and I hate it. I hate it all.

And in the back of my mind, I'm thinking. . . is this what it was like with Aimee? My memories of our past life are being altered almost. . . changed. . . for the worse.

I can't handle any more of this.

I don't know how long it's been, when finally Lawrence and Mr. Adams return, switch the lights on, and turn off the screen. Immediately, as my eyes adjust to the sudden brightness and the absence of the video, I feel better, my stomach feels calm, my lungs are normal. I can think clearly and there's no longer a burn coming from my heart. My skin feels cool and relieved. *Was it all just in my head? How is that possible?*

One boy, about my age, stands up immediately. He is sweating all over, and his face is contorted with rage. "You!" He points a light brown finger at Lawrence. "What the fuck is wrong with you? How could you do this to us?"

Lawrence sighs. "George, please return to your seat."

George doesn't sit. He looks around at us, pleading at us to join his little rebellion. And I want to stand up too and point my finger at this evil doctor.

But. . .

I can't. Me suffering like this ensures that Janice is safe, at home. Away from this horror. Away from this insanity.

Innocent, sweet Janice. There was once a time when I had to babysit her on a Friday night, on a *Friday* night out of all nights. When I could have been cuddled up with Aimee and my friends, watching some soapy drama, but my parents had a date night and the babysitter we usually have was sick.

So I took care of Janice. I forgot to make mac and cheese for the two of us, so we just had ice cream sundaes and chocolate chip cookies and sprinkles and popsicles. We were on a sugar high, having pillow fights, and listening to old pop music like "Call Me Maybe." Singing horribly along with Carly, dancing wildly to the music. "Hey, I just met you" and pointing at each other, "and this is crazy, but here's my number, so call me maybe!" making a telephone gesture by our ears at "call me."

We laughed and laughed until we couldn't breathe, we did each other's nails and I braided her hair, and she told me that when she got older, she wanted to do that.

She wanted to flounce around in her cute jean mini skirt, red blouse, dark pink lipstick and just hand out her number to cute boys she sees on the street.

I can't let anything happen to her innocence. A place like this *will* destroy her.

She's too young. Nothing bad can happen to her.

Because if something bad does happen to her, she will never recover.

And my parents will not only have to deal with one destroyed girl, but two destroyed girls. . . I can't let that happen to them. They are the bestest of parents that sacrificed so much for us to have a happy life. I can't bear to see them see Janice, broken, hair frayed, dark bags under her eyes. . . I'm shaking.

I look at George, he is pleading with me silently, staring at me with innocent eyes like Janice's, and I shake my head. What's the point? Rebelling only means we will be punished, and those we care about destroyed. What do you gain from trying and failing? What do you really gain in a kind of situation like this?

"I'm sorry," I mouth at him.

"Sit back down, George," Lawrence says steadily.

George looks around, come'on, come'on, he's probably thinking, but everyone here has something, someone to lose, even George probably has someone back home. . . and I see it in his face as he realizes there's no point, the hope inside him dies out as he slowly sits back down, staring at the ground.

"Good." Lawrence rubs his hands. "Now, how was that experience for everyone?"

People raise their hands and answer, each phrase or word the same: "horrible," "disgusting." And Lawrence nods, proudly. His special whateverthefuck cocktail pill worked. No wonder he has a 100 percent success rate.

"This is great. It's working. Now!" He picks up the vial of the bright pink pills and looks around the room. "Now, for the reward." He calls me and I quickly come with my water bottle. He hands me ten bright pink pills and I swallow them with the water, not all at once of course, I swallow five and then five more. He checks me, and then has me sit down. He repeats the process to everyone else in the room, and leaves with Mr. Adams, the lights turn off, and a video clip plays on the TV screen.

This time, a pretty young girl and a thirty something year old man are sitting on some fancy rooftop, overlooking the city lights and skyscrapers. I recognize the Empire State Building and immediately think of home.

Of the city that never sleeps, where at night, my lullaby would come from the open window, the cars honking and drunk people hollering, creating a nice, soothing rhythm. It's calming, thinking of home, but the image of home is immediately ruined by the couple or whatever kissing on a lawn chair, the man's hands under her tight orange skirt.

I feel a bit dizzy but focus on the footage in front of me.

And then their clothes are off, the night air rustling the girl's hair, and his penis throbbing. . .and I don't feel disgusted by it like I usually did in the past videos.

The girl smiles, and I feel like smiling with her.

Butterflies are flying in my stomach; each flutter of their wings sends a wave of pleasure throughout my whole body.

I feel giddy, joyful happy, I'm in Candyland and I find myself smiling, I feel my eyes enlarging, glued to the TV screen, watching them. . . watching their bodies joyfully join together, in harmony, becoming as one!

My teeth are showing in my wide smile. I don't think I've smiled like this in such a long time. . .

The moans are loud and beautiful. . .like a church choir. I feel my nipples harden, and. . . I'm wet?

I look down, I didn't pee or anything. . . I. . .

I shake my head and turn back to the screen. My heart races a million beats per minute, I find my hand dragging toward between my legs, but have enough force to not do that here in public. When I'm in the shower, I'll think back to this glorious rooftop sex scene and. . .

WHAT IS WRONG WITH ME.

THIS CAN'T BE HAPPENING.

Those horrid thoughts wash away and away and away and away, and all that's left is candy and bright colors, and sunsets, and cake frosting, the smell of lemon and lavender and Mister Softee's ice cream. . . my mouth waters as I stare at the man's beautiful pure lips. I look around, and I see the others, just like me, enthralled and seduced by the video. They are tempted to touch themselves, but do not. Still aware of everyone around them and the cameras watching.

I am in love.

\* \* \*

The lights rise, and immediately I regret everything that I felt, everything that I almost did, all the emotions. . . all the. . . what the hell is wrong with me? What was in those pills that made me love it all? And what happens when I'm not on the pills and I see something like this? Will I still become addicted to it?

Dr. Lawrence nods at all of us, like a proud parent who just taught his kid how to ride their bike for the first time. Without training wheels of course.

And this is not the end.

The whole process gets repeated.

The pain with gay porn.

The pleasure with straight porn.

I'm revolted at what I *should* love.

And I'm drooling over something I've always hated.

What is wrong with me?

\* \* \*

The grueling three hours are over. I quickly leave the room, without looking back. Diana follows close behind me.

We have like very little time before we have to go to the next thing on our schedule. I have work and Diana has "Rigorous Training."

"You okay?" I ask her.

"I'll be fine," she replies, "You?"

I pause. I don't know how I am. I'm just so confused. Thank God that's the last time we'll see Dr. Lawrence. He said he'd be busy elsewhere, where he has many other patients he needs to "save." But despite the fact that we won't ever see him again, I still feel like whatever he did left a permanent mark on me. It's a tattoo that changes and shifts with my emotions, overriding my basic human rights.

"I don't know," I say, shaking. I look at Diana, her pretty eyes, her black hair short. She's so pretty. . . I feel something in the back of my throat, threatening to burst in tiny, glass shards. . . "I should go," I mutter, and I run to the laundry building. I don't look back. I can't look at anyone today.

I pass by the trees in the hot, dry, summer heat, and I don't know how to feel anymore. I feel. . . I am gross, and at the same time I feel relieved. Relieved that the class is over, that what happened will never happen again. . . that the only people to see my reaction to those videos were the people in the room and whoever might have been watching through the security cameras.

My parents, my family, Janice will never see what kind of person I've become here, or like. . . they'll see the result of this place—but they won't see what *actually* happened to me. . . I don't know. I'm shaking my head, rubbing my face, moving my stupid hair out of my face, when I bump into Crystal.

"Oh, hey Crystal," I smile as we walk to the laundry building.

"Hey," she almost whispers.

"Are you okay?" I question, the sun shines brightly and bounces against her blonde hair.

"Yeah," she says.

I turn to her, and step in front of her, blocking the way. She looks at me. Tears are all over her face. "What's wrong?"

Crystal eyes the soldiers. I make a point not to actually touch her, and just laugh, making it look like we are just having a healthy banter.

"Nothing," she moves around me, and heads in front of me. The laundry building becomes louder as we are closer to it. I walk toward her fast, and we see the other kids from the previous shift exit the building.

Ruby, a girl with a small face and acne along the bridge of her nose looks at me. "We just put some stuff in the dryer," she tells me.

"Thanks," I smile.

We enter the stuffy room, and immediately begin sorting the dirty clothes into darks and whites. Two more kids should be coming soon and helping us.

I dig my hand in the dirty laundry basket and begin sorting. My hands find something squishy, and I pull it out. Some gross, brown stuff on someone's underwear. Yuk.

I quickly toss the dirty underwear in the trash can and slather my hands in laundry soap and find a half empty water canister and hurry outside and begin washing my hands with the old water. One of the soldiers eyes me and smirks. I ignore him and continue cleaning my hand. I rub my hands against the dry grass and bring them to my nose to check if it's still there. It still smells disgusting.

Crystal comes out with a piece of wet rag. "Here, let me help."

I stand up and she takes my dirty hand and begins to rub my hand with the rag which seems to have more laundry soap then I used. The soldier walks toward us. "No touching!"

"I'm just cleaning her fucking hand, OKAY!" Crystal yells.

He stops abruptly, clearly shocked. He shakes his head, and just watches us silently. She is an innocent girl who never curses.

My hands feel nice as she continues rubbing it hard, making sure all the molecules are gone. Then she takes out a water bottle, with what looks to be clean water and pours it over my hands. I rinse well, and she takes a handkerchief from her pocket and hands it to me.

"Thanks," I say.

"Yes, of course. Can't let you clean clothes with dirty hands," she whispers. I have a feeling she's not only talking about laundry. We head back inside.

I'm glad I've got a good friend I can rely on.

# 23

We don't ever get a break. There's no vacation, no rest day. . . nothing. . . it's a never-ending cycle because they think the best way to "cure" us is to relentlessly push our limits, routine after routine, change after change.

They think that if we go through these ordeals enough times, we will break.

I feel like it's working.

# 24

The next week, at breakfast, I am a bit late, and the noise is as usual, the chaotic music of voices.

I sit at my usual spot with my friends, and they all seem sad and are not eating their food. I'm hungry, so I dig in right away.

I look at everyone. I'm sitting between Penelope and Yola. Sam, Jade, and Diana are sitting across from me.

I swallow the bite of powdered eggs and it goes slowly down my throat. I drink some water. Much better. "What's going on?" I mumble. I look at everyone. "Where is Crystal?"

No one says anything.

Did something happen to her? Is she being punished? "What's going on?"

Sam looks at Diana. "Tell her what you told me."

Diana shakes her head; she looks like she is going to vomit. She breathes slowly. I wish someone could just tell me already and rip off the Band-Aid.

"What is it?" I look around, my eyes getting wet. I look down at my food and want to eat, but not before they say something.

"Crystal was in my cabin. She worked the early shift before breakfast, helping to prepare the food and so forth."

I freeze. She "was," she "worked"?

"She. . . she left early as usual, but after her shift, we usually meet up before breakfast here, just to chat a bit."

"Okay. . .So. . ."

"She didn't show up today."

"What happened?"

"She killed herself, Maia," Diana says, her voice clear, but what she said cannot be true. It cannot be true, so it becomes wavy and wobbly in my mind.

"What are you *talking* about? She probably. . . just got taken by the soldiers to be interrogated or something."

"I saw a body bag being pulled from the bathroom by the kitchen," Diana says. She rubs her face hard so that it becomes red and puffed. "I talked to the others at the station. They said she went in the bathroom and was there for a long time. They assumed she had an upset stomach or something, but when the soldiers pounded the door, and there was no response, they opened the bathroom using a special key, and there was blood everywhere."

My eyes widen. No, she can't be dead. She. Just. Can't. I just saw her. She was here, yesterday, at dinner. We were just having a normal conversation, as if we were a family. A family that's going through struggling times. She seemed fine. She seemed. . . There was no indication that she would have wanted to end her life.

"There must be a mistake." But everyone shakes their head. I know they are telling the truth. They must have discussed this before I arrived. She was just preparing break—I feel the eggs in my stomach, and I feel the acid building up around the eggs, and I feel it coming back through my digestive system to my mouth. I swallow it back down. I don't want to make a scene.

"How. . ."

"We. . ." Sam shakes his head. "We think she must have grabbed the kitchen knife and slit her wrists. The bleeding must have been so bad that they couldn't do anything to save her, even if they *did* want to save her."

"But. . . why?"

"Why do you think, Maia?" Yola snaps. "It's because of this place. This place must have *gotten* to her."

I stop eating. I don't feel like eating.

To think this food was being cooked in the same place where Crystal grabbed the knife and went to the bathroom—just like that. How did she even get the knife, wasn't anyone watching her, didn't the guards see? Or maybe they were okay with letting her die . . one less person to look after.

She was right. She never did get to "leave" this place, maybe she left when she died. But she never got to leave this place alive.

My eyes are boiling, they hurt so much. I haven't blinked in a while, and they are so dry even though I feel like crying a waterfall. My fingers are shaking and the acid in my stomach is burning through my insides.

She was so innocent. So kind, with her beautiful, blue eyes. She had so much potential.

She wanted to be a doctor, specifically an ER doctor. She wanted to save lives.

All she did to end up here was like girls. She didn't even act on her crushes. She just had the crushes and told others about them. She was never in a relationship. She had never even kissed a girl or had sex with a girl. She just felt something toward girls.

Just because of that, she was thrown in this fucked-up prison and labeled and paraded around like a goat, and spit on and told that she was dirty.

First Aimee, then Conor and Alyssa, then my soul, then Crystal.

I have no idea when this will end. I don't even know if it even began. Are all these tortures just a start? Who knows how much more they have up their sleeves? I don't know if this is the beginning, middle or end. I don't I don't know if this is. . . what have I become? What are they doing to me?

Who am I really? How am I supposed to know myself truly if who I thought I was is *wrong* to society, is *wrong* to the authority—to the people in charge telling me I'm wrong, telling me my mindset is wrong, telling me that everything I am and everything that I am made out of is not right, but I really did believe that I was right. But now, I don't even know if that part of who I was—I don't even know if I can trust myself to know myself completely. How can I rely on myself? How can I become somebody if I can't even trust who I am? If I can't even trust who I thought I was.

I don't know anymore, and this new change in me or realization, this reckoning, is an act of betrayal to my dead girlfriend. She would have never let anyone change her—she was resilient; she had purpose. Nothing could stop her except death.

She is dead because she refused to follow these arbitrary rules, ridiculous laws, these soldiers who thought that they were in the right, and she was in the wrong. If she hadn't died on the bus, she would have died here. She wouldn't have put up with this. She would have died like Conor and Alyssa.

And I—and what is left of who she is—of who she was, I knew her completely. The memories we shared together are her, so me changing who I am is in fact also changing who she was and what she left on this planet, and she would hate me for that. She would hate that I'm changing—that I am complying with *these* rules. That I am following these people who make absolutely no sense at all but yet make sense to the people who are in charge.

I can't live with myself.

If I am letting myself be changed. I am tarnishing her memory. I am tarnishing what she loved on this Earth.

I'm gonna end up like Crystal. I know it. I am too weak to keep living and stabbing who I love—loved—in the back. I don't know how I'm gonna do it, or where I'm gonna do it, or when I'm gonna do it, but I know I am gonna do it.

Maybe Crystal was right. Maybe she did the smart thing. She removed herself from the equation. She chose to die. She chose to leave this place on her own terms, not being changed, not turned by the tyranny. She rebelled against them by breaking their rules and choosing to die.

Now she doesn't have to witness others being hurt.

Now she doesn't have to be in pain.

Now she no longer has to be ashamed of her feelings.

She is finally free. That's all we've ever wanted.

To be free.

And *me*. . . maybe in freedom, I can join Aimee wherever death sends us. Even if those biblical freaks are right, and gays go to hell, then maybe I can be in hell with her. I can spend eternity in pain, but I will get to be in her arms every night—well, if hell does have a night; I'm not really sure how that works. I'll figure out a *way*.

It is so tempting to just end things here, so very tempting. It's like standing on the edge of a cliff and looking at the landscape before you, at the shiny, glittery rush of water at the bottom, and the very blue sky with hints of white, fluffy clouds, at how big everything looks, the vast pile of rocks right at your fingertips. . . the temptation to just jump and have that feeling of the wind rushing past you—as if you are flying, and then, the world will end in your eyes—your mind will black with a glitter of stars. . . and then you will be nothing. You will be merely a body, without a pumping heart and a without set of lungs that expand and contract. You will be a mass of cells, and blood will stop, and you will be at the bottom of some crevice, or being pushed by the heavy river currents, or you will be eaten by some animal that thanks the Gods for sending them a meal from the sky.

It is so tempting, so very tempting, and I just. . . I just. . .

I just want to jump.

But I can't leave my family. . . my friends. . . my new friends. . . my life. . . my future. . . my hopes and dreams. I have so much going on, even if I'm stuck in this never-ending, fucked-up world.

Eventually, we'll be let out. Yes, we have to go through the toughest things we will ever experience in our lives. We will be tortured to be "normal," we'll be cured or whatever. But we will get to live our lives again. It won't be our lives, but we will get to live some kind of life. And maybe things will change back. Eventually.

Or maybe. . . just maybe. . . maybe. . . we can get out earlier. No, not by "curing" ourselves in six months. But byleaving this place—by. . . *escaping*.

They want us here, but why do we have to do what they say? Why do we have to follow their commands? Why are they the boss of us? Why are they the boss of me?

If we escape. . . we can save our families and then. . .

We will be free. And we can spend our time in hiding, waiting for the government to wake up and realize how much pain they are causing, or there will be a new President. . . or we can help others escape and rebel against these evil people. Make the change. Make it like our ancestors, our *gay* ancestors, did. I don't know. There are so many possibilities. And I know I'm just trying to talk myself out of it, but I know I have to live. I have to live. I have to live for not only my life and the living people in my life; I have to live for those that died. Because If I don't live, then they'll just be corpses.

I have to make their life worth something.

That means I have to live.

But I can't, I won't continue *this* kind of life.

This life where I am changing and betraying my one love in this world.

So now I am left with three options.

**One.** I continue living while being changed and end up killing myself.

**Two.** I can try and escape and maybe fail. Janice will be punished for my actions, but at least I tried, and I'll be able to live with myself.

**Three.** I escape and succeed. I will hide Janice somewhere, and I will live life knowing that Aimee is looking from wherever she is right now, beaming with pride—knowing that I did the right thing.

In the beginning, I had no choice.

But now, I have a choice.

My parents are not going to save me. It's been forever. And nothing has happened. I'm sure they're working really hard, and I don't blame them for the fact that whatever they're doing is *not* working. Because I know they are trying their best. I know it in my heart.

I wish I could rely on them longer, hold out onto hope that they *will* save me *soon*. But it hasn't happened yet. And I see no evidence that they will succeed in getting me out of here in the future.

So right now, the now is all I have.

I have to rely on myself to get out of this mess.

I have to escape.

I hope that I can escape.

And not just "I," anymore. It must be "We."

# 25

We have to escape.

I don't know how, or when, or what, or who, but I do know *why*.

I think of home, but *that* only brings pain. Pain, so unimaginable, and I can't. . . I can't. . .

It's a gunshot to my heart.

I'm here in this fucking place because of what I did and wanted to be in my life.

Because I was open about my life.

Because I barely had any secrets and expressed myself freely in front of others.

I resent myself for it. And I hate myself for resenting myself. And I hate that I hate that I resent. It goes on and on and on.

I fall into this loop, this loop of self-hatred and hating myself for hating myself, and it repeats, and it's a downward spiral, and I don't know how to deal with it, I don't know how to think, I don't know how to deal with it, I don't know how to escape, because every time I do think about escaping this downward spiral, I think about hating myself over and over again. Hating myself that I can never have the strength to overcome this challenge, and I hate it so much, I absolutely hate it.

Is this what they want? Is this their goal, to make me hate myself so that I can become a new person?

*Does* this actually work?

*Can* this actually work on me?

I don't know. It seems to be working.

I don't want it to, but I've already lost myself, so I don't know what they're capable of doing.

The bell rings and I pick up my tray and put it in its proper place.

Penelope is next to me.

For a quick second, I lean into her ear and whisper: "We have to get out of here."

Her eyes widen, scared, and filled with uncertainty.

Before she can protest, I say one more thing to her, before giving her the good-enough distance that is *allowed* here.

"Look who we're becoming," I snap. "I already feel myself being brainwashed. I can't stand to be here longer and being even more brainwashed. I can't do that to myself, my family. . ." I stop and give her distance and time to think.

A thought stops me cold: But *how* will we escape?

We are trapped, and we are just teenagers, with no skills whatsoever. Maybe the most, almost criminal thing I have done is look on my phone in secret in high school, during class.

But how can that help me now?

I don't know what to do.

I'm not a hero.

I'm no leader.

I am just a seventeen-year-old girl, with no idea what life really is.

# 26

I have never been a leader before. I never had this much responsibility to take care of this many people before.

Okay, I was the captain of the basketball team in middle school, and I was in charge of some home science experiment with my friends during freshman year, and I was a planner for several awesome, epic dates with Aimee. But leading an escape from prison, that I have obviously never done, nor expected to do ever in my entire life.

I'm a rule follower. I don't see any point in breaking the laws to get a high, and I definitely don't see myself as committing a crime that would land me in prison. Probably protesting would be the highest level of resistance that I would reach in my life.

I didn't break any laws to be trapped in this prison camp, though. I just loved someone.

But no one seems to be doing *anything* here *anymore*, so it's my job to be the leader. And I am known for my rebellious bursts when I arrived here. And I'm flying under the radar because they think they've broken me.

And yes, they may have broken me, but they have also given me the tools of hope. To hope for a way out of here. To hope that there will be a life once I get out of here.

We'll probably be on the run, but anything, *anything*, is better than becoming someone we're not.

I've read some YA books, watched several TV shows and movies that have to do with breaking out of a prison. I know they're not reliable sources, but I have to try. I have to *do* something.

First thing: We need to have a gathering, in a secret place, of those who want to escape and who are capable of escaping.

The problem: there are no secret places.

They have made it impossible to gather where no one is watching. All I can do is just deliver whispers to the people I trust the most.

You never know who's going to betray you.

I am in the shower line, in front of Sam. It's dark outside and many of the soldiers that linger about don't really seem to be that focused on us. It's been a long time, and they have gotten used to the fact that we are *good little girls and boys.*

I turn and lean into his ear: "I'm gathering people to escape."

I can't see his face, but I'm gonna guess his eyes are widening right about now. "What?" he whispers back.

"You want in?"

The line moves forward.

"Yes."

"Spread the word. And we need to find a place to figure the details out."

"Got it."

Silence.

The line moves forward.

"Maia?"

"Yeah?"

"How are you going to pull this?"

"I don't know." I place my hand on his shoulder. "I don't know what I'm doing, Sam, to be honest."

He places his hand on my hand. "*They* don't know what they're doing either," Sam whispers, his breath like crickets dancing in my ear. "We have the advantage because they won't know what's coming."

The line moves forward, and we part. I smile at him, but I doubt he can see it.

\* \* \*

The next day, I catch Penelope, she says she's in, and I tell her to spread the word. She is scared, but I really trust her. I know she is capable of handling this.

\* \* \*

Over the next week, word has spread. It goes around slowly, but we want to be careful. It's better to be safe than sorry.

Sam found a place where we can meet in private. He spread the word to everyone on our team.

It's during movie night.

Usually, everyone "good" is gathered where orientation was and has buttery popcorn and watches some boring rom-com movie.

It's a reward.

If you don't have any offenses on your record, you get to go to movie night.

But if you *do* have some offences, you have to go back to your cabins and sleep, knowing you are definitely missing out on these fabulous movies.

I've been sitting through *Titanic*, *A Man and a Woman*, *The Lake House*, *You've Got Mail*, and more.

I've never liked those kinds of romantic movies. They are so unrealistic and unconvincing. Like why watch a movie that doesn't convince you it's real? How can I escape into a world when there's a blaring sign that says: "This is fiction"?

I've been trying to teach myself to sleep with my eyes open. It takes a lot of work. You have to just stare at a point in the room and just focus on it, not trying to blink at all. And then you stop focusing on what's in front of you, and you roll your eyes inward so they're facing your brain, and eventually you space out.

Haven't gotten there yet, but I hope I won't have another chance to do try it again.

I hope this escape can work so I can never have to act like I am having a *good* time.

The others already have offenses on their record.

I pissed a soldier off yesterday—I made a crack about his ugly face, thinking he couldn't hear me, but he did hear—and now I have an offense on my record, and I'm banned from the movie.

I am in the cabin. Sam is there as well. Normally there's always a soldier sitting there, reading his magazines, but tonight he's nowhere to be seen. I'm guessing he's at the movie.

I get off my bunk and I quickly head to the bathroom and shower area. There are no cameras there.

Diana, Penelope, Jack, and Yola are there already, talking quietly to each other. Their eyes are wide, and they motion me to come over.

Jack and I have reconciled. He knows where my head space was, back when his friends died in front of him.

He's a warrior. Attempting to escape, again, even after who knows what kind of torture he had to face.

I nod at him.

They make room for me to lean on the wall. I'm next to Penelope. Black bags sag under her eyes, and her hair is frayed and split.

"Thanks, guys," I say, my voice shaking as if there is an earthquake in the center of my throat.

"So, Maia," Jack says. "You have some sort of plan or are you just winging it?"

I don't know what to say.

I have been winging it.

I open my mouth to say something, but nothing comes out.

"She got us together, that's what matters," Sam says as he enters.

The team is almost together. He stands in front of the toilet doors and faces us.

"Yeah, but it'll all be for nothing if we just don't think of anything *good*."

"I. . . was hoping some of you had ideas," I say. "I wasn't thinking about the next steps. I'm. . . I. . ." I look at the ground. Penelope grabs my hand and squeezes it. I look up at her and smile. She is very pretty here, weirdly, because the lighting is very bad. It's just the typical plastic kind of light that is on the ceiling.

Jade, the last one of our team, enters, tiptoeing, and stands across from Sam.

Her eyes are clear, and she nods at me.

And before we continue discussing whatever we were discussing, Jade speaks up: "Someone else is coming."

"Who?" Sam questions. They all eye her, trying to figure out who she brought, if they can trust this new member of the team.

"His name is Zach, and he should be here any minute now," Jade says.

And then a tall, lanky dude with sharp, dark eyelashes and slick black hair that fits on his head perfectly enters. His eyes are dark gray, his nose perking upward, and his lips full. He has an olive shade to his skin. He looks like he could be a model, or maybe he *is* a model.

I remember him instantly. I had to insult him at the name-calling game.

We make room for him, even though we are cramped already.

"Hey, everyone." He sets his eyes on me, and I look at my feet. He is attractive; I would know what to say about him if we had to do the weird hetero practice together because those eyelashes and lips are obviously sexy, but I don't see myself with him in a million years. He's a guy. Simple, right? "You must be the Maia everyone is talking about."

I roll my eyes and look at him and then look at Jade. "Who is this guy?"

"I think he'll help us with our plan," Jade tells me, then she looks at him. "Zach, tell them what you know."

"My parents sent me a letter. They coded it very carefully so that those pricks wouldn't cross things out," Zach says, his eyes finding each of us. "They knew I'd understand the code because cryptography is my hobby. Basically, the letter said that there is a group outside that is trying to help us get out. They are a radical organization made up of many people with different occupations who are willing to break the law to help us. Unlike other organizations that think protests and lawsuits will work."

I nod. This is what we need; this is the breakthrough we need to get out of here.

Why didn't *my parents* do anything? Why didn't they contact this organization and send a code through the letter? Were they afraid of getting caught?

No. They must have had a reason. Maybe they were trying to protect Janice as well. Maybe the risks were too high. They didn't want to lose the both of us.

Or maybe they were desperate to do something but just had no idea how.

Or maybe they *did* contact the group, maybe they *did* try everything that's humanly possible--but nothing worked. In a way, that's the worst possibility of all, because it means there's no hope.

"This organization can help us," Zach is saying, "but"—of course there is a but—"we have no way of communicating with them. They've tried communicating with us but have failed. We don't have access to technology anymore, so they've been trying many different techniques, sending messages with the food that comes in, attaching notes to pigeons, but nothing has gotten through."

"So, what?" Sam says. "Is there anything you can do?"

Zach closes his eyes and then opens them. I notice he fidgets with his hand. "Unfortunately, for now, there isn't a solution."

I cross my arms, disappointed.

"We might as well just quit now," Yola says, scratching her head where her dark hair is starting to grow back, from where they shaved it before because it was pink.

"We have people on the outside; that's got to be something," Penelope says, optimistic as ever.

"There. . . has to be a way. . ." I say, more talking to myself than to them.

"There might be a way," Diana says, her voice rising, and everyone looks at her for the oh, miracle-of-life answer. "I know this girl—no, guy—at my cabin." We all give her a confused look and she explains, "He identifies as a male, but is a *girl* according to the government. The name he calls himself is Lucas, but they call him Edith. And we think that he is pregnant. He has been getting the signs and is definingly chubbier than when we first got here. . ." I'm trying to wrap my mind around this new information, and it makes sense, kind of.

"Wait, what?" Yola creaks. "How. . . *why*?"

"A few weeks before the government brought him here, he was with his buddies, and they got attacked. When the attackers realized he was trans, they gang-raped him. He never talked about it to anyone, not to the police, not to his parents, and now, he can't even say *anything* now."

"That's. . . sad, but what does he have to do with our mission?"

"He has to go to the doctor, right, to get checkups and stuff? They can't do that here because they're not set up for it, and they wouldn't even think about not taking care of an unborn baby, because they're religious. . ."

"He can get a message out when he's at the doctor's office. He'd be out of this place," I finish for her, and she nods.

"Yes, that's what I'm thinking." She looks at Zach. "You think that could work?"

"Yeah, I think it could. He'd need to figure out how to communicate with the people from the organization, but I'm sure they'll think of a way. My parents' letter said they have people watching the camp all the time. Maybe they have someone in the hospital. That way we'd have a line of communication, and. . ." Zach smiles for the first time and it makes his eyes glow with life.

No. . . Why do I. . . are all those fucked up lessons really working? Have I really been brainwashed? Why am I feeling attracted to him?

They are making me think that I find him attractive, when really I don't find him attractive.

I have to get out of here before they mess up more of my mind.

We continue talking more about the details and the plan slowly begins to unfold.

Diana and Zach will tell Lucas about the plan, and hopefully he'll be on board.

This world seemed dark and hopeless and eternal.

But now, there are possibilities.

Possibilities.

Good things can finally happen.

# 27

The days go slow as we anxiously wait for Diana and Zach to ask Lucas to help us communicate with the outside world. I just go through the motions, hoping, hoping for something. I know hope is bad, because most of the time, when you hope and hope—you just end up getting disappointed and being disappointed hurts more than not hoping and expecting the worst. But I can't help but hope. Because hope is all I have.

# 28

I never really noticed Lucas before I heard of him.

But now I'm seeing him around the camp.

He must be feeling horrible, forced to carry a baby that is a constant reminder of his rapes, and even worse—he is forced to be someone he is not.

They make him wear a skirt; they make him grow his hair out and tie it in pigtails; they force him to smile and walk like a woman.

I see Diana and Zach with him, and they talk in hushed whispers. And I'm only hoping that they are telling Lucas the plan, and I hope he agrees to the plan. Yes, he is at risk of getting caught and punished, but he is vital to our plan.

And if he wants, he can escape with us.

To be honest, I'm not sure if he will want to escape.

He is pregnant and showing.

I'm not sure if I want him to come. He'll just slow us down. I just want to think of the goal at hand: everyone escaping. We have to act fast, and we can't have anyone dragging us down.

I know it's horrible of me to say that, but what else am I supposed to say? I have to think of the group and what's best for the group.

I shouldn't think too much about it. It's his choice.

\* \* \*

We meet again in our usual spot on Sunday. And finally, finally, there is good news.

Lucas is on board. He is part of our group now. He is going to try to help us communicate with the outside world. He has an appointment next week for an ultrasound, and hopefully, someone will come in contact with him.

Lucas looks miserable.

His hair has started to grow past his shoulders; he wears a long dress, with tight shoes, and you can already see the baby bump.

This is fucked up.

He was planning on getting an abortion, but the government picked him up before he could.

A new member of our crew, a transgender teen whose name is Clara, but forced to be someone she is not, Max, comforts Lucas.

When we become settled in the bathroom area, everyone looks at Lucas.

He looks up at us and starts to speak. He is very uncomfortable in his body. "I guess we should just skip all the formalities and get right to it." He nods and looks at each of us, who are sick with worry and afraid of getting caught. "So. I'm with you. What's next?"

We discuss the plan, tell him what he has to do.

We are crossing our fingers. There's a very slim chance that this could actually work, but we have to cling to the small things. Because there is nothing else.

We have to hope, because if we don't, then what's the point in living?

We have a bit of time before "lights out." The whole team—Lucas included—has discussed all we could of our escape plan, so we go back to our cabins one by one, so as to not raise suspicion.

Now it's just Lucas and I in the bathroom area. We are sitting next to each other, leaning against the wall.

He's attempting to tie a ponytail but his hands are shaking too much. "Here let me help." I tell him.

He turns around and I take his hair into a bundle and tie it into a decent ponytail with a hair tie he handed me.

"Hair is absolutely ridiculous," he says.

"Yeah, that's why I kept it short most of the time," I chuckle. We are side by side now, and I notice the heaviness of my growing hair, resting on my shoulders.

Lucas turns to face me. "Yes, definitely I can imagine short hair looks good on you."

I look at him. "Thanks."

"I feel like we'd be good friends if we met. . . you know, under *normal* circumstances," Lucas says out of the blue.

"Why did this happen to us?" I mutter. We have to get going soon, but I like this peacefulness with Lucas, the fragile aura he brings.

"I know, right," Lucas says, "but you know, in a couple of decades, when this is all history, we will look back at it as if it were nothing."

"You don't think that there will be permanent damage?"

Lucas shakes his head. "Just keep focusing on who you are and what you love, and nothing can change you."

I look at Lucas, at his hard-set eyes. "How. . . how are you so. . ."

"So what?" He takes my hand and grips it hard, once, and then fiddles with his dress.

"I don't know. . . I just feel like you'd be angrier. . . mad. . . like. . . after everything that has been done to you. . ."

"That I was raped by a bunch of dudes and forced to have one of their babies? That I don't even know which one of those fucktards is the actual father? That I have to be someone I'm not and become a mother, when instead I wanna live as a bachelor till my eighties. . . how am I so optimistic all the time?"

"I nod. . . I'm sorry if. . ."

"I have to stay positive, Maia. I have to keep my hopes up." His chest is heaving. He stands up and holds his hand out. I grab it and he helps pull me up. "I'd be drowning in hopelessness if I wasn't so hopeful about my situation, about all of our situations."

I hug him tight, swimming in his warmth. "It's just so hard. . ." I say between sobs. "This place. . . I just. . . can't help but feel so hopeless, and any way out, I don't know. . . I don't even know if this escape will work."

He pats my back, and each pat sends a million candle lights to my heart.

"If we were never hopeless, there would be no hope."

It takes me a while to understand that.

# THREE

There's a difference between feeling happy and being happy.

# 29

I remember a recurring dream I used to have when I first started dating Aimee.

It was an idiotic, cheesy romance dream that felt so real, I swear I thought it was real as I was experiencing it. Like I didn't question how it could be "real," I was just enjoying it as it went along.

The dream was slightly different every time.

I knew it was bad to have these dreams when I woke up in the morning, but the night before, I would prime myself to have the dream by telling myself like a mantra: "I will have the wedding dream tonight. I will."

I know, wedding dreams give false hope and put ideas in my head that should not be in my head in the first place. I mean, we had just started dating, and I shouldn't think about *our wedding*, but I couldn't help it. It was so magical and felt so good to have this kind of dream.

And sometimes—when you meet a person, you just know that person is "the one." That this person is the one who will be in your life forever and will support you and you will trust them, and they will trust you. You know this person can be your best friend and your partner in every challenge you face.

Of course, I never told her this. I should have told her. I should have told her something. I didn't because it'd make things awkward, and it might scare her off. She wasn't a person who wanted to be tied down. She wanted to be free, completely free.

I should have told her this when she was alive. I should have given her hints that I saw her as a future bride; I should have, I should. . . There are so many things I should have done, and I regret deeply not doing them.

Because really I knew she wouldn't leave me for that. Even though we never said anything, we both knew that we loved each other.

She probably would have laughed at the dream, or her hand would lightly brush against my thigh. Or she would have added to the dream, adding the things that she wanted at her wedding. She'd probably want to lean away from tradition, go for a more modern approach.

Things like pop music instead of the classic melodies.

Instead of a church, she'd want the wedding to be in an underwater glass structure, where you'd be walking on glass, seeing the fish underneath you. Something like that.

And no cake, but maybe everyone would be sharing a joint or something.

My dream was completely traditional, perfect really, and it had a different plot each time, but would be resolved by the end of the dream. Like a rom-com movie, which I despise, but secretly, deep down I *love* that stuff when it comes to what I'd want to do with her.

I remember it so clearly.

Neither of us liked suits, so both of us would be wearing dresses. Maybe mine light gray, or a bit different than hers, which would be white. White as pearls and vanilla frosting flairs over it.

A white dress was the one traditional thing she'd like to keep. She never told me this, but I'd always see her eyes widen in awe at wedding dress window displays. That was a secret she kept deep within her.

And it'd look so beautiful on her. It'd drape down her legs, and her shoes wouldn't be those painful heels, they'd be the ones that are just elevated slightly, so there isn't a strain on your toes.

And her beautiful long wavy brown and purple hair in a beautiful bun. A white carnation would be at the perfect angle in her hair, and her face would have natural makeup. And she would look so, so, so, beautiful. So beautiful that no one could keep their eyes off her. She'd be glowing, and every ounce of her would just shriek glamour and beauty.

Oh, I could stare at her for the rest of my life. She's *that* beautiful. It's not like her image gave me some pleasure or gratification or whatever, it's more that I just felt at peace with myself and so lucky to be her girlfriend.

I never remembered what I looked like.

I'd never look in the mirror in my dreams. I heard from someone that if you do, your dream will become a nightmare.

That is something that I did not want.

It's one of those cool dreams where I knew I was dreaming and at the same time thinking it's real and could have some control of what I did and said. Not complete control, though. I'm not an expert in lucid dreaming.

I was probably wearing something a bit similar, but not exactly, and she would look at me like I was beautiful. She would look at me as if I were from heaven, as if I was some sort of enchanted princess.

There'd always be a problem in my dream wedding.

People went to the wrong location; our car got stuck in traffic; we'd get split up because some gangsters crashed the wedding. That dream was weirdly heart-racing, and I just loved the adrenaline. It's something I'd never want to happen in real life, but in this dream, since it was *my* dream, I was this almighty force who would win every fist fight as if I was some martial arts expert.

Like the bad guys who feed on destruction came from all sides and wanted to steal my bride to be, but I would stop them. I punched and kicked their nuts so many times, that there'd just be a bloody mess on the floor, but thankfully the blood didn't get on my dress or my bride's dress at all.

There was another one, where we both had cold feet and needed some time to ourselves. And because this was *our* wedding, we could do what we wanted. Even though everyone was waiting for the ceremony to begin, we made them wait. We went to Central Park in our dresses, all dolled up, holding hands, and sat on some rocks, overlooking one of the many large lakes with the ducks and the baby ducks and the mom leading the way. And her eyes would glimmer at that picture of life, of hope. And we'd just be laughing. And we weren't technically supposed to see each other in our dresses before the ceremony because of the superstition, but we did, and all this daring and breaking and rules and making people wait just made the whole event even better.

We rushed back to the wedding but stopped at a bookshop to buy books to read to each other on our honeymoon. And we went to the place of ceremony and couldn't decide who would stand at the altar, and who would walk down the aisle. But we went, and she like quickly went to the end of the altar and so the wedding began.

I used to literally have tears of joy when I woke up, and it combined with the eye boogers, and I would wipe it all away and quickly write everything down in my dream journal.

I loved having those dreams.

She is truly. . . was truly. . . the best person in my whole entire life. I have so much to thank her for, and I can't believe she is gone from my life. Forever gone.

And the dreams are gone too. And my memories of them are memories of something that never happened.

It is not even something that can become a real memory because it will never happen.

She is dead, and I have to move forward, but it is so hard to move forward because I never got to say goodbye. I am stuck in the past and. . . I don't know what to do.

Some days, I'm just gliding along, looking forward to sleep, other days I can't stop thinking about her, and now. . . I don't know. . .

I feel like I am slowly losing her, but isn't that what I want? I don't know what I *want* anymore. I don't know what I want because I do not even know who I am.

They have erased who I am, and all that remains is a blank sheet of paper. Now it's easy to mold me into something, to fold me into a crane or crumple me into a ball.

They can color me, put lines on me, cut me, shape me, do whatever they want.

All I have are memories, but those are slowly washing away.

Now, they are all blurry, the colors faded, the shapes disfigured, and even the memories of the dreams are slipping away.

But isn't this what I wanted?

She is mist, slowly leaving me, but leaving cold chills down the back of my spine, water droplets across my cheek.

I still feel her, but before I know it, she is gone.

\* \* \*

As I head to lunch, I see a nice black SUV roll in through the gates, its tires scrunching on the gravel drive. Quickly the gates close again as the car pulls up next to Headquarters.

Two soldiers emerge from the building, gripping Lucas by the elbows. He no longer has the band on his wrist, but he is in cuffs and there is a black bag over his head.

The soldiers bend his neck and shove him in the car and get in after him.

The gates swing open again as the car approaches. It rumbles through and they close behind it.

Some soldiers shove me along, and I smile in my mind. It's working. It's working. They are taking Lucas to the hospital.

But even though I *feel* happy, I am *not* happy.

There's a difference between feeling happy and being happy.

It's an emotion verse a state of being.

I still have lost so many people. Even myself.

How can I ever be happy again?

\* \* \*

I'm on the line to dinner, and Zach approaches me from behind. "Can we talk privately?" I look at him, at his firm face, "Uhh. . . sure . . . there's no harm to that, right?" Just a girl and a guy, that's what they promote. We get the food, cold rice and slices of ham, and head to a table, in the corner, away from everyone else. My friends who I usually eat with eye us suspiciously but continue with their conversation.

"What's up?" I nibble on the ham. It's slimy and tastes like rotten milk. We can't look suspicious, so I fake laugh, as if we were just two people getting along.

"I'm starting to have some doubts. . . with the whole, *thing*," he says in a whisper. He's talking about the escape. "Like, how hasn't anyone caught on? How are we getting away with meeting up in the bathroom area? Maybe they know what's going on, and they're onto us. After all, we're still wearing *these*. . ." He raises his left arm to show the electronic bracelet that we've all been wearing since we got here. "Won't these give us away?"

I squint. I haven't really thought of that. Maybe the bracelets sound an alarm somewhere, in a control room or something, when a lot of them are in one place? Or. . . maybe they don't. Maybe some guards are supposed to monitor the bracelets' locations at all times, but they're getting lazy. Maybe when *we're* meeting, *they're* at the movies. That kinda makes sense. The soldiers do love these sappy movies, I've noticed. They absolutely *love* them.

Anyway, we're all still here, aren't we?

Never mind. I don't have space in my head for doubts and worries. I just have a focus: escape.

"We are already too far in it to quit," I say simply. "If you don't want to participate, you can leave. If we get caught, we won't say that you were a part of it in the beginning."

"No, I'm with you on the escape and everything. I just. . ."

"Just what?" I gobble the cold rice; it goes slowly down my throat. I take some water and sip it down.

"I just hope that you know what you're getting into, and what you're getting everyone in. You have to take responsibility *if* something *does* happen."

I slam the cup down and clear my throat. "You think I don't know that?"

I feel bad for talking back like this, but his attitude, man, he's just so. . . what's the word? *Condescending.*

"I know what happens if the escape doesn't work, if we get caught," I say. "I've seen it with my own eyes. People died because of a failed escape attempt. And there's no justice for them. There's no funeral for them. But. . . we have thought about this, we have a plan . . ." I don't know if I even believe this myself.

"Everyone is in it, and they know of the risks. But especially. . . especially *I* know about the risks. This was my idea, and if anyone gets hurts or. . . dies," I shudder, the rice is still taking their grand time going down my throat, "it will be my fault. Because this is my . . . I have become responsible for them. I can't. . ." I squeeze my eyes. "I can't let anyone else die. It's too much for me to handle." I look him straight in the eyes. "But what choice do I have?" Finally, the rice settle in my stomach.

Zach looks at me, his eyes are almost trembling. "Right, yeah, of course, just making sure," he mumbles and puts food in his mouth, to give him a reason to not say any more stupid stuff to me, because, now he knows, how I react to stupid stuff. . . .

I smile, I don't want us to be on bad terms, we have to escape, we are a team, we can't be enemies. We must be comrades.

I think back to the insult game.

"I'm sorry about what I said at that game," I blurt out. I've been meaning to apologize to him. I did the other day to the gay guy I had insulted. He understood completely.

"What game?"

"The insult game, before the hike?"

"Oh," he brushes me off, "it's no big deal."

"Okay. . ." I nod. I can't help but be curious. "How did you know . . . that you are asexual?"

He smiles. "I just never. . . had that. . . want, that need. . . and when I got my first girlfriend. . . we just loved each other, for each other. . . we were just happy together."

"Is she here too?" I ask softly.

"No. . .She never really defined herself as asexual, but she was always accepting that I was. . . It's good she's not here. I miss her deeply, but. . ."

"This place is hell. We would not want any of our loved ones here." I understand. I don't want my dear little sis here, and if Aimee was alive, I would do whatever it took to save her. Is it better she's dead than facing this torture day in, day out? I shake my head. I don't want to think of that.

"One of the reasons why I want to escape. I want to see her. . . I need to see her."

It's nice he still has a girlfriend to go back to.

# 30

Lucas came back the same way he left, still pregnant, and we're waiting to hear from him. He left on a Monday, came back the next day, and now it's Thursday.

I find myself staring at nature whenever I can. The trees are still bright, green, and full of life. The leaves are so fresh, and I just wanna gobble one down, even though I know it'd taste horrible.

The bark is so brown and rough, and the birds are chirping away. They are so free; they can fly wherever they want, and they can do whatever they want.

I'm pretty sure if some birds of the same gender started mating, the other birds wouldn't even care.

\* \* \*

On Friday, Lucas screws up his courage and whispers a message to one of us, who passes it on, like the telephone game, and by Sunday, which is movie night, we've all gotten the word. We meet in our usual spot.

Lucas updates us. "A nurse spoke to me while she was taking my blood. We didn't have a lot of time, but the soldier who was guarding my room went out for a moment to take a piss, and then she told me that one of the guards here can help us. He is a corrupt guy, and our friends on the outside paid him off."

"What's his name?" Diana asks.

"It's McDonald."

I hold back a snicker. Our fate depends on a guy with the same name as a *hamburger*, I think giddily.

"He works the morning shifts in the kitchen and the night shifts at Housing 15. He has a spiky brown mustache."

Sam and I look at each other. We know this guy. I've seen him around. Kind of a sleazebag, was my impression.

"The code word is *nightmare disease*."

We all nod. Kind of appropriate, that is. They say we have a disease, and we're living a nightmare.

Diana looks at Sam. "You live in Housing 15, right?

Sam nods. "Yeah, and Maia does too."

"So," Lucas goes on. "One of you says the code word to him, and he'll tell you how to get the bands off. . . And then. . . "

Lucas takes a deep breath. "The nurse told me one other thing, for after we jump the fence. Outside the gate there's a road that goes straight for about a mile and then comes to a fork. We have to cover that distance fast because it's out in the open. No one can help us there because it's too visible.

"At the fork, she said to bear right. The road gets curvy there and there are a lot of trees. A few hundred yards down that way we need to look for a driveway on the left with a white sign next to it. The name on the sign is 'Freeman.' Just up the driveway there'll be a dark-colored van parked behind some bushes. Tell the driver the passcode and she'll get you to safety. She'll be there every Tuesday night starting at midnight. So the breakout has to happen on a Tuesday."

Lucas stops, breathing heavily, and looks around at all of us. "Can you remember that?"

"I got it," says Sam.

"We have a plan," I chime in.

"Way to go!" someone else murmurs.

I can almost feel the buzz of excitement in the air.

*We have a plan!*

\* \* \*

As we part, after sharing a lot of planning and words of advice, I catch up to Sam.

"I can talk to Big Mac," I tell him.

"No, Maia, I can do it."

I grab his arm, holding him back. "You might get caught. This could be a trap. It was my idea to escape, so I should be the one to take the risk."

"You don't have to be a hero all the time, Maia." He shakes off my arm and continues walking back to our cabin. "If this really is a trap, it's better that I get punished than you," he says—in a low voice, because several guards near the cabin are watching us now. "You're more important to this group, Maia. You are the glue."

I'm flattered. My cheeks blush at his compliment.

Just as we're heading into the cabin, Sam glances back at the three guards. They are looking at us intently now, suspiciously. They must think we are *plotting* something. One of them steps forward. Sam stops and looks straight at me. "I apologize for what I'm about to do," he murmurs in my ear, and he bends forward and takes my face in his hands. His delicate fingers warm me, and his face is close to mine, and his lips brush mine, and for a second, I just stand still. I don't know how to respond. All I feel are his warm, tender lips against mine, which are not moving at all.

I'm not enjoying the kiss itself; I'm enjoying the comfort and knowledge of having someone who is willing to touch me and embrace me. . . instead of treating me like I'm sick with disease. He is treating me like a human being.

I hear a low whistle. It's the guard who was watching us. He makes a thumbs-up gesture and rejoins his friends.

They laugh. Obviously we are no threat, we are not conspirators. We are just a boy and girl in the bloom of youth, falling in love and stealing a kiss. That's exactly what the authorities want, isn't it?

# 31

I fall asleep while trying to stay awake. I was trying to stay awake to watch Sam creep out of his bed and approach McDonald. But the day quickly falls on top of me, and I tumble to another dreamless sleep.

The next thing I know is the usual morning routine.

The day slugs forward.

I see Sam from time to time in the distance, and I don't know how to approach him without raising suspicion.

I am in the line to take a shower in the evening, minding my own business, eavesdropping on a conversation between two people whom I barely know: Kendra (her name, according to *them*, is Michael) and April (a bisexual girl) are talking about some pop songs.

I don't know what's going on in the world right now, but I have a feeling that nothing is actually *getting done*. For us, I mean. Maybe some celebrities are expressing their concerns about these new regulations and rules, and about all the people who disappeared, but if there is any outcry about our fate, it's not having any effect.

There *must* be some protest out there. From the ACLU and Human Rights Watch, people like that, plus all of President Miller's political enemies. But if whatever they're doing was *really* working, if their petitions and Instagram posts and TikTok videos are really making a difference, we wouldn't be here.

And yet we are.

Because no matter how much money and status you have. . .

Sometimes you cannot change the system.

Most of America is probably going about their daily lives. Because we, the ones that are suffering, are only a minority.

I wonder where the celebrities who are "diseased" are. I haven't seen any, except for Yola, if you count her. Are they in a separate camp. . . Were they murdered?

What happened to the famous political couple Pete and Chasten Buttigieg? The nation's sweethearts and their adorable children?

I remember watching the news when their marriage license was revoked, just the day before the Pride March. They were facing the cameras grimly, vowing to fight for their rights, our rights. . . Where are they now? . . I hope their love and their family have survived.

And what's happened too, by the way, to those gay right-wing types who actually supported Miller? Like they supported Trump before. I never understood what was going on with them. Was it that their ideology was stronger than their identity, or the money was too good, or they just hated themselves? There were only a few of these guys, but the press made a big deal of them. Like what's-his-name, Peter something, who owned the company that made the equipment that was used to comb social media and identify everyone's sexual orientation. What was he thinking? And where is he now? Did Miller build a five-star luxury camp just for him and his chums? Or did he jump in his jet when the shit hit the fan, and skedaddle away to his estate in New Zealand?

Well anyhow, fuck those guys.

Sam comes up next to me, sweat on his forehead. His clammy hand reaches my hand and pulls me away from the line. I look at him with concern. The guards are watching. They are always watching. "What are you doing?" I say in a hushed whisper. "They're *looking*."

"I know." He smiles, pulling me in the direction of the cabin. "They're going to let us do what we want, Maia. Remember?" He smirks. "They encourage straight hookups."

"They encourage maybe being a heterosexual couple but not sneaking around like *this*."

"It's entertaining to the soldiers. Their job is very boring; they need a distraction like this once in a while."

I nod. We're at the cabin. No one is here. The guards are really giving us space.

I look at him. "What's going on? Did you talk to that guy? Mc-Donald?"

He nods. "Yes, that's what I want to talk to you about." He looks at the ground, his feet shuffle around, as if he is trying to dance or something.

"What happened? What's the plan?"

"He knows a way to get the metal bracelets off," he gestures to his left wrist, "but, it's. . . he's corrupt. . . so it comes at a price."

"Okay, so what do we have to do? I thought our *friends* on the outside already paid him off. What more does he want?"

He looks into my eyes; his eyes are watering slightly. "It's not money he wants, Maia."

"What does he want?"

He is taking forever to answer. People are going to wander in soon.

"It's something sexual."

I shudder at the word. *Why does everything have to be about sex?*

"Okay. . ." I don't know what to say.

"I offered. . . my. . . services, but he wants it from a girl."

I swallow my saliva. "Yeah. . . okay, I'll do it. Whatever it takes." I'm surprised at how quickly I respond. But I am really desperate.

I mean, it can't be that bad, right? Like what we have to face every day in this fucking place is a hundred times worse than a sexual act. *Right?*

"You. . ." He shakes his head. "No, Maia. It shouldn't be *you*."

I scrunch my eyebrows. "Why not? It has to be someone. I may as well do it, this whole thing is my idea, I must. . ." It's a sacrifice I'm willing to take.

"You're too innocent, Maia. . . This. . . this will destroy you."

"We are all innocent, Sam. And this place has already destroyed me." My eyes tear. "They killed the love of my life, Sam. I will always feel lost without her." I bang my chest with my fist. I don't want to cry anymore. It hurts too much.

"Maia. . ."

"Sam. . . let me do this. Please. . ." I won't let anyone else suffer. I'll do it all if that's what it takes. "I wasn't able to save her, but maybe I can help save the others."

He closes his eyes in contemplation and sighs. "Okay, okay." He looks at me, pity drowning him. "Tomorrow, after lights out, stay up, and when you hear three car honks, go to the bath house, and he'll be there. He'll tell you how to take off the bracelet. All you have to do. . ."

A kid comes in, hair wet and goes to his bed, we scurry back outside, and I look at him. "Thank you," I whisper.

One of the guards looks at us, his smile sly. We ignore him and get back on the line. I shiver. Oh my God, what have I gotten myself into? I feel like collapsing, but instead I compose myself. I straighten and take a deep breath.

This is something that I have to do.

* * *

The next night, the crickets are loud. I lie on my bed, on top of the covers, my fingers shaking, my mind numb, and anxiety riding up from my chest to my head. I don't know what he'll want from me, but I know it's going to be bad.

I am so tired, it's hard to keep my eyes open, but I do. I have to be strong. Being strong means that you have to be vulnerable to all the bad things in the world and know you'll survive them. I feel like I am naked, and I am about to be thrown into a black pit that goes on forever, so I'll always be falling, always be afraid of cracking my head on the bottom like an egg, the cracks uneven and wary, and the black swarms around me like mosquitoes feasting on a live brain and—

HONK.

HONK.

HONK.

I sit up quickly.

I slowly get off the bed, the bed squeaking slightly, and put on my shoes. The guard looks at me from his chair, nods, and then goes back to his magazine. Does he know? I feel cold, really cold. My legs are shaking. I hear a rustle, and look, Sam is awake. He nods and watches me leave the cabin.

This will be quick.

It will be done with.

Then we can escape.

And I'll be with my little sister and parents, and I won't ever have to deal with any of this shit ever again.

The door opens swiftly. I see another guard, and he nods slightly. This McDonald guy must have some power or something to tell all of these guards to stand down at the girl breaking curfew.

I slowly walk over to the bathrooms. I am shaking. I feel like a walking vibrator.

The crickets are not loud anymore. It's like. . . it's like they are having a moment of silence for me, like they know what's going to happen, and they fear for me. I approach the bathrooms. The light is on, and I head inside. The door slams shut behind me and I see, at the end of the place, a man, shorter than me. He looks to be in his forties. He has oily brown and silver hair that drapes down to his shoulders, a spiky dark brown mustache, and his lips curl when he sees me. He is ugly. Hideous. It doesn't matter. I quickly tell him the code word.

"Maia, right?" His voice is heavy and sulky.

I take a step back, my back hitting the door. *How does he know my name?* But that's a stupid question; of course they know our names. They are always watching us; they've read our files, they've. . . I quickly nod. I have to get this over with. I don't want this to happen. I don't want to go through with this, but it must be done.

"Shame," he slithers.

I gulp. What does he mean by that?

Does he feel bad that someone like me is in this kind of situation?

"Okay, let's do this." He smiles and approaches me. My back is hard against the door, and I look around. I want to escape, but I have to do this. We have to be able to get these bracelets off; we have to escape. "Don't look so scared, dear; you may even come to enjoy it."

He is closer and closer. I can smell his breath—pepperoni and onion.

"What do you want from me?"

He smiles harder and he is in front of me. He doesn't seem to care that he is shorter than me; he may even be turned on by it.

"I want to stare at your beautiful eyes while you. . ." he takes my shaking hand, and he unbuttons his pants with his other hand. His dark gray boxers are showing, and his thing there, gross, gross. He guides my hand under his boxers, and I can feel his heat, the sweat, the disgusting slime, the hardness. The thing grows and grows and grows under my hands, like a monster evolving.

\* \* \*

I run out of the bathroom quickly and go to a patch of grass and wipe my hands on the grass over and over and over and over again. I feel like vomiting. But I should get back to bed soon.

I can still feel his thing on my fingers, I can't believe. . . I can smell him everywhere, that disgusting pit-of-the-stomach smell, the smell of piss and semen mixed together, the stale bitterness of the molecules, the forever lasting image of his glittering eyes exploding in pleasure.

But it was worth it.

He told me how to take off the metal bracelets. It's really quite simple.

Like cat collars, the bracelets have a safety catch. They are designed to fall apart if they sense a hot flame nearby. The idea is, if there's a fire, and we all have to evacuate quickly, we'll be able to pass through the death zone at the fence without the bracelets zapping us.

That's what he told me, anyway. It was some legal thing they had to do, he claimed. I'm not sure that makes sense—do these torturers really worry their heads about *fire safety?*—but nothing here makes any sense, really, and what choice do we have but to believe it?

We'll just have to try it and see.

I stand up shakily. Soon, this will all be part of the past, soon, soon, soon.

I head toward the cabin and open the door. I see Sam's eyes, and I quickly look away from him, ashamed of what I had to do. He notices my discomfort and immediately leaves his bed and heads toward me. The guard looks up from his newspaper, peering at us with curious eyes.

"Give me a second," Sam says quickly. He looks at me. "Are you all right. . .did—"

"Yeah, I got it," I whisper. "I'll tell you when we meet on Sunday."

He nods, takes my gross disgusting hands, and squeezes them

tightly. "Thank you, Maia." Then he lets go and goes back to his bed. I head to my bed and slop on the covers.

I close my eyes, but my mind stays on high alert.

I feel worse than naked.

I have been skinned, from head to toe, the redness of the muscles revealed, the bones jutted out.

I no longer feel human.

# 32

Finally, Sunday comes again.

It was a hard week, but I did it. I got through it, and now we can plan our escape.

During movie night, our group gathers again in the bath house. I shiver, the familiar aura of the lights and the walls reminding of me of what I had to endure. But it's over. Soon all this pain and ache will go away, and we can finally be free.

I wonder why we haven't been caught. Are they so sure they have us chained that they don't realize the metal is rusting?

"Maia?" Penelope asks.

I nod, awaking from my trance. "Yes."

"So. . ."

"Ah, right." I look at the rest of the group. Sam, Clara, Lucas, Jade, Diana, Jack, Penelope, Zach, and Yola. "These things," I gesture to the metal bracelets, "unlock when they sense fire." I explain about the safety catch. "That's the only way to unlock them, without the General's master key."

I've never seen her use that key, but she must have unlocked Lucas when he left the camp.

"So. . ," Zach muses, "we have to put our hands in fire to be free?"

I nod. "Or near it, anyway. There's some kind of thermal sensor in these things. Or infrared, I don't know."

Zach looks at me carefully. "You sure you remembered right?"

"Excuse me?"

"I mean, I don't know, Maia, but this seems rather farfetched, don't you think? Why would they make the bands pop open like that when all we have to do, if there's a fire in one of the buildings, is run to the big field, or jump in the lake? We wouldn't have to go outside the fence and cross the death zone at all."

"I thought of that," I retort. "A lot of these camps, and regular prisons too, are all in one building or compound. Especially the ones in cities. And they have the death strips right outside the exits. The bracelets were designed for that. And the company that makes them, only makes one model. Luckily for us!

"Anyway, that's what McDo . . ." I don't want to say his name. "That's what the guard told me."

Zach doesn't give up. "Maybe the guard was wrong, or lying, or he said something different, and you just didn't hear him correctly, or. . ."

I'm getting pissed off now. "Do you know what I *had* to do to get this information?!"

Sam looks at me. "Maia."

I ignore him. "This is the only way, all right?" My voice is getting louder. "If you are not willing to join, then just fuck off."

"Maia," Sam says again.

I look at him. His eyes plead with me to quiet down. We can't let the guards hear us.

"Okay, okay," Zach mumbles. "I'm with you. Sorry."

I cross my arms. "Okay. Good." I sigh. "Let's plan this."

* * *

During lunch the next day, Lucas tells me that he doesn't want to participate in the actual escape. I drop my fork on my plate, it still has a piece of meatloaf stuck to it.

I quickly pick it up. "What?" I remember what I said, he'd only slow us down. But he got us *this* far, it would be horrible for him to be stuck here while the rest of us go free. Of course, we plan on somehow getting everyone else out once *we* get out—we haven't really planned that part out—we'll figure it out later, when we actually escape and meet up with the underground group that's supposed to be helping us. . . *if* we actually escape, and *if* we find them. I shouldn't doubt our success, but I can't help it. "You *can't* stay here," I tell Lucas, "it's. . ."

Lucas looks down at his pregnant belly, "I can barely get up in the morning, Maia. If I go with you, I'd just slow you down."

I shake my head; it doesn't feel right.

"What happens if you're stuck here, and you have the baby? Will they even let you keep *her*?" The nurse in the hospital, the one who's helping us, told him the results of the ultrasound. A girl!

"I'll be fine, Maia."

I hate being so God damn stubborn. "Really, Lucas. . ."

"I can handle myself." Lucas says firmly. "All my life. . . I got through it all. I've had to live in the wrong body throughout my childhood. . . especially during puberty it was the hardest—seeing things develop, seeing the body you didn't want changing. . . to something even more. . . *wrong*. . . it was horrifying—and now this. . ." He gestures down at his body, his swollen breasts and strained legs. "It's like a scene from *Alien*. Something alien is growing inside of me. Every time I think of this thing—I will remember the rapists' eyes as they. . ." Lucas shakes his head, his eyes wet. "But I can deal with this. . . and I won't under any circumstance make your, all of you," he looks at the rest of the group, "your chance of escaping less than it already is."

He takes a deep breath, wipes his tears with the back of his hand.

"I won't be the reason that you guys get caught. I can't live with myself if that happens." He continues eating his food, like he didn't just say an awesome bad ass speech.

"Okay," I say. "All right, then."

After we escape, and meet up with our allies, and win more people to our side and grow in strength, we'll come back for him and his little girl.

Meanwhile, we can escape.

Oh yes!

We *will* escape!

. . . And you know something funny? They're still giving us the pills. Every morning we have to pop them in our mouths and wash them down. It's such a routine now, I don't even think about it anymore. But I'm starting to wonder, are they even *working?*

Did they *ever?*

I always figured the pills were tranquilizers, to keep us in a low-energy state so we won't even think of, like, *escaping.*

I burst out laughing at a sudden thought. The others at the table eye me curiously.

What if the pills were *placeboes* the whole time?

What if they worked only so long as we *believed* they did.

What if we stop believing it?

I'm feeling better already.

# 33

I feel like we are in some movie, some high-action thriller, like music should be playing in the background, that action-y type music with the thumping and the energizing hum. But this is *reality*.

And yet, it doesn't feel like reality. Like none of this should have happened to any of us, all the pain and fear, we never deserved *any* of this. We didn't do anything wrong.

But it happened, and there's nothing we can do to change what happened to us; we can only change *what will* happen to us.

It's rather beautiful tonight. It's Tuesday, the day the nurse told Lucas we'll find help outside. The night sky is bright, the stars glittering in awe, blinking as if to tell us that fate is on our side. There's a half moon low in the sky. The trees rustle, creating a nice, distant rhythm that matches the night crickets. The air is wet, the aftermath of a rainstorm creating a slick of water that drips from the rooftop edges.

I climb out of the bed quietly. The guard is sound asleep, upright in his chair. We drugged his water. Yola had pretended to sprain her ankle, and yelled so loud they took her to the camp infirmary, where she managed to pocket some painkillers and sneak them out. When our guard stepped out for a moment, Sam crumbled the pills and dropped the powder into his water bottle and shook it well, like he was making a martini. The guard never noticed, and now he's snoring gently.

I tiptoe to his chair and gently take away the newspaper he's been reading.

It's the *New York Post*.

On the front page there's a big photo of President Miller, clasping his hands in prayer, and the headline:

### PRAYS FOR GAYS
**Forgive Them, Says Prez,
But Cure The Sickos First**

Just the right kind of paper, I'm thinking, to start a fire with!

Sam joins me and starts searching the guy's pockets. We know he's a smoker, he's always stepping outside for a puff, he must have a lighter or some matches. We're counting on that. Sam finds a pack of Camels and tosses it aside. And he pulls out something else. . . yes! It's a matchbook, the old-fashioned kind they hand out at restaurants and bars, with a row of stiff paper matches under a folding cardboard lid, and a brown strip at the bottom for striking them. He holds it up in the dim light. The cover, believe it or not, says Miller Time! The beer, not the President. There are only, like, five or six matches still in it. They'd better work. . . Sam gathers up some more paper stuff, some magazines he'd scrounged up, and a couple of books they gave us, all about morality and clean living, and we quietly leave the cabin.

I feel bad about leaving the others, but we'll come back for them, I'm sure of it. We can't bring everyone with us; we are only teenagers. Our plan has a lot of holes in it, but it should work. It has to work, because if it doesn't, then I have no idea what will happen to us. We quietly hurry to the bath house. There are soldiers in the distance, but they don't notice as we sneak behind the cabins.

We head into the musty bathroom, and Sam nods at me. I nod back. We crumple the newspapers and magazines and pile them on the floor, next to one of the stalls. We take all the rolls of toilet paper out of the stalls and add them to the pile.

Sam pulls the matchbook from his pocket, tugs out one of the matches, and strikes it. It glows red for a moment and goes pffft and I smell smoke, but that's all it does.

Shit!

He strikes another and this time it bursts into flame. He holds it to the edge of the pile of paper. It flares up quickly.

The fire is red and looming and becomes bigger and bigger. We throw in the morality books. They crackle and spit glowing ashes into the air. I can smell the smoke billowing around us. "You ready?" Sam murmurs. I nod. We bend closer to the fire, extending our left arms, getting the bands close to the flames.

Right away Sam's bracelet clicks and falls off.

It works! It really works!

But mine is still fastened. There's something wrong with it!

I hold it closer. Still nothing. The heat creeps up around my hand. It hurts! I reflexively pull back but Sam grabs my arm and pushes it deeper. I want to scream. . . but then suddenly, mercifully, the metal clicks and falls into the fire and instantly I pull back and rush to the sink and turn on the cold water with my good hand and hold my seared hand under the streaming cold water.

The pain is intense but the rushing water soothes it. There's a towel by the sink and I wet it and wrap it around where the pain is.

The fire is still blazing. Paint is blistering and peeling off the door of the nearest stall and suddenly the dry wood bursts into flames.

Time to go! We run out. I'm still clutching the wet towel to my burnt skin.

We're heading toward a bunch of trees in a little hollow near the fence, where the others are supposed to be waiting for us with the makings of a second fire. The plan is to get their bracelets off while the guards are distracted by the bigger fire we've started in the bath house behind us.

That's blazing gloriously, I note as I glance quickly behind me. Flames are licking from the windows, and suddenly a part of the roof caves in, sending a cloud of sparks billowing into the sky.

Sure enough, we hear the guards shouting and running toward the conflagration. Somewhere a siren wails.

Otherwise the camp looks deserted. Sam takes my arm. We've arrived at the clump of trees. Down in the hollow, Yola and Zach are waiting, ready.

But where are the others?

In the darkness we can see the two of them have collected some papers and branches and leaves. Sam pulls out the matchbook. We're down to three matches, but thankfully the first works this time, and we quickly have a merry little blaze. Hopefully the guards won't notice it, down where we are, as they run to the other fire.

Yola and Zach extend their arms toward the flames, gasping as they feel the heat, and like Sam, they're in luck. The bracelets on their wrists immediately click and pop open, falling to the ground.

"Where are the others?" I ask. "They should already be here." I look around, but all I see is darkness, except for the pink glow of the bath house fire in the distance.

Yola bites her lip: "Maybe they got caught. We should just go."

I shake my head. "We can't leave them."

The seconds tick by. The fire is ebbing, so Sam hastily gathers some more branches and tosses them in.

An alarm blares through the outdoor speakers. Guards are shouting louder and louder. I wonder if they'll call in a fire department from outside. No, they wouldn't dare. They wouldn't want outsiders to see what goes on here, or take the chance that the prisoners might swarm the firemen, begging for help, crying for freedom.

"Maia!" Zach hisses. "We can't wait for them any longer. We have to get out of here NOW!"

No, I can't leave the others. Clara, Jade, Diana, Jack, and Penelope. We can't just leave them.

"You can go!" I shout. Sam breaks some more branches and puts them in the fire. He looks at me, worried. "I'll stay here and wait for them. You can get a head start," I roar like the fire, its blacks and oranges dueling, like my mind and heart. Luckily no one else can hear me above the clamor of shouts and sirens. I know leaving is the smart thing to do, but I can't leave people I care about. I *can't* do that again.

"I'll wait with you," Sam says. He nods at the others, gesturing for them to go ahead, but they don't move.

"Ah, fuck," Yola growls. "We'll wait together."

Just then we hear a pattering of footsteps. Clara, Jade, Diana, Jack, and Penelope come stumbling toward us.

"They. . ." Penelope pants, but there is no time for explanations.

The four of us pull the other five toward the fire and push their hands over the flames, letting the bracelets crackle and fall.

Just in time. Our fire dwindles and sputters and fades to embers. I look at Sam, and then at the others. And my eyes land on Penelope. I grin.

Freedom is near.

My legs seem to be moving on their own accord over the driveway, I can hear the footsteps of the others crunching on the gravel behind me, and I climb the gate, and as I land on the other side I wait to be shocked to smithereens, but nothing happens. I'm alive! I let out a gasp of relief and the others follow.

We start running down the road, the moon lighting our way. We pass an illuminated sign that says "Welcome to Camp 17." My lungs are burning. The others must feel the strain too, but we can't stop. Soon the guards will realize we are gone and come after us. They cannot let us get away. If we succeed, we can tell the truth to the world and everyone will realize the horror that really happens in these camps.

The moonlight glistens on the road ahead.

No one is following us. . . yet.

A gentle wind is blowing, like the breath of freedom, and it feels fresh against my forehead and for the first time, for the first time in a long while, I start to smile, *to smile*, to smile out of pure joy.

# 34

It is dark, the moon is setting toward the horizon, and as we run we can see several streetlamps ahead, one close, the others far away. They are like beacons of hope.

We reach the first one and I stop for breath, clutching the lamp post, feeling my bare hands around the metal. I feel the coolness and I smile. I gleam. The very fact that I'm able to touch something so ordinary gives me joy. I've been trapped for so long, stuck in the same routine every single day, that one small change, that one normal thing can bring me happiness.

We. Are. Free.

I want to stop and just roll on the ground, and laugh from the pit of my stomach, laugh in the joy of freedom, but I know I can't.

We start running again. Back at the camp, they are probably counting the prisoners to make sure we're all there. The fire must be out by now. We should be tucked in our beds, fast asleep so we can wake up and do the same shitting thing tomorrow as we've been doing all the other days. Keep doing it and doing it day after day until we're all certified as *cured*.

But we are not in our beds.

We are free.

We are not going to be *cured*.

They must have figured this out by now. General Wilson is probably ordering her soldiers to survey the surrounding country and corral us back. They could send out a drone or call out to the local police to track us with dogs.

We haven't really thought that far. All we know is that we have to meet someone at the rendezvous point, someone who'll help us, and then they'll take us to a safe place.

We pass another streetlamp. I'm running next to Penelope and she turns to me and laughs. Her teeth gleam in the night, and I grab her hand, interlock her fingers with mine, and we run and run and run and run. Sam is leading us like he knows the way.

I hear a faint rumble of engines far behind us. I glance back over my shoulders and see headlights.

They are still distant and we must be almost at the fork in the road where the nurse said to turn right. After that, the driveway with the sign that says "Freeman." And the van that will take us to safety. We are almost there, I feel it, I know it, we are about to make it.

I hear a gunshot, then another. Is someone firing in the air, to warn us to stop? Or are they shooting *at us*? Shooting to *kill*? Are they that desperate to make sure no one gets out that *they'd kill us*?

The roar of engines is getting louder, the headlights brighter, closer. We are panting really hard, our mouths open. I look at Sam, running ahead, and see him looking back at me. I'm looking at him for a solution, and he is looking at me for a solution.

We don't have a solution.

*And then we do.*

There's a third streetlamp ahead, illuminating the spot where the road forks. To the right, a smaller road curves up a hill into the darkness. To the left, it goes straight downhill toward some buildings. Straight ahead, beyond the fork, a hill rises sharply, covered in dense shrubbery.

Forcing the words out between gasps of breath, I shout to the others, "Go left here!"

"No, Maia," Sam protests. "We're supposed to go right!"

"I know!" I stop and grab him by the lapels. He bumps into me and stops too. As we steady ourselves I stare into his eyes, which in the light of the streetlamp are wide with surprise. "If we go right they'll follow and catch us all. Let's go left while they can see us." I point to the streetlamp. "Then a little bit downhill, where it's dark, you guys turn off, head up this hill, into the bushes, and double back to the other road and head for the rendezvous point without me."

The others have stopped and gathered around us, all breathing heavily.

"I'll go on down this hill into the town and hopefully they'll all follow me. I'll try to make it look like you've gone on ahead. Anyhow, I'm the one they really want."

"No, Maia," Penelope says. Wet streaks her cheek, and the lamplight glows on her, making an angel out of her.

"You can't do this, Maia," Sam says, his voice low.

"I'm doing this." I give him a smile. "We don't have much time. Let's move it!"

The trucks are still far behind us, but they're getting closer. I have to lead them down towards those buildings, where I'll scream and make a scene and wake everyone up, do everything I can to distract our pursuers while the others run to safety. It's the only way. This escape plan was my idea, and if we all get captured, their pain and death and everything bad that could possibly happen to them will be on me.

I can't let that happen. They have to be free, and if it costs me *my* life, *my* pain—

Then, so be it.

So, the fuck be it.

"Please, Maia." Penelope runs to me and clings tight. It's the first time we've truly, really, touched. Her touch feels amazing. I try to pull myself away.

"Let go," I say.

"No!" She hugs me closer. I can feel her warmth, her sweet breath, the point of her nose next to my ear. "Penelope, let go!" I almost scream.

The trucks are close enough now that I can see our shadows from the glare of their headlights. That means the guards can see us too. There are two trucks, one behind the other. That's good. Only two.

I push Penelope away and yank my hand out of her grip. As I turn away I hear another gunshot and, at almost same instant, a loud *ting!* as the bullet glances off the lamp post.

That does it. "Come!" I scream and start running to the left down the hill. "No more words!" And the others run after me, instantly, like it's an *instinct* and they have to follow me because I'm the leader, the alpha.

About fifty feet down I can see the faint gleam of a sandy path on the right, leading up the hill. "Go! Go!" I push Sam onto the path, then Penelope. Sam gives me a desperate look. "Go!" I scream again. After what seems an infinitely long moment, but is probably just a split second, he nods and extends a hand to Penelope, pulling her along. They run up the path and disappear into the darkness.

Zach is next. He hugs me tight.

"Wait, Zach," I say. "When you make it to freedom, if you can get to New York, please go find my family for me. 81 Irving Place, Apartment 9E. Tell them I love them, I love them so much! And warn them, they must take Janice to somewhere safe!"

He nods and tries to say something but I shake my head, tears in my eyes, and push him away. He turns and runs after Sam and Penelope. After a moment's hesitation the others follow. I take a deep breath, turn toward the town, and run.

I don't look back.

I just hope to fucking God that they'll make it to safety, that they'll finally be free.

* * *

I run and run.

After a minute I hear the roar of the engines dip to a growl as the trucks slow down and stop at the fork in the road. They idle briefly and then rev back into a roar. I glance back and see a pair of headlights turning my way, and then another.

Good! Both trucks are following me.

My heart is hammering against my skeletal chest. I am not thinking anymore, I am just running, my feet hard against the road, as the roar of the army trucks grows behind me.

I keep running down the main road. I don't know where I'm going, but I have to keep on as long as I can, to give the others, who are running in the opposite direction, more time to escape.

I am among buildings now. The lights shine bright. And I run, harder and harder, faster, and faster. Those training sessions paid off.

Ha!

Take that!

I'm giddy with exhaustion. I feel like laughing but I am too out of breath.

As I keep running and running I'm passing a gas station and a deli, silent and empty in the night, and I pass houses and more houses. Suburban houses, with navy blue and red mailboxes and perfectly cut lawns.

The army trucks are close behind me, both of them, and I hope that those two are all there are, and there aren't others chasing my friends. The trucks are so close that their headlights are casting shadows of me running ahead of them, long grey Maia forms skittering on the road. Again I hear a shot, and a whistle as the bullet whizzes past my ear.

Suddenly, without even thinking about it, like my body is telling me what to do, I dart to the right, across a lawn toward a cute yellow house with a brown rooftop and French doors. I find a rock and throw it through the glass of the door and immediately an alarm sounds. I reach through the door, between the shards still attached to the frame, and open it from the inside, scraping my arm on the glass.

I run into the house. An alarm is blaring and lights are turning on. There's a stairwell ahead. I have no idea what I'm doing, but I have to buy time for the others to finish their race to freedom. I run up the stairs and find myself in a hallway with three white doors. One of them opens and a man in his fifties appears, wearing a bathrobe. "What do you want?" he demands in a shaky voice.

"Please," I start to say.

He gives me a closer look, sees my clothes, takes in my exhausted panting and the desperate expression on my face.

"You're *from the camp*, aren't you?"

"I. . ."

"You're *one of them!*" He retreats to his bedroom. I see him reach for a phone and jab it with his finger—calling 911, I'm sure.

"Stop," I gasp. "Please, help me."

He gives me a look of disgust, like I'm some *parasite* that infiltrated his home. He turns back to his phone. "Yes, I have a break in." I take a few steps back and open one of the other doors. I stumble through it and lock it behind me.

In the dim light I see a bed. There's a girl on the bed, about my age, with silky blond hair. She sits up and gazes at me with wide eyes.

"It's okay," I say.

The door bangs. "Don't you dare hurt my daughter!"

"I *won't!*" I shriek back. What does he think I am? Some criminal? But *of course* he thinks that.

People are going to believe whatever the President says. Whatever the person in authority says. That's just how the world works nowadays.

I hear the roar of the army trucks and the shouts of the guards.

I go to the window, push aside the pink curtains, and look outside. There are lights everywhere and about a dozen soldiers are approaching the house. A voice over a loudspeaker calls: "MAIA ROBINSON, COME OUT WITH YOUR HANDS IN THE AIR. WE HAVE THE PLACE SURROUNDED."

How do they know it's me?

But this is good. It means they are focused on me and not the others. Maybe, hopefully, they think I'm the only one who escaped, but that can't be true because they would have counted us by now, taken note of who's missing.

"What do you want from me?" The girl is standing up, scrutinizing me as I stare out the window. She edges toward the door.

"I just want to go home," I say, tears falling from my eyes, and she looks at me with pity. But then her face becomes stone cold.

"You should have never sinned in the first place if home means *that* much to you."

I take a step forward. She backs away, almost near the door.

"What are you talking about?"

"All of you are corrupting America. You are shredding the very roots that make this country great."

Oh my god, it's like she *memorized* this crap.

"I'm just *loving* people, that's all," I plead.

"That's not love," she spits, and she quickly darts to the door, opens it, and rushes out into her father's arms. I kick the door shut and lock it again.

I look outside the window.

The noise is louder than before.

I recognize the voice coming from the speaker.

General Wilson.

"Maia," she says. "You're only making this harder for yourself. The more you resist, the worse it will be for you."

Well, duh.

"Think about your sister, Maia. What you do now affects what happens to her."

I freeze.

What will they do to her?

But. . .

*Zach will find my family and warn them.* . . . I can only hope.

"We have the place surrounded." It's General Wilson's voice again. "We will not stop until we have you in our hands."

I open the window, pushing it up, and I poke my head out. Immediately the guards and soldiers point their guns at me. "WHAT ARE YOU GOING TO DO?" I shout. "SHOOT ME? IN SOMEONE'S HOME? HOW'S THAT GONNA LOOK FOR YOU?" I turn my head and notice there's a balcony above me. The wall of the house slopes toward it. I can climb this.

There's a white wooden ledge outside the window. I sling my legs out and step on the ledge, my back to the wall, and look down at the people gathering there. A dozen soldiers stare up at me wide-eyed, guns drawn, but I haven't heard any more shots. General Wilson is standing behind them, clutching a megaphone. I climb up to the balcony, my hands gripping the wood hard. Splinters pierce my skin but I ignore them. I use my upper body strength to pull myself up onto the balcony.

I quickly stand up. I'm on the roof of the house, with a low railing in front of me, and a little door behind. It's like a crow's nest. Now, I have a better view of what's happening. It's not just soldiers down there anymore. People have come out of their houses and are staring around at the commotion. Phones are out, recording everything. I hear sirens, and a regular police car pulls up behind the army trucks, followed by a second police car and an ambulance. And trundling down the road behind them, here comes a press van! It pulls up in front of the house, disgorging reporters and their cameras.

Maybe I can make the most of this situation.

I look down at the cameras and hope to God that they can hear me:

"MY NAME IS MAIA ROBINSON," I yell. "I AM GAY AND BECAUSE OF THAT, THE GOVERNMENT KILLED MY GIRL-FRIEND AND IMPRISONED PEOPLE LIKE ME.

"EVERY DAY, THEY TORMENT US, THEY BRAINWASH US. THEY TRY TO MAKE US BELIEVE WE ARE DISEASED. THEY THINK THEY ARE CURING US. THEY THINK THEY ARE CLEANSING US OF OUR SINS. BUT I HAVE SOME-THING TO SAY."

I smile.

I hear the soldiers and guards crashing into the home, thumping on the floor and steps.

"I WILL ALWAYS BE GAY."

The shouts are growing and growing and growing.

"NOTHING CAN CHANGE THAT."

The guards are bursting into the room below me.

"NO MATTER WHAT THEY DO TO US," I shout. "THEY CAN *NEVER* CHANGE WHO WE ARE."

Hands reach from the window below and grab my legs and I kick them away. I lean forward, out over the growing crowd. Maybe I can jump off and die. That will make a statement! I'm about to hurl my body off the balcony, but the door behind me bursts open and mus-cular arms are pulling me and twisting my arms behind my back. I can't move. There are a bunch of guards around me, dragging me in-side. One of the guards produces a syringe and plunges it in my arm.

I feel the special sauce toss through my veins, and consciousness falls swiftly away.

# 35

I remember the first time that I went into a sex shop. In New York, you're supposed to be at least eighteen years old to enter, by law. Me and my girlfriend weren't, but there were plenty of places that let us in anyway. Because it's not like it's a gun shop or anything. It's a harmless shop filled with things that may seem taboo to the outside world but that can expand your sexuality, let you go on a sexual adventure to who knows where.

Sex is a human thing.

A shop for sex stuff is a human thing.

I was freaked out. Aimee had been there before but this was my first time.

I remember the ceiling video camera pointing at us. The camera was next to a TV screen that showed us what it was recording, and immediately the atmosphere was different.

It was full of joy; it was like a secret club for adults.

A cheerful woman with curly hair and an accent I was not sure of greeted us at the entrance and asked for our IDs. We gave them, and winked and she gave them back to us.

We were just two girls in love, almost eighteen; the law didn't matter.

She asked us if we needed any help, but Aimee was already walking ahead of us. I looked at the woman and shook my head. "No, thank you," I said quietly and darted forward to catch up with my girlfriend.

It was a bit embarrassing that she seemed to know where to go like she was some expert, but she's a free spirit. She always knew what she wanted.

The shop itself was pretty narrow, so I squeezed myself next to her, our shoulders touching, and she grabbed my hand tightly, and oh my God—there was a whole shelf of dildos just towering over us at the end, all in different colors, some really big. I couldn't believe that people actually *used* them, like it'd probably hurt a—

"When is she going to wake up?" I hear someone to my left—or right—or in front of me? I have a huge headache; the bones in my skull seem to be grinding together. Are they supposed to be doing that? I don't want to open my eyes because they hurt, like the pupils are drowning in acid.

"Should be any minute now," a deep, down-to-the-earth voice says.

"Maia." The voice is vaguely familiar. I heard her somewhere. . . sometime. . . some. . . A slap on my cheek, and my skin tightens in pain. "Wake up!"

"I wouldn't do that."

"She's awake, I know she is." This person is like a snake, I know that much. "She's just pretending," the voice slithers on. "That's what she does, that's what you always do, isn't it, Maia?" General Wilson! That's who this person is. I feel like her hand will attack me again, so I open my eyes quickly, and there she is in her perfect general uniform, tidy and *straight,* her hair tied back in a bun, not a strand of hair out of place.

She is glaring at me. She looks to the person on the other side of me, a thirtyish man with loose skin around his nose and a huge mole next to his right eye. "See, I told you, she's awake."

I try to sit up, but find I can't. I'm on some sort of stretcher, and there are these bandages wrapped tightly around my body, binding me to the stretcher. The place we're in looks like an ambulance. Medical kits and CPR things are around. Sturdy shelves on the walls.

The ambulance jostles.

We are going somewhere.

"You've really caused a big mess for yourself, Maia."

I try to spit, but my mouth is dry. "Fuck you."

General Wilson sighs. "I really thought you learned something."

"You can never change me."

She laughs. "Yeah, I know that." Weirdly, she *admits* it now, admits she can't change me. "That's why you're going to be in someone else's hands now."

"I'm going home?" I say, hopefully.

"Noooo, I never said that."

I take a deep breath. Anywhere *away* from General Wilson *has* to be better.

"You're going to a camp for adults." She smiles. "They are going to be much, much, much harder on you than I was." She shakes her head pityingly. "I tried, Maia, I tried really hard to give you as many opportunities to redeem yourself as I could, but I guess you're too set in your sinful ways to ever be changed using our *benevolent* program."

"What are you talking about?"

"We have obtained a judicial order, Maia. You clearly are a danger and a bad influence on everyone at Camp 17. You burned up an entire structure and the fire could have spread to the other cabins and burned those *children* when they were asleep." She gestures to both of my hands, and my elbow, which are now bandaged. They feel numb now that I'm thinking about it. I must have cut myself on the glass when I broke into that house. "And you hurt yourself. Clearly, you need more help than we can possibly give you."

"You can't. . . I'm seventeen, I'm not an adult yet."

"The judge approved it. You are almost eighteen. That is sufficient."

"No! My parents."

"Your parents have no control over this situation."

"This. . . this is *illegal*! You fucking can't. . ." I try to move against the bonds, but they are tightly wrapped around my body. "People are going to find out. . ." I think back to what I said on the balcony. "People saw! They heard what I said! There were TV cameras! There will be investigations. . . soon all of America will. . . and. . . my friends. . ."

"Believe whatever you want to believe, Maia. Dream on!"

I smile. "They made it out, didn't they? You can't find them."

"They're dead," she says simply. My heart drops. "They're dead. And no one believed your *stupid* speech. We announced that you were off your medications. . . and hallucinating."

She's lying. She has to be lying. "You're. . . lying."

She looks at me closely but doesn't say anything more.

I'm not sure what to think. There's no way of knowing if my friends really *did* make it out. I mean this is the government we're up against. Maybe they had more soldiers ready to search for them. Maybe they didn't hide that well. Maybe the people who said they were helping were just spies or. . . I shake my head.

*Or else she's lying. That's what she does, that's what you always do, isn't it, General Wilson?*

And my speech on the balcony, so dramatic, with the press below, pointing their cameras—it *must have* been on TV. Not everyone is going to believe what *they* say.

People will start to doubt the government.

I have planted the seeds.

General Wilson smiles, her face crinkling like there are little spiders all over it. "You want to know something, Maia?"

I want to tune her out; I can't let her get in my head. But all I see is her face, and all I hear is her slimy slithery voice.

"Dr. Diamond told me how much your sister means to you. . ." Her smiles gets wider as my heart gets colder.

"Stay away from her," I spit.

"Why should I?"

I gulp. I knew this was a risk, but I had to take it. I had to get the fuck away.

"You can't. . ." I don't know what to say. I was warned, but. . . at the time it seemed like escape was the only option. Any longer and I would have ended up like Crystal. But now, my sister is at stake.

Zach might be alive and coming with our friends to warn my family, to save them. . . but what if she's telling the truth? What if they all died, and Janice is still in danger. . . I have to do whatever I can to save her.

Even beg. "Please. . . Please don't take her away from my parents," I cry.

"But you were warned, Maia. You knew the stakes."

"Please, I'll do anything. . . please. . ."

"I wish there was something you could give us, Maia." General Wilson shakes her head, as if she were actually sad about what is going to happen to my sweet, young, innocent sister.

"I'll. . ." I tumble over my words, the sounds leaving my mouth before I even had a chance to think them, "I'll tell you how we escaped, I'll. . ."

"We've already figured out all that. You left behind little breadcrumbs, and your pregnant friend was helpful once she was threatened."

I want to scream "*he, not she*" but I don't. I know that I am at the end of the road.

She smiles, "Oh, Maia, the things you did to attempt your little escape!" She towers over me, sucking in her power. "While we've been on this pleasant ride together, while you've been sleeping off the morphine we gave you, I've had time for a Zoom conference with my associates back at the camp." She picks up an iPad from somewhere beside her and waves it over my face, grinning. "They have been conducting quite a *thorough* investigation. And it didn't take long, either. We do have our methods. Oh yes! I know *everything!*"

I want to open my mouth and scream.

I want. . .

I need. . .

I need to curse at her, ruin the world, kill the people in charge, murder them in their sleep.

"You know, for a girl who says you only fuck women, you really know how to please a man."

I gulp. She can't be saying this. . . she can't. . .

"It's a good skill to have, you know!"

Whatever. I don't care what she thinks of me. Fuck her. "Just stay away from my sister, please."

"I'm sorry, Maia. This is what happens when you break the rules, you must know that by now. There are rules and *punishments* put in place. I hope you can finally learn that at the camp for adults." I want to fucking ruin her. "Don't worry," she smiles, "if your sister doesn't show any signs of the *disease* at the camp, it should be an easy ride."

I imagine the General's bare neck.

I imagine whipping a knife over her soft skin, slitting the veins, seeing the blood spill and spill and pour over her twitching body.

But I can't move.

I can't speak.
I can't scream.
I can't think.

# FOUR

# Solitude of my heart

# 36

After what seems like hours, I don't know how long, the ambulance stops. I hear rumbling from the front, and metal grating against metal, and the vehicle jerks forward again. More metal grating and then a clang. We stop again and the engine cuts off with a final grunt and sputter.

We have arrived.

I have no idea what to expect. I am *terrified* of what lies ahead. Why can't they just let me go home? General Wilson looks down at me, smiling.

I hear the doors open and I feel the clattering of footsteps.

"You're from Camp 17?"

"Yes, I'm General Wilson, here to oversee the transport."

*I'm luggage.*

I feel the gurney moving backwards, down a slope, and I see a gray-blue sky. Just sky, nothing else. The sight makes my eyes water, and there is a swift change of wind that beats against my splayed hair.

"Will she make a scene?"

"Probably." General Wilson is standing over me again. "She *likes* to do that."

A man appears, standing next to her. His face is clean-shaven, pale, and he has an army hat on. I feel his hands moving around my body, and the bonds are unlatched.

I immediately sit up and look around. It's that early-morning time when everything is still tinged with gray. I see the ambulance to my left, and to my right there is a soaring gray-brown brick building, probably about five stories, with fancy windows that have white pillars on each side. At its base is an arch of that gray brick, and beneath the arch is a bright red door.

A clock tower juts above the center of the building. It's tall and mighty and has a midnight blue square clock with gold Roman numerals etched in.

I am dizzy, but I jump off the gurney quickly. There are soldiers everywhere, armed and alert. They're all wearing that familiar red arm patch, with the blue cross and the golden sword, and the gold letters that stand for United States Morality Guard.

A chill runs down my spine.

"Whoa, steady there," says the soldier who untied me, approaching me softly. I take a step backward, consider making a run for it, but the soldiers are forming a circle around me. I have no way out. Sweat collects on my forehead, and. . .

I'm so tired, I'm so fucking tired.

I almost feel like fainting again, but I don't. I widen my eyes, shake the insides of my brain, and I stand still. I don't want to give them an excuse to tie me up again. I don't know what's going to happen.

The soldier looks at General Wilson. "We can take it from here."

General Wilson nods, and she puts her hands in her pocket and takes out some folded papers. She unfolds them carefully and hands them to the soldier. "These are her files."

But he shakes his head, and she folds them and puts them back in her pocket. "No need. We only need *her*."

*What is this place?*

General Wilson nods, looks at me, and her eyes wrinkle in on themselves, like she almost pities me.

If she gave me hell, and she is afraid for me *here*, then I guess I really have arrived at the ninth circle of hell.

She climbs into the ambulance beside the driver and slams the door. The engine rumbles to life and the ambulance backs up, makes a U-turn, and heads for the gate, to the outside world. As it passes me the passenger window rolls down and I see General Wilson staring at me.

She's smiling.

And waving at me, this cutesy little wave, like you'd wave at a little kid that you're dropping off at school.

And then the ambulance is out the gate and General Wilson is gone. . .

And I am here.

Will I ever leave this place?

\* \* \*

The soldiers push me through the arch, open the red door, and I smell the old wood and stone. It is very calming inside. There is a large sort of lobby area, filled with more soldiers standing around a counter on the edge of the room with an empty chair behind it. I don't see much of the space, as I'm hurried down a hallway, on creaking wooden floors, past sturdy wooden doors on each side, with signs next to each, all blurred. They don't give me time to look.

And at the end of the hall is a vast timber door, and one of the soldiers knocks quietly.

A deep voice replies: "One minute!"

We stand idly by the door.

A minute later it opens. A twenty-something man in a blue button-up shirt, a midnight blue tie, and dark blue khaki pants comes out, hands in his pockets, his face freshly shaven, his smile grim. He looks at me, another look of pity, shakes his head, and hurries out.

"Yes?" comes the deep voice inside.

The soldier next to me quickly replies, "Professor Milborn, we have a new one."

"Come in."

The soldier pushes me through the door, and immediately my eyes light upon a man in his late sixties with a round white face, clean, combed white hair, and dark blue eyes. He looks me over.

He is behind a desk that has an office phone on it, along with several books, some black pens and sharpened pencils, and a notebook open to some scribbles that I can't read from this angle. In front of the desk is a single chair with white cushions. The wood is painted white.

"Come, sit."

I hesitate.

"Are you going to be fussy? You seem like a smart girl; you must know by now what happens if you disobey."

I glance around the room. There is a bright window to his right, and a cabinet to his left. Other than that, it's a pretty simple setup. The soldier stands behind me, blocking me from the door.

I don't really have a choice.

I sit down on the chair and the old man looks at the soldier. "You may go."

"Professor. . ." the soldier says and points at me. "She's has a record of *acting out*. I recommend I stay here in case she decides to . . ."

"I'll deal with that if that happens," he replies simply, and then looks at me. "But you're not going to, right?"

I squeeze my eyes. I'm really confused at his vibe. I'm not sure what to think of him. I shake my head.

The soldier nods. "I'll be right outside if you need me." And he leaves and closes the door behind him.

The old man looks at me and clasps his hands together.

Then he looks at his notepad. "So, Maia Anna Robinson, born December 14, 2008. Social Security Number: 156-44-092. Is that correct?"

I'm not surprised that he knows all this. Nothing surprises me anymore. I nod.

"I am Professor Milborn. It's very nice to meet you." He holds out his hand across the desk.

I really. . . can't. . . fathom his strange kindness. It must be some kind of ruse. But whatever, I'll play along. I reach my bandaged hand to his and shake it slightly. He smiles and we let go. Okay. . .

"So, Maia, tell me why you're here."

A laugh bubbles at my lips. *What the fuck.*

"What?"

"Why are you here?" he repeats.

"Why are you talking as if I came here *voluntarily?*" That's messed up. "You dicks fucking kidnapped me, killed my girlfriend, forced me into some brainwashing camp, tortured us. . . and then you probably sent my innocent sister to a junior camp, just because I am different *than you.*" He is scribbling something on his notepad with his pencil.

I push my head forward, looking at what he's writing with his stupid, pointed pencil.

*Anger management issues, intemperate language, acute concern for girlfriend, sister*

I lean back and chuckle slightly. Another shrink. He stops scribbling and looks at me.

"You mentioned your girlfriend. Have you engaged in any sexual activity since she died?"

My face becomes still and cold. How can he have the audacity to talk like that? I grind my teeth and try squeezing my fists but realize it is almost impossible because they are still sore.

I want his face to just fall off his body. How can he say this to me?

And I realize, he is not expecting me to answer these questions. The only thing he cares about is my reaction to them. I already gave him too much information; I can't give him anything else. I decide not to say anything. I close my lips and stare silently at the window. The sky is still so blue, and I can see a green field with little people walking across it.

He looks at me and then looks at his notebook and scribbles more stuff down.

"Let me ask you this, Maia, do you love your parents?"

I look at him. My parents?

My parents.

They drift in and out of my mind. I want their arms wrapped around me. I want them to whisper in my ear that everything is going to be all right, that they are going to take care of me, that they will make sure nothing evil happens to me. I want my mom to kiss all the bruises and scrapes and burns on my body, healing them instantly. My eyes water and my chin trembles.

He scribbles more stuff down. I don't want to see what he has written down.

He looks again, his face holding the same still expression of a psychopath.

"They must be worried sick for you."

"Yeah, of course they are." I let that slip out. *I thought I was not going to say anything.* It's like he has a superpower, just pulling stuff out of me. I can't help but continue speaking. "You people took me away from them. They are probably going to die from the stress."

"So, you should go back to them as soon as possible. And. . . you have a younger sister."

I breath in, nauseous.

"She's being sent to a junior camp, how precious."

Fuck him. Fuck everyone. Anger boils inside me. I feel hot and sticky. My heart beats so fast it might explode.

"I'm sure she'll do fine. They aren't that bad, trust me. Can't cause trauma at such a young age."

My anger dims a bit. Is he right? Why would he lie about this? I don't know what to believe.

I can't believe anyone anymore. All I can do is trust my gut.

"You should do everything in your power to see your parents and younger sister, once she is out, as soon as possible." And he continues scribbling something on his notepad.

He's a freak.

A mind reader.

A mind reader freak.

"Then let me go," I grumble. "Let me and my sister go."

He shakes his head and places his pencil down. "I'm afraid I can't do that."

I gulp. "Why can't you people just *accept* that some people are going to be *different*, do different things, *love* a different way then you? This is not how it's supposed to be."

"It's not about accepting people, Maia. It is about putting America first, and the individual second."

"Then I'll move to Canada."

"And spread the disease there."

I bang my hands on the desk, and it hurts like hell. But he is *so* frustrating. Delusional.

"You're going to have to control your temper while you're here, Maia."

I stand up. I can't deal with *him* anymore. "WHY CAN'T YOU JUST LEAVE ME AND MY SISTER THE FUCK ALONE?!"

I can't do this.

The guilt, the pain, the. . . everything. My sister will be in a place *like this.*

His eyes widen. "Maia, sit!"

I'm not a fucking dog.

I run the tips of my fingers through my hair. My bandaged fingers get caught and tangled in the knots, and I pull hard, and it hurts, but I pull and pull and pull, and my hands fling forward with clumps of my messy hair. "Just. . . Just. . ." My eyes well with tears. A wave of horror crashes into me, leaving me breathless, even weaker than before. "Just leave me and my sister alone. . ." I shake my head over and over and over again. The tears sting my eyes and cling to my eyelashes; my face is hot and fluffy. "I didn't *do* anything wrong. My sister didn't *do* anything wrong."

I am falling off the face of the Earth, into some black hole far, far away. But I can't fall apart now; I can't fall apart in front of this man. I don't even know who he is and how much power he holds over my life, this man who seems to know everything about me from my bursts of anger, his needy, greasy fingers grabbing inside the privacy of my heart and extracting my very core.

I don't hear him calling the soldier. I don't hear the soldier and then more soldiers coming in and pushing me down to the table. I don't feel my head slamming on the wood, I don't hear the screaming or the yelling or the anything.

But I do see the professor close in on me. His face is the only thing that I see, his voice all that I hear, and he is looking down on me, arms crossed like a disappointed father, shaking his head. "Maia, Maia, Maia."

I want to spit at him, but I can't muster enough saliva in my mouth.

"Things only go downhill if you choose to go downhill."

That doesn't make any sense.

"What happens to you next is because of *your* actions and *your* words today."

"Fuck you," I mumble.

"We do things differently here, Maia. Everyone is an adult here, Maia, and the punishments are severe. Back at your kiddie camp, they'd take away privileges, right? Make you *uncomfortable*? Maybe a little pain *here* and *there*, but here, you will learn your place. The measures we take will make you the person *we* want you to be." He chuckles, "Now, Maia, go to sleep." He puts his hand on my cheek, and I feel a prick in the back of my neck, and he continues to pet me like I'm a puppy, and his plump, old, smelly hands are weirdly comforting in a way, in a way, in a way, and blackness prevails.

\* \* \*

I am cold. I am really cold. The hairs all over my body are standing on their own. I don't want to open my eyes. I'm not sure what the punishment is, or if it's even started, but I don't want to know. I squeeze my eyes tighter, but the cold takes control of me. I have to find a way to be warm.

I open my eyes. My back—my *naked* back is on something hard and cold. I look up; there's the night sky, with the moon in it, gently lighting me and my surroundings—but there's something between the sky and me. I quickly stand up on my bare feet, almost losing my balance, and reach my bandaged hands upward and hit a piece of glass. I feel cool air on my belly. I look down, I am not wearing clothes.

I wrap my arms around my chest, I am not wearing any clothes on my upper body, either.

I am not wearing any clothes at all.

All I have are the bandages on my hands and elbow.

I am naked. Like a baby.

And then I look around at where I am.

On all sides of me, all six sides of me—wall, ceiling, and floor—is glass. Just glass. See-through glass.

I am in a glass box.

The glass floor is on the ground. Dimly in the moonlight, I can see grass crushed beneath it. I'm outside. *I'm outside.*

I look around. It looks like I'm in some sort of outdoor hangout area, like a college quad. There are benches nearby, trees, and gravel sidewalks going in all directions. Surrounding the whole quad are more of those old-fashioned gray buildings that seem to reach the sky.

I put my hands around the glass walls, trying to find an exit. There is a kind of doorway dent, and I try pushing and pulling, but nothing works. I am trapped. What the fuck. What the fuck. What the fuck.

I have to get out of here.

It's nighttime, and people are not around, but if people come here, they'll see my naked body. My tears well. I start to bang the glass hard with my fists, my already bandaged wrists, and it hurts. I bang them harder. The pain is ridiculous— it's a rattling of disaster, it's a constant—

And how am I breathing? I look around and find some tiny breathing holes in the ceiling. I start banging there. Nothing works. And then I'm banging my head against the glass doorway, and a headache flares from my temples, and I see a soldier appearing from the distance. He is quickly approaching, and I try and cover myself as best as possible with my hands, leaning on the opposite side of the wall, my ass and back pressed against the cold.

He shines a flashlight at me and shouts, "Don't hurt yourself or we'll have to tie you down." And then he gets closer to the glass, pointing the flashlight at my curves, and my legs, at *me*, and I sink to the ground still covering myself up and I feel so humiliated. I am an animal in a zoo.

And then I hear a distant voice, and he looks away. He gives me one last glance and leaves.

I lean harder against the wall, and I move on my side. My back still against the wall, I bend my legs so they cover my thighs and I wrap my arms around my boobs tightly, and I'm hoping this is only a nightmare.

# 37

I don't know when I fell asleep, but apparently I did. And when I wake up, to the bright sunlight streaming through the glass and warming my skin, my eyes snap open. I am huddled in a corner, trying to cover most of my body with my limbs, but it barely works. All the walls are transparent, and my limbs are not long enough to cover up everything. I have to decide which area to cover.

Do I value the privacy of my vagina more than my ass and boobs?

I curl onto my side and try to lean against the corner, but the glass is hot. The only cool glass is the bottom. So, I'm stuck in the middle, curled on my side, my legs closest to my vagina, my arms trying to wrap around my boobs and ass, and I see that there are people.

People.

People with eyes.

People with eyes and mouths and...

They see me.

They *see* me.

They walk through the quad, getting from point A to B and vice versa. A couple of soldiers are standing and staring, but the rest walk past, which is a bit better than what the soldiers are doing. But they still glance at me. They still *glance* at me.

The people, these strange people, are all adults.

The men dress in shades of blue like that guy who left the old man's office.

And the women are wearing all pink. Pink shirt, pink skirt, pink bows in their hair.

What the fuck. What the fuck.

It looks like a human dollhouse where a child dressed real people up like dolls. A sexist child.

All shades of blue:—navy blue, dark blue, sky blue, baby blue—blend in with the flamingo pink, magenta, bright pink, peach pink as more and more of these people pass though the quad, glancing idly at my bare skin, their eyes drifting from the tips of my toes to my dirtied knees, hairy legs to my pubic mound, over the curves of my body, my perked nipples to the nape of my neck to my bandaged hands to my face, disheveled and oily. . .

No no no no no no.

I want to stand up and try again to get out of this box, but I don't want to stand up. If I stand up, I'll be in full view. Everyone will see all my parts, every part of me together and full and. . . This can't be happening. This can't be happening.

I close my eyes, I cannot bear. . .

This humiliation.

Eyes linger on my naked body, and I can feel the pity in them, and I can feel the stares. They tear apart my insides. I cannot even begin to describe my emotions, what I'm feeling, what this is doing . . .

I squeeze my eyes shut, trying to force myself back to sleep.

But I cannot sleep, I cannot, I cannot—

\* \* \*

Naked, vulnerable, I squeeze myself in the corner, shutting my eyes so tight that my eyelids hurt. I can't do this. I can't. . .

I can't. . . .

Everyone is looking at me.

*Everyone* is looking at me.

Their eyes wander around my body.

People who are older than me pity me.

People who have more power than me abuse my body on display. Molesting me with their eyes.

* * *

I think of my sister sometimes.

I still grasp at the hope that somehow she and our parents made it to a safe place, that Zach and Penelope and the others are safe too, that the professor is lying, like General Wilson was lying before. . . .

But what if it's true? What if she's suffering in the same fate as me? Because of me?

I love her so much but. . . I can't think of her now. I have to believe that she is doing all right, that she is okay. . . even if she's captured, taken prisoner like me. . . but she's not *diseased* like me; they'll treat her with respect, right?

They have to. They must.

* * *

I don't eat for days.

Do I drink water? I can't remember.

I do my business in the far corner. I wait until dark to do it. People see that too, in the morning, like I'm an animal. I can't clean myself.

* * *

The sun is harsh, and the night is cold.

I don't know how long it's been, and when the doors open, when the doors officially open, arms grabbing me, blanket over my torn body--one of them making a joke about the smell--I feel disgusting. I feel ashamed. I feel embarrassed. I am horrified. I am terrified.

I am a broken body, about to be broken even more.

\* \* \*

I wake up.

My brain is foggy. There's a dull sensation on my shoulders, and my mouth is so dry. I smell something acidic.

My eyes open, and I see a strip of overhead lights glaring on me. I turn my head. My head is on a cushion and my body is on a mattress.

I sit up.

I am in a bed.

On white sheets, covered with a white blanket, the bed frame cloud-white. I am disoriented. Everything in front of me moves up and down, dizzily in motion.

There are other beds like mine.

A row of beds on the side I am on, and a row of beds opposite. But I am alone.

I turn right. My neck cracks and I cringe at the noise.

There's a white wall with white shelves.

To the left, there's another white wall with a white door. Above the beds are just the same old white walls.

White privacy curtains are pulled to the back of the wall.

There are metal poles by each bed, and weird motionless devices next to each of them.

I notice I'm wearing simple white clothes.

Too much white. It's too bright.

A white clip is attached to my finger. I hear beeping.

I look down at my arm. There's a needle in it with a tube attached to a bag hanging on the metal pole next to my bed. I want to pull this fucking thing out. I want to, I want to. But I am too tired to.

My head aches. The energy in my body is slowly seeping away from my mind. My body my body my body

\* \* \*

I wake up to the patter of footsteps. My eyes open and I sit up.

Huh. . . I must have slept.

The needle in my arm is gone.

A woman, wearing a simple light aqua-blue nurse uniform, comes shuffling in, holding a pale-yellow tray piled high with food.

It smells good.

Behind her is a soldier, keeping watch. He is very tall.

And I immediately shiver. I remember the soldiers. Their eyes watching me, staring me down, looking as if I was some slut splayed open in a porn magazine. I could almost smell their saliva dripping from their mouths; I could sense the temptation in their bodies, in their muscles. I could see the way my naked body makes their body react, makes their eyes iron and my body a magnet. I know this will haunt me for the rest of my life. It will creep into my dreams; it'll ruin every future relationship; it will steal my simple pleasures away. It will it will it will—

The nurse smiles at me and places the tray on my lap. I look down.

Mashed potatoes with cut carrots in them, beef dipped in juicy sauce, tiramisu, a cup of orange juice and a plastic spoon on a folded napkin shaped into a flower.

I am soooo hungry.

I feel my stomach churning and rumbling

But I can't eat. I can't eat *their* food.

I can't have the soldier watch me eat. I can't have him watch me do anything anymore.

All I want to do is grab the fucking plastic spoon and eat the meal in one gulp.

But my pride won't let me.

Tears well in my eyes as I watch my hands shove the tray. It slams upside down on the floor. The food—maybe I'll just crawl on my knees and eat it from the floor. I am so hungry.

The nurse goes tsk-tsk. And she turns around and leaves the room.

The soldier remains standing there. Watching me.

The rush of rebellion starts up in my veins, and I feel a tiny bit of energy seeping up from what's left of my reservoir of life force.

I sit up straight. I swing my legs on the other side of my bed. My bare feet touch the cold floor, and I quickly stand up, but my legs get wobbly, and I fall on my ass. "Fuck."

The soldier doesn't help me up.

I don't want him to.

I try standing up again.

My legs are shaky, and I fall again.

I try again, and finally this time, while also leaning on the bed frame, I stand up, my whole body shivering as if I were cold.

The soldier just watches me.

And I take a step forward, and then another, still leaning on the frame, trailing my fingers against the sheets, the soldier just watching me. And then I'm at the end of my bed, my ass leaning on the railing. I take a deep breath. I have to get to the door. I have to get out of here. I don't know how I've gone so far without having the soldier stop me, but I must take this chance. Even if it's a small chance of escape. Or whatever.

I lean my right foot in front and am about to bring my left foot forward, but the soldier quickly comes to me and grabs my arms, pulling me away from the bedframe, and there I am, dangling, my feet trying to gain balance. He pulls my arms up high, and I am tiptoeing. And then with a strength I didn't suspect, he picks me up and flings me onto the bed, my feet hitting the frame. I hear a crack and feel a bruise start to blossom.

But he does not scare me.

This only fuels me.

I quickly get up again, and I am about to punch that fucker in the face, but then the door opens.

Professor Milborn enters.

He shakes his head as he walks toward me.

The soldier takes advantage of my distraction and pulls me back to the bed.

The professor's arms are crossed over his chest.

I quickly sit back up.

This man. This man. He humiliated me.

He put me in that glass box.

He exposed my inner secrets, my body, my treasure, to outsiders. To people who *don't* deserve to see me like that.

"Fuck you." I stand up again and stumble toward Professor Milborn.

I can tackle this old man, I think, but then the soldier grabs me again from behind and pulls my wrists together behind my back, squeezing them tight. I can feel his presence all over my body. I can feel him enjoy it.

I try in vain to pull my arms away. I kick his legs. "Fuck you fuck you fuck you."

"I thought you learned your lesson," the professor says, shaking his head, stepping closer to me. "Would you like to be in the glass box again?"

I freeze.

The glass box.

"Because that can certainly be arranged. I can make your stay last longer this time, and I can even make you feel more pain in there. On top of the mental distress, I can arrange for physical pain. We have instruments for that. I can shatter your brain into little pieces. You see, dear Maia, my success rate is 100 percent! I convert you insects so perfectly that people from all over the world come to me to be reconstructed according to my designs, to be *restored* to normality. And, even if you are in a million pieces, I will change each one of those pieces. . . It's really up to you, you know. Would you rather be in a million bits? Or would you rather be whole?"

I am already broken. I am already shattered into bits.

Do I want to be broken even more?

I don't know what to do.

My arms slack in the soldier's grip.

"I. . ."

The professor nods at the soldier, and he lets go.

My arms fall slack to my sides.

I slump forward. I feel my body weaving in and out, moving against my will, I am shaking, I am withering in my own body.

I don't want to end up in that glass box again.

I can't.

I should be stronger than this.

I should be. I can't let him change me. I can't be changed. I won't be changed. Change is not possible for me, anyway, because I was born this way.

I can't let them win.

Because if I let them win, they will stay in power and control *all of us.*

A thought flits through my mind: I really hope my friends made it out. I hope they didn't suffer the same fate I did.

"So, what will it be, Maia?" Professor Milborn grins.

He sounds so sure, he sounds so. . .

I feel a bubble of tears trapped in my throat. I feel the dam about to be broken, the river about to be let loose. But I can't let him win.

I can't let him win anymore.

I can't let *them* win anymore.

I have gone too far for them to win.

My mind works. My mind is a clock, ticking faster and faster.

The wheels turn and turn and turn, grinding the core of my brain, grinding the core of who I am.

Who I long to be.

What I am.

I don't know where my mind is. I don't know where I'm going. I am soaring through the air, static whispers, many different voices come at me at from all directions of my mind. Whispering things that I cannot comprehend. A million mosquitos in my mind. I start to collapse.

I don't know.

Three words.

I feel myself drifting away.

I feel my mind losing its body and my body lose its mind.

I don't know what's happening to me.

I see the top of my head, and I look at myself from above, and then at the soldier and then at the professor. My back is to the ceiling. I have floated up like a balloon, but I am trapped in this room, unable to move, just staring down at my actual body shake and shiver.

"I don't want to go back there." I hear a voice, my voice, but coming from that body below me, whisper and quiver.

The professor smiles.

NO. I DON'T WANT TO GIVE IN.

But I can't *do* myself. It's like I'm possessed by another being, another form of myself, another facet of my being has taken over my mind in order to save me. To choose the most reasonable solution to keep my mind intact.

I don't know shit or words to describe it.

The ghost of me, that thing below, tells the professor, yes I want to be whole, please don't put me back in the box.

NO, I WILL CHOOSE TO GO BACK TO THE GLASS BOX. I WILL NOT BECOME HIS PUPPET. I WILL NOT BECOME HIS BARBIE DOLL.

"Eat the food off the floor then," the professor says, eyeing the food that got slopped by my bed.

NO DON'T DO IT, MAIA. DON'T DO IT.

The ghost of me goes on to the floor, on her knees, flips the tray over, trying to fling the food onto the tray, but failing to do so. She looks for the plastic spoon, but the professor hisses, "Use your hands."

The ghost pauses.

I feel a bit of control, but then the control gets stolen away from me again, and my back is harder up against the ceiling.

And I see her, I see the ghost take a glob of the food with her clean fucking fingers and put it in her mouth. The food seeping into her bandages.

She stops, eyes watering, tears falling.

NO NO NO NO N
WHAT THE FUCK IS WRONG WITH ME
I TRY TO GAIN BACK CONTROL. I TRY AND MOVE AND GO BACK INSIDE MY OWN BODY, BUT I CAN'T. EVERY-THING IS NUMB. I AM JUST WATCHING THE GHOST OF MYSELF, THE GHOST OF ME EAT THE FOOD.

"Keep going."

And I am just watching the ghost clean the floor, clean the tray, swallow the food.

I feel the energy seeping in, but I cannot move. I cannot bring myself to stop eating the food, and then I feel myself drifting down, toward that ghost thing on the floor.

I realize I am no longer the balloon stuck to the ceiling.

I am back inside my body looking up at the professor.

I have become the ghost.

And I don't know if I ever want to be something that is not a ghost ever again.

Maybe being a ghost will save me.

Because as a ghost, I don't have to be myself. I don't have to deal with pain.

As a ghost, things are fine.

# 38

I am back in my body; I can feel my fingers and my toes. I ache everywhere. My mind is foggy, my thoughts are a rapid, festering mess.

I am sitting in Professor's Milborn's office, twiddling my thumbs, looking at him, answering his questions. I don't really have a choice, honestly.

"Do you remember your dreams?"

"What are the themes of the dreams that you remember?"

"Any sex dreams?"

"With girls? Guys? Both?"

Question after question, penetrating my privacy, stealing away my insides, making me someone that I'm not. It's like I'm some lab rat.

"What do you do when you see a pretty girl across the room?"

"What do you feel?"

"What about a handsome guy?"

"Do you have any desire to have sexual intercourse with a male?"

"Do you have any urge to reproduce?"

I don't want to go back in the glass box. I don't. I don't. I don't.

But I don't want to answer his questions.

I have no choice.

I am trapped.

"Where do you see yourself in five years?"

"Who do you want to become?"

"What are your dreams? Aspirations?"

He scribbles on his notepad, and a pounding starts knocking in the inside of my head. I just, I don't feel human anymore.

He smiles. "Thank you, Maia, for your candor."

I nod. I want to go home. I want to get out of here. My mind is a blob, a blob of nothingness.

He taps on his office phone and puts the receiver to his ear. "Can you please bring in Stella?"

He puts the receiver back in its place and looks at me. He smiles. "If you keep up the good behavior, you should be out of here in a couple of months."

I freeze. I take a deep breath.

"Are you. . . are you serious? I'll get to go home?"

He nods, his smile full of teeth. "Yes. Of course I am. Just follow these five simple rules: One," he counts them off with his fingers, "do what we say. Two, do not fight back. Three, do not *try to escape.* Four, get along with the others but do not fraternize with them. I will not let your filth stunt their process."

My eyes water.

*Filth.*

That's what I am.

Because I love women, because I have sex with women, because I fuck women, because I kiss women, because I flirt with women, because because because because. . .

Loving women is part of my identity.

But I don't want to be filth. I don't deserve to be filth.

I can't. . .

"Five, no sinful acts are allowed. If you follow the rules, things will be good for you. Do you understand?"

I don't know what to say.

"Maia?"

I quickly nod.

There's a knock on the door, and he says sweetly, "Come in." The door opens, and I turn.

It's a woman, wearing the usual all pink outfit: flamingo-pink high heels, candy-pink pencil skirt, ruffled icing-pink blouse, and a pink beret with a magenta cotton ball bobbing on it.

Even her touch of makeup is pink-themed. Her pretty, honey mustard hair is flowing on both sides of her face. Her eyes are big and crystal blue, and her legs are long and shaved.

"Ah, Stella," Professor Milborn says. He gestures to me. "This is Maia."

He looks at me. "Stella will be your mentor, your friend here. She will show you the ropes of the place."

No. I want to go home. But I don't say anything.

"Hi, Maia," Stella says perkily. "Let's get you settled in your dorm. And then let's get you into some proper clothes."

I taste vomit in my mouth. I swallow it back, forcing the acid back down my throat. I don't want to wear what *she's* wearing. It's sick. But I don't want to end up in the glass box again.

I stand up, my legs shaking.

"Okay. Good." She smiles. It's so fake. Like fake fruit flavoring.

She turns to the door, but Professor Milborn in his sweet voice calls out to her: "Oh, Stella." She turns and looks at him, dipping her head slightly so she doesn't meet his eyes directly.

"Yes, sir?"

"Let me know if she disobeys or does *anything* out of the ordinary. She came from the kiddie camp and made a mess."

"Understood."

I look at Professor Milborn. I want to poke his eyes out with his pencil. I want to see the blood drip. I want him to struggle. I want him to feel the pain of knowing that he will never see again.

He smiles. "Be good, Maia."

And I smile back, teeth showing, my docile response masking my hate.

Stella opens the door and walks out. I follow her down the hallway and a soldier follows close behind me.

Stella looks at the soldier. "We're good here." She looks at me. "Right, Maia?"

I nod quickly. I don't want to be near soldiers anymore. They are toxic. They bleed pain into my bones. I follow her as we go outside and turn right onto a path that goes downhill. There are neat college buildings on each side, old-fashioned, fancy. Well, not a college anymore. Some have new plastic signs on them that say "Classroom," "Nurse's Ward," "Demo Room."

There are trees everywhere, their colors auburn, garbage truck green, bright yellow, marking the beginning or middle of autumn? I've totally lost track of time.

I smell the fresh scent of flowers in the distance, and I feel like smiling, despite everything, at the luxurious beauty. Whatever this college was, it indeed was a beautiful campus. I probably would have considered applying here. *Would have considered.* I almost stop. Not *will consider.* Have I lost hope in my future entirely? I want to stop and just sit on the ground and never get up, but Stella is scurrying ahead of me and I must keep up.

It's hard to keep up. My legs are wobbly; I haven't used them in days.

The cement pavement feels hard and rough against my shoes.

I notice there aren't a lot of soldiers around. There are security cameras here and there, but soldiers seem to be clustered around the gates at the edge of the campus.

And finally, a large, red brick building stands before us.

Around us, actually. There's a neat little garden in the middle, with the red building surrounding it on three sides.

We stop for a moment in the garden, gaping. At its center is a beautiful swirling sculpture of metal scraps that looks oddly familiar.

On the far side of the garden are a few shallow steps leading to a blue wooden door. Stella heads up the steps. A sign next to the door says "Dormitory B."

Inside, there is a loud air conditioner that booms and blows thick heavy cool air throughout the rooms. There's a large lounge area with bookshelves filled with books. I see "Romeo and Juliet," "The Great Gatsby," "Women in Love," and others.

All classics.

Heterosexual classics.

We go through an orange door to an elevator. I feel even more trapped than before.

Stella presses the button and the elevator dings. Some people exit. They nod at Stella respectfully and look at me briefly. Pity in their eyes. They recognize me.

The men wear all blue, and the women wear all pink. Fuck. This is so sexist.

We enter and she presses the number six, and a couple of seconds later, we exit into another long white hallway, lined with orange doors parallel to each other, and she finds room eight.

Dormitory B.

Floor six.

Room eight.

I have to remember where I live. I'm going to be here for a long time. I feel sure of that.

I can't do this. My eyes well up again.

Stella knocks on the door slightly, and a man's voice, gruff and stoic, says: "Come in."

Stella opens the door, and we enter what I would imagine a college two-person dorm room to look like. I've only seen pictures. I was planning to visit some colleges soon, but that's all kaput.

It's a medium-sized room with a small window overlooking more of the pretty campus buildings. There are ugly metal bars nailed in front of the window, presumably to prevent us from jumping, and to the right is a bed with a man in it, a man in blue, a big man in blue, leaning on a pillow, reading something. In front of the bed is a blue chest.

I look to the left. I presume that's my bed. White sheets folded and a pillow on an empty cream-colored mattress. A pink chest in front of the bed. And that's it. All the walls are plain beige. Boring and boring. The man looks up, and he eyes me and then looks at Stella. "Come on, Stella, they promised I could have the room to myself since Julie left."

"We're running out of space, Stanley. You have to understand. And she's a special case. No one was expecting her until recently."

He looks at me. "How old are you?"

"Seventeen."

He tsks. "So young. You should still be in a kiddie camp. What brings you here? Everyone says the kiddie camps are *heaven* compared to here."

I gulp.

"Well, well," Stella smiles. She goes to my chest and opens it. She rifles through it. There are light pink sneakers, bright pink flats with purple bows, pastel pink high heels. All sorts of skirts, all different shapes and material, but all of them pink. Some have purple or white stripes or ruffles on them. There are shirts, blouses, t-shirts, all pink. Dresses, all shades of pink, some super short, some long gowns, long sleeved. Even the bras and panties are pink, with little pink bows on them. She sifts through, snags some pink leggings. She looks at me, but I don't care a fuck. She smiles. I step closer. At the bottom, there is a plastic bag with the necessities: even the tooth-brush, soaps, toothpaste, and shampoo bottles are pink. There is another plastic bag with *what the fuck*. Pink tampons and pink pads.

"Where do they get all this?" I wonder out loud. "How do they have the money to buy all this pink crap?"

"We have a lot of donors who are very loyal to the cause," Stella replies primly.

Who the fuck would donate money to a place like this? They will definitely go to hell.

"Okay," Stella says, smiling. "Now you can change, get settled in, and then meet me back at the entrance to the dormitory."

"Where's the bathroom?"

I can't change with *him* there. Even though he probably already saw me in the glass box, I still feel *some* need for privacy. Or do I? I'm not rebelling anymore, am I? I'm not fighting back.

"It's around the corner, by the elevator. I'll show you."

I quickly pick some clothes at random, grab some bathroom necessities, and follow her out.

We head back toward the elevator and turn a corner, and there's the bathroom. The women's bathroom. The sign on the white door is stark, it's says "WOMEN" in bright pink letters, and clearly it's plastered over the original sign, which I'm guessing might say "All-Gender Bathroom" or something like that.

Before Miller, colleges were preparing the world for a better future, creating an inclusive environment where everyone, regardless of gender or sexual orientation, was accepted and could learn and be happy.

Now they serve a different purpose.

I enter the medium-sized bathroom quickly and head to the showers. There is a security camera in the corner above the sinks and mirror, but luckily not in the actual shower space. I stretch the shower curtain as far is it can go so whoever's behind the camera can't take a peek. I shed my weird hospital clothes and toss them on the other side and hang my new clothes on top of the curtain. I hope they won't get wet. I turn on the shower, take out the bathroom necessities, quickly soaping my body, as if I could wash away the terrors of the past. I try and try and try to clean off everything, try to make myself feel better on the inside, but no matter how fiercely I scrub, I still feel disgusting inside.

I feel my strength flowing back, from the nutritious food that the ghost of me scraped off the floor. . .

But I still feel filthy.

No matter how hard I wash my skin, I will always feel the filth of my disgusting self.

Guilt pours into my heart and I long just to erase myself from the world.

Just to erase myself from existence, or better yet—erase myself from ever having been born. If I were never born, my sister, my friends, maybe even possibly my girlfriend would be happy and alive.

\* \* \*

I meet Stella by the entrance, wearing a light pink t-shirt, a musty pink medium loose skirt, and light pink sneakers. I don't wear a hat. I didn't have any hats in my chest. Thank God. They just look fucking ridiculous.

I left my old clothes and toiletry back in my room, where Stanley was still reading his book.

"So, it's really easy navigating around here. I'll give you a quick tour, and we can stop back at the administration building to get you your schedule."

"Schedule?" I shudder. My schedule back at the "kiddie" army camp was filled with useless shit.

"Yeah, kind of, like it's just mandatory appointments every day.

But it's totally easy. The rest of the time you can either do some volunteering, join some clubs, or you can use that time to just take a mental break. Like reading, exercising, or eating. Whatever you desire. The dining hall is open from six a.m. to nine p.m. And you have to be in your dorms by ten. Eleven is lights out. It's very chill."

Right. I roll my eyes without her noticing.

Chill.

So chill, soldiers still wander in and out, there are security cameras on poles and on the sides of the buildings. The call boxes with emergency buttons that used to be all over campuses, to call the campus security, aren't there anymore.

I cannot call for help.

I may never be given that option ever again.

# 39

We are back at the main building where Professor Milborn's office is.

But this time we are in another room, on the floor above. It's a medium-sized office, with potted cactus plants by the windowsill, a desktop computer, and papers on the table. A woman with long jet-black hair and summer gray eyes looks at me. Rectangular glasses rest on the tip of her pointy nose. Silver bangles dangle from her ear, like she's some sort of hip model.

But hip means someone who is modern, or ahead of their time. A cool person. She is definitely not hip. If she is working in this sick, psycho-land place, that means her mind is very, very old-fashioned, despite her age, which is probably twenty-five by the looks of it. She must firmly believe in the old ideas—that being gay, being different, is a sin.

Or maybe, deep down, she believes we were all born like this and there is nothing anyone can do to change who we are, but she is just doing this for money. A job.

She clacks away on her computer with her long, light purple fingernails. Unlike me and Stella and all of the women here who are forced to be here, she does not wear pink. Instead, she wears slim black jeans, a light blue shirt, and a white, open-collared shirt on top. She's trying to look professional, trying to fit into the *man's* world. Ironic.

Isn't that a form of sin, trying to dress like a man? Isn't that illegal nowadays?

Maybe she's the daughter of an official and that's why she gets away with this.

I chuckle softly. What? I can't help it.

She stops clacking away and looks at me sternly. "Do you find something funny, Miss Robinson?"

Yes, she calls me that. Sick fucker.

I shake my head and mumble an apology. And she continues clacking on her computer.

"And. . ." She quickly types the last bit. "Done." She stops and looks at me. And then presses a button, and a printer whirs. It's under her desk. I look at the black box, and then I notice her shoes. Black high heels, shiny with perfection. I see a piece of paper flow out, and she watches me watching the paper sliding out of the printer with fascination.

I just haven't seen something like that in a while.

When the printing is done, she takes it and laminates it with another device I didn't see before, hidden behind her chair on the top of the shelf, and then she hands it to me.

"Today's Monday by the way. It's almost four o'clock."

It's my schedule. I look it over. Stella eyes it as well.

"I recommend you memorize it, so you don't have to bring that everywhere with you. You don't need to bring anything with you to your classes, not really."

Stella nods. "I can show you where your class or session is now, and when you're done for the day, I'll give you the official tour. . ." She smiles.

I study my schedule. I can't believe I have to do this all over again.

I see that I do have some free time every day where I can eat or join a club or whatever, as Stella had told me before, but I still have to go to all these appointments and classes and shit shows.

I thought I had escaped all this.

Maia Anna Robinson
**Condition:** attracted to the same sex
**Schedule:**

**Monday**
10:00am-12: Group conversion therapy. Smith's Auditorium.
2:00pm-4: "Straightening yourself" class. Room 105. Administrative Building.
4pm-6: Intro Session. Room 305. Fall Building.
**Tuesday**
8:30am-10: David's Closet class. Room 506. Summer Building.
10:00am-12: Real World lecture. Room 422. Summer Building.
2:00pm-4: Group conversion therapy.
**Wednesday**
6:30am-9:30pm: Mimi's all-day relaxation technique class. Room 202. Fall Building
**Thursday**
5:00pm-7: Intro to Family Values. Room 329. Winter Building.
9:00pm-10:30: Group conversion therapy.
**Friday**
10:00am-12: "Straightening yourself" class
5:00pm-7: Intro to Family Values.
**Saturday**
11:30am-2: Group conversion therapy.
2:00pm-4: Real World lecture.
6:00pm-8: Intro Session.
**Sunday**
10:00am-12: Group conversion therapy.
1:30pm-5: Progress Reviews. Room 332. Administrative Building.
7:00pm-9:30: Assembly. Smith's Auditorium.

I check where I have to go now. The Fall Building. Wherever the fuck that is.

I look at Stella. I grip the schedule tightly, my hands shaking. I'm not sure what this is. Intro? I don't want an introduction because that would mean this is really starting over again. I have to go through another layer of hell.

"What is this?" I ask, my voice wavering and shaking. "What is this?"

I feel bubbles in my chest pop one by one. As if I were in an airplane, and my ears are popped due to the pressure changes. But instead of feeling it in my ear, I feel it in my chest, popping and popping, destroying my chest cavity in its wake.

My mind is muddy, and the voices around me are distant waves roaring in the ocean, sliding away and away from the sinking ship that is my mind.

I feel a hand on my back, warm fingers. I turn my cloudy mind to the body holding the arms, holding the fingers. It's Stella. She's tapping softly on my back. "Just breathe. Just breathe," she says. "Take slow breaths. In through the nose." She breaths through her nose, guiding me. I copy. "Out through the mouth." I blow the horrid breath of pain out, and I feel better. "In. . ." In, sucking the air, sucking the feeling of warmth, the perfume coming from the administrative lady. Did she say her name? Or did I simply forget it?

"Out. . ." I breath out, the stench of being trapped, the crippling fortitude of my mind leaving my body, the. . . My vision clears. I am bent over, my face on my lap, my hands over the back of my neck. I sit up quickly and look at Stella, who is looking at the administrative lady, who eyes Stella's hand on my back.

Oh, for fuck's sake.

She quickly takes her hand off my back.

The administrative lady moves her mouse around, typing, typing.

"Please don't report me to Professor Milborn. I'm making really good progress." She fakes another smile. Cringey. "I'm volunteering to be a mentor. Mentoring Maia and others who came before her."

"I'm sorry."

"She was just having a panic attack, that's all. I was just trying to help."

The administrative lady looks at Stella, pity in her eyes. "I'm sorry. It's my job. . ." She clacks away and then looks at me. "And you. Mild panic attack. I think we can get you some pills for that." She smiles.

*More unknown pills. More unknown medicine.*

I shake my head, but I'm not going to say no to the administrative lady. I want to. But what would that bring? She would report me to Professor Milborn, and he would put me in that glass box. . . . And I don't want to be in that glass box. I just want to go home.

Maybe I can just go through the actions, pretend like I'm "being cured," and go home earlier than a couple months.

But this is part of my identity. This is who I am.

And what if I fake it so well that I start to believe my own bullshit? What then? How will I ever get back to who I am?

Who knows what the outside world is like. Who knows how many restrictions they put out there. Who knows, who knows, who knows. . .

"What is your name?" I ask. "I'm sorry, I think I've forgotten."

"I'm Lavender."

Lavender. Pretty name.

Lavender looks at her watch, and then looks at me. "You better hurry, now, before you're late."

Stella stands, coldly staring at me, angry that I got her in trouble.

I stand up quickly, schedule in my hand, and follow Stella out through the hallway, through the second-floor lobby, down the rickety steps, letting my fingers feel the smoothness of the wooden railing, and out the door. We are in a rush, so she runs, passing people in their "appropriate colors," passing more college buildings, and then we arrive at a small, flat-roofed, light blue building, probably only three floors, with pixelated glass windows.

A sign says: "Fall Building."

"Okay, I'll meet you at six. We can have the official tour and then we can head to dinner together." She smiles. Her eyes tell a different story, though. After I got her in trouble, the last thing she wants to do is show me around.

I do the math. Two hours long?! My mouth gapes open, and then she's off and I'm alone, well, not alone, but for the first time in probably a week, I'm awake and don't have a chaperone with me. I consider just not going into the building, finding a way out, but I shiver. I saw the soldiers.

They will catch me. And I don't even know where I am. There are no maps anywhere. I don't have my phone to use Google Maps.

And I will get put in the glass box.

And *things* will happen to my sister.

But. . .

I'm contemplating what to do when I hear a deep voice, low and steady.

"*Maia?*"

I turn around and I see a familiar face. A face I have not seen in months.

It's Jacob, my neighbor from *before*.

With new glasses, stubble on his chin, he wears the blue uniform, and his eyes, his eyes are soulless.

"Jacob! . . . What. . .?"

He approaches me with hasty steps. "What are *you* doing here? Why. . . ?" He gestures to my clothes, my goddamned pink clothes. "*You're not supposed to be here!*"

I want to hug him, but I'm not sure if that's allowed.

We used to invite Jacob and his family over for dinner. They'd bring over wine and some cranberry pie that was so delicious. Perfect touch of crust, sweet but tangy. Their three kids are the cutest. They're siblings, one year apart. They'd be playing with their Nerf guns. The oldest would pull my hair, teasing me. I hope they're okay. I hope they are better off than. . . their parents.

"Where's Cason?" I ask. "Is he all right?" He and his husband Cason had adopted those three beautiful children.

He shakes his head. Tears cover his cheeks. "I haven't seen or heard from him since that wretched night."

I saw Jacob and Cason the night we got taken from our homes. They were beaten and bruised, and a fucking social worker was taking their kids away from them, sending them to foster care or something.

He steps forward, placing his hands on my shoulders, and looks at me sorrowfully. He's only a couple of inches taller than me. "Maia, you were in the youth camp, what. . . what did you do? Why did they send you *here?*" He shakes his head. "Not. . . . I hope you didn't try and. . . escape. . . ?"

"I didn't just *try*," I say, almost scolding him. "I actually escaped with some others. . . who . . . I think they might have made it out. I'm not sure."

"Oh, Maia, you should have kept your head down; you should have done what they said. . . anything to stay there. You don't want to be here. This place is. . ." He shudders.

"What, just stay there and let them do all that to me?! Let them *change* me into someone I'm not? I had to *try*. I had to *try!*" My eyes are tearing. He doesn't understand. If he did understand, he wouldn't still be here. He would have tried to escape too.

"This place is a hundred times worse than where you were," he tells me. "Whatever pain you had there is a hundred times worse here. . . And their techniques here, they are on the other end of the spectrum! Maybe there, you could have stayed strong, look like you let them make you into someone you're not, but then bounce back, become your old, normal, loving self again. But here. . ." He shivers, tears pouring down his face. His hands tremble on my shoulder. "The changes they make here are permanent. The techniques. . . they strip away who you are and build you back up again, with their own pieces. They turn your desires into death wishes. They make what you want what you hate. And you can never go back."

"They can't *really* change us," I insist. "You know *that*. They can try to, but who we are, *what* we are, we were born like this. It's in our genetics; it's in our code." I shake my head, not sure I really believe what I'm saying, but hoping I can convince myself.

"Maia," he says in a low voice. "You can be born with brown eyes, but your eyes can be scooped out of you and replaced with blue eyes. You can be rewired. They make it out to be a cure for a disease, but really it's just a solution to what they think is a problem. And unfortunately, it works."

"*What the fuck are you saying?!*" I shake his hands off my shoulders. I step back. Oh, Jacob, Jacob, Jacob.

Jacob and Cason were a couple before I was even born. I grew up watching them hug each other and hold hands and smile and love each other. They were the first gay couple I ever knew. Because of them, I was able to understand what gay is, what *being* gay is; they helped me recognize that I am gay myself. Without them, I would be hopeless. "*Jacob, are you fucking hearing yourself?!*"

"Lower your voice, Maia." His eyes flit around. Some soldiers are watching us from a distance, alert. But I'm so fucking mad. I'm so fucking mad. Anger boils in my veins, and I know I shouldn't take it out on Jacob. I know I should take it out on the real enemies, but he is the only person I can take it out on right now.

I slap him.

He steps back, shocked. Before Miller, I'd never shown any of my anger to anyone I cared about besides my family. And to my family, only on rare, rare occasions.

Even with my family, I never hit or shoved them. Certainly I never slapped anyone. What's happened to me?

"*What happened to you?*" I shout. "Did they make you say this?! Did they threaten your kids? To become this *slave?*"

The soldiers approach us. I hear their footsteps on the gravel, their batons swishing against their legs.

Jacob eyes them and then he looks at me. "Listen! Get down on your knees now, Maia."

"What?"

"Go on your knees, ask for forgiveness. So they don't report you for fighting."

"What the fuck? I'm—" He puts his hands on my shoulders and pushes me down, forcing me to my knees. And now he is on the ground too, kneeling. I try to stand but he holds my arm tight. At this moment, he is stronger than me. Danger has energized him.

I want to punch his fucking face.

His beautiful, gorgeous, stubbled chin, and those lips that used to part in such a glorious smile; no wonder Cason fell for him hard. He was just so goddamn gorgeous.

"Do you want to end up back in the glass cage?"

My eyes widen, and I freeze. How does he know. *Did he see me. . . naked?*

"I heard there was a young girl there," he says, "but I didn't want to see, so I always took a different path instead of passing through the quad. I never thought it'd be *you.*"

My eyes well with tears. "I don't want to end up back there," I sob.

I feel my shoulders light again, and his hands are pressed into his legs. I am still bending, on my knees. The soldiers are closer.

"Just let me handle things. I'll make sure they don't tell Professor

Milborn. Just go to your session and tell them you were late because you got lost."

"What about the cameras?"

"I'll ask them to delete this part. Just let me talk. Play along." He looks up.

There are five burly soldiers, they hover above us and grin. They are in their usual uniform. I see their guns. Maybe I should just snatch one from them, but I know if I try, they will tackle me before I can do anything. "Hey there, boys," Jacob says in a bantering tone, like he'd use to get a bargain on something he wanted to buy. He smiles his flashing smile.

"Jacob. . . with. . ." One of the soldiers, apparently their leader, grabs my chin with his cold fingers and forces my head to look up at him. "The troubled one. She's already made a big fucking headache for the bosses . . . what are *you* doing arguing with her? This is definitely against the rules. No fights or fucks!" He snickers.

"She was my neighbor *before*," Jacob smiles, "and I was just telling her how she needs to *start behaving*. Just trying to help you guys out, doing a favor for Dr. Milborn." Jacob looks at me, his eyes sliding over me, condescending as all fuck. "Right?"

I don't want to end up in the glass box, so I play along like he said. I manage a smile and nod slightly, which is hard, because the soldier still grips my chin hard.

He lets go and looks at Jacob. "This is gonna *cost* you."

"Right, of course," Jacob says, "you won't tell Professor Milborn, thank you, and. . . and would you mind erasing the security footage?"

"That's going to cost extra."

"Yes, of course."

"You're gonna have to do more than give us cash." The soldier smiles, a sly fucking smile I'm ever so familiar with. That guard at Camp 17 had that same smile.

I shiver. "No, don't." I look at Jacob and then at the soldiers. "Just tell Professor Milborn whatever you saw. Don't make him pay."

Jacob gives me a look, his head twisting to look me dead in the eyes. "Maia, *please*," he says under his breath.

The soldier brings his hand to his chin, as if he is combing his fingers through an imaginary beard. "Hmmmm."

"She's not thinking straight," Jacob goes on. "You know how girls are." I feel like shit. But he's saying it so I won't have to face worse.

The head soldier looks at the others. They mumble to each other.

He nods and then looks at Jacob. "You have more to offer, so let's go. And *you*," he says to me, "you stay out of trouble now!"

Jacob immediately stands up. I stand too.

"No!" I shout. "I'll do whatever it is."

Why would they take Jacob? Why are they choosing a man? Are they gay? Would they *dare*? Or is it something that's not sexual? Do they just want to humiliate him more, have power over him? I can't imagine what it is they want from him, what he can possibly offer them. . . . But whatever it is. . . I should be the one to take the fall. I'm the *troublemaker*.

"What can you possibly do?" The head soldier eyes me, his eyes going up and down my body. "We've already *seen everything*." He smirks. "It's not enough."

I freeze. I'm just standing there now, watching the soldiers leave with Jacob, and I can't move.

*. . . I wasn't enough.*

*My body. . . wasn't enough.*

But why the fuck do I care if they are attracted to me? Why do I fucking care?

Like I know *Aimee* was attracted to me. She loved my body. She loved how I looked in the school hallways, or in the subway, or in bed, naked and sleek with sweat on every curve.

She was the one true person that not only loved the inside of me but also the outside of me. And not just like she loved my body sexually, but like it was more than sex for her. I was a work of art, I was a symphony, I was a goddess to her.

And I never felt someone look at me like she did, after . . . I haven't felt someone attracted to me in a long time. Maybe Penelope could have looked at me like that. . . but she's not *her*. She's not Aimee. . . We never had enough time by ourselves to reach that point. . .

I hope Penelope made it out. I hope she's free, regardless.

I don't find myself attractive either, any more.

If I don't find myself attractive, and even a man doesn't find me attractive. . . then. . .

*Who am I?*

And why are my thoughts so centered around what a man thinks of my fucking body? I shouldn't care. I shouldn't give a fuck. I'm not attracted to men, so why should I care?

Have I already been changed? Without me knowing?

Was Jacob right?

Have they changed me forever?

Have they changed me into *wanting* attention and *wanting* to be liked by men?

By any man? All men?

So then what's next?

# 40

I walk through the white doors of the Fall Building, and instantly the scent of pine needles hits me hard. My nose crinkles. It reminds me of the smell of Christmas, that time in New York City where, on every couple of blocks, you'll see a bunch of Christmas trees leaning on each other, the workers with their scarves over their mouths, asking if you'd like to buy a tree.

My family has a tradition of giving a name to the tree we have chosen, like Taylor Branch or Iris Tree, and spending the day before Christmas decorating him or her or them, eating oatmeal cookies, smelling the fresh pine needles, feeling the needles under our bare feet.

Will I be home in time for Christmas?

Inside the Fall Building, I am in a large room, with plush, dark navy-blue sofas lining the walls, the window looking out on a patch of grass underneath the shimmering light blue sky. There are tables with paper origamis: green frogs, light blue cranes, pink flowers.

It's rather cozy, and at one end of the room, there is a brown door, and that seems to be the way, so I open it, and there are different doors on each side of the hallway with different numbers next to them. "101," "102," "103," et cetera. Evens on the left side and odds on the right.

I hear a mumble of voices behind each door.

I walk to the end of the hallway, turn a corner, and there is a stairway at the end of the hallway. I pass by more doors, and then head up the stairs.

I enter the third floor and quickly find "305." My palms are sweaty, and a slow, steady headache arrives. I don't want to do this, whatever it is, this *Intro*.

But what choice do I have?

I softly knock on the door, rata-tat-tat.

"Come in."

I open the door and find myself in a medium-sized room. There is no window.

It's a simple room, with mirrors on the left and right sides.

In the middle, there is a grey metal office chair, the kind that swivels, and farther back, facing toward me, there's a white armchair where a man sits languidly, legs crossed.

He has slender fingers, tight muscles, a black, tight t-shirt, and light blue pants. His eyebrows are knitted together, and his eyes are so. . . soft. They are pebbles tossed in the sky. The color is an intense dark blue, one I have never seen before. He has spiky blonde hair, and a small mouth. He looks to be about thirty years old; he could be a high school teacher.

In his lap is an iPad, one of those jumbo-sized tablets that visual arts professionals use. There's a white clip-on at the top of it, like the one I saw at the nurses' place.

There's a camera in the corner of the room, watching us, its red light blinking steadily.

"You're late," he says, clearly pissed.

*Oh, how we wasted precious minutes to fucking make me someone I'm not. How sorry I am.*

"Sorry. . . I got lost," I mumble.

"Close the door and sit," he commands, pointing to the office chair.

I don't like the way he is commanding me. It's sick, like he gets off ordering me around like a dog. The same way Dr. Milborn did.

I hover by the door, pausing, testing him almost.

And then I give in. I don't want to cause any trouble. I gulp, close the door, and sit on the office chair, facing the man in his armchair, closing my legs tight, trying to sit up straight, but that's so uncomfortable I end up leaning back in the chair. I place my hands on my lap and glance up at the security camera. There's probably a soldier watching a monitor, outside somewhere, at the ready to burst in and attack me if I do anything wrong.

"My name is Chaz Raymond. I will be conducting your Intro Sessions."

He gives me the clip. I take it with my tender fingers. "Put it on your right index finger." I do so. My hands and elbows are still bandaged, but my fingers are not. It hurts as the clip wraps around my finger, but soon it grows numb.

"What is your name?"

He looks at his iPad. I try to look at it as well, but he angles it towards him so I can't see it unless I stand up to look. Which would get me in trouble.

"Don't you know my name?"

He looks up quickly. "You're going to answer my questions and participate, correct?" he says in an even tone. "I can ask the doctor to get the words out of you if you'd like. It'll cause you a wee bit of pain, but we must proceed with our program."

I'm not sure which doctor he's talking about, and which program, but I am afraid of him. In the past couple of months, I have feared doctors and scientists and people in authority, instead of looking up to them like I did in the past.

"Maia Anna Robinson," I quickly say.

"Age?"

"Seventeen."

He nods. And continues looking at the iPad.

"Parents' names?"

"Carl David Robinson and Hana Mae Robinson." I miss them deeply. I say their names slowly because the sound of them gives me a moment's peace.

He smiles.

"Okay. Now the next couple of questions, I want you to answer truthfully. And if you don't, I will know," he says.

"Know?" What the fuck is he talking about?

He flips the iPad to show me the screen, and I see that half of it is black, except for some white wiggly lines, and underneath is a white square, probably some kind of notepad app. Now empty but I'm sure it will soon be filled with his invasive notes about me. "Your heart rate remained the same when you answered the previous questions truthfully. If it picks up, I know you're lying."

I see a spike.

"How will you be able to tell the difference between a lie and me just being nervous?"

"I'll know. They didn't hire me just for my looks." He smirks.

I gave no indication that I thought him good-looking. By the way, he's not. If I *were* attracted to men, I *still* wouldn't find him attractive. Not if he was the last person on the planet and it was our job to repopulate the Earth.

I sigh. He turns the iPad around.

"Tell me about the first time you fornicated with a girl."

Fornicate. What a weird, old-fashioned word. "Why don't you just say *have sex*?" I ask him.

"Sex, like the phrase *making love*, is only to be used for when *a man and a woman* are having intercourse."

I roll my eyes.

"Are you going to answer my questions, Maia, or are you going to object? I can get the soldiers to help us here, or the doctor, anyone I like. I can force the answers out of your mouth, like I said." He heaves a sigh. "I don't like repeating myself."

He puts his hand in his pocket and pulls out a little silver box with a red button. It must be to call them. I can't let that happen, so I quickly reply, "Okay, okay, I'll tell you."

I gulp. I have never told anyone what I did with Aimee. Never. It was a silent promise between us. We just knew that what we did together was our secret. Only between us. No one can ever know what we did. Because our love, our love was just for each other.

He looks at me: "I'm waiting."

I look at my lap. "I. . . I was at her place. And we talked a bunch before about when and what, and how much, and how far we were going to go. She'd had sex with people before, and we went shopping together at a sex shop to get. . . to get like a bunch of stuff, like we weren't planning on using *everything* we bought. And we wanted to be careful, so we got dental dams. . ." I look down at my fingers. I am unconsciously scratching the back of my fingers over and over again. I might even draw blood. I feel like I'm going into too much detail, but I'm afraid if I quickly just summarize it, it would not be *enough* for him. I have to give him what he wants.

"Continue. And look at me when you tell me."

Sick psycho-bastard. I look up at his soft eyes, just focusing on the softness, and continue. "It was. . . interesting. . . I don't know. Like everyone says your first time is not going to be as magical as they make it out to be in the movies, but there was something pulling me to her, this new love that was born from our touch; it was magical for both of us."

"Go into more detail. Describe it for me so I can visualize it."

I glance up at the camera.

Do they *hear* what he is telling me to do?

Do they know he is taking advantage of the situation, exploiting his power over me, using this session to satisfy his own weird sexual desires?

Men do get turned on by the thought of lesbian sex; that's a tale as old as time. On porn websites, I've heard, lesbian porn is always the highest rated out of all the other shit.

And for these guys to get off on watching, isn't that itself a sin? And yet they get away with it.

The actual participants are getting punished.

While the real sinners get to take advantage of us.

I curl my left fingers into a fist, my misshapen nails digging into my bandaged palms.

I have no choice, though.

I hate that I remember every detail of our first time.

I used to love re-watching it over and over in my head.

But now, I wish I had just forgotten it. That it just blended in with the rest of my sexual experiences with her. Because if I did, I could tell him the truth and say I don't remember anything.

"We watched a soapy movie on her laptop, about two girls falling in love, while curling next to each other on her bed. And when the credits rolled, I became really nervous, because our plans were to watch a movie and then have sex." I think back to that moment. I was so nervous, my whole body shaking. "And she hugged me tightly." I would do anything to be in her arms again. My eyes become wet, but I push the feeling away with all my might.

"And half of me wanted to get this over with because first times are always weird and suck." He smiles as I say the word suck, sick fucking bastard. I just want to squeeze my fingers around his bare neck. "We were kissing and touching each other, all over, it felt really good." I declare my memory to him, that this love, this moment was real. It was not a sin. It was not a disease. It was something deep and profound that no one person can replicate. "We stripped naked, and her eyes were glossy as she looked over my body as if I were something she had never seen before. And we were kissing deeply with tongue and all." Am I saying too much? Why am I saying too much?

*Because I am afraid.*

"And she touched me all over, kissing me, fingering me. . ."

"Show me how," he says, his voice drooping.

"What?"

"Show me how she touched you. Show me what she did to you with your fingers, on your body," he says. Devil sick bastard.

"No. . ." I tumble over my words. "No, I didn't. . . this is not. . . You can't do this. You can't make me."

"I can make you do whatever I want."

"This is illegal."

"Says who?"

I look at the security camera. "Them. They're watching. They won't let you do this to me."

He leans forward, smiling. "One, I'm not doing anything to you. I want you to show me yourself, on your body. I am not breaking any laws or intruding on your privacy." Yes you are, yes you are. "And two, no one is watching us. Yes, it's being recorded, but I will delete the footage later.

"And I will have you know, young lady," he adds, "that I happen to be a *personal friend* of our esteemed President Doug Miller, who has done so much for our nation. And for that reason if for no other, I would strongly advise you, don't even *think* about messing with me!"

And he grins, staring at my body, his eyes roving up and down.

"Just *fuck* you!" I tell him.

One by one, the memories of Aimee dissolve, leaving me with the memory of telling this evil turd our deepest love for each other.

"Oh my pretty one, don't say *that*," he titters, licking his lips with his fat, sluggish tongue. "You have to understand, Maia. I am only doing all this to help you."

"FUCK YOU!" I stand up. "If you're helping me, then why delete the footage? Why would you be afraid of them judging how you *change* me?"

"Sometimes people don't understand." He smiles and stands up, towering over me. "Sometimes the right way is the wrong way in some eyes. That's life, you know. But I know, deep down, that this, that *I* will put you on the right path, in the right way. So. . . show me!"

The memory of her is gone, replaced by the sight of this evil man. Now every time I look back at my first time with Aimee, I will think of this piece of shit. He has ruined it. He has ruined the memory.

"Show me!" he says, louder. He takes a step forward and then he grasps my chin. "Show me, or I'll just have to do it myself." He trails his other fingers around my shoulders, over the collarbone, down and down, feeling my boobs through my shirt.

Fuck him.

Fuck all this.

I take a deep breath, summoning up all my strength, and I push him back and stand up. His eyes widen. He wasn't expecting that. I shove him again, harder. He stumbles back and falls in a heap into the armchair, dropping his iPad. "You slut," he shouts and gropes in his pocket for the help button. Without even thinking about what I'm doing, I turn and grasp the metal office chair by its armrests, and with strength I didn't know I had, I lift it up and I turn back toward the man as he scrambles in his chair, groping in his pocket for the button, which he won't find in time, because with all my might I bring the heavy chair crashing down on him.

"Fuck!" he screams as the chair tumbles off to one side. He puts his hand to his forehead where blood is now spurting. "You will fucking pay." The iPad is at my feet, it will be my next weapon, and I pick it up and raise it high. He's looking at the blood on his hand. I bang the iPad down over the top of his head, hitting him hard with the edge of it, like it was a cleaver. It makes a sound like a muffled squishy thump.

"Die," I hiss. "Die. Fucker. Die."

I don't know all of what happens next. But I know I'm hitting him hard in the head over and over again with the corner of the iPad against his temple. And I don't hear him anymore. I don't hear the thumping anymore. The iPad in my hands is broken, the screen shattered. I drop it and look at him. *Chaz*. What a stupid name. There's blood all over his face. I kick him. He doesn't react. I look at his chest. It isn't moving.

Did I just kill him?

I don't wait around to figure this out. I drop the iPad at his feet, turn, and head to the door. I open it and bolt. I have to get out of here.

I probably just killed a man, but this fucker deserved it. Who knows how many people he took advantage of?

He can't get away with ruining the most precious memory of my whole entire life.

I run and run and run.

I don't stop.

I don't see where I'm going but then all of a sudden, I feel a rush of soldiers behind me.

They tackle me and I fall.

They pile up on me, as heavy as the seven elements.

Something pricks my arm and I'm knocked out in seconds.

The last thing I see is the splatter of *his* blood all over my oh-so-cute pink outfit.

# 41

I wake up with a sudden urge to pee. My bladder really hurts. It pulses in my pelvis.

Pelvis, right? Is the bladder located in the pelvis?

I should Google it.

I open my eyes and reach to where my back pants pocket should be, reaching for my phone, but instead I cup my ass, my squishy ass cheek. What? I continue feeling up my own body, groping around, and I realize I'm staring at a reflection of myself. A reflection of my naked body. I am in a closet, and the sides. . . I feel around the sides. Hard plastic, unbreakable. Somehow the mirror, which is on all four sides of me, is outside of the plastic, but attached to the plastic.

I turn around and around and see my naked self everywhere.

I don't want to see my slumped, naked body.

I crouch and wrap my arms around my head.

I close my eyes, but after a couple of seconds, a banging infiltrates my brain. So painful, so menacing that the pain immediately breaks open my eyelids once more.

I hear a voice. "Don't try to sleep, Maia. A special drug is in your system that will deliver pain if you try and close your eyes." I stand up. I don't know where the voice is coming from.

There is a small hole on the top of the plastic closet. I try to reach for it, it's too far. I bang hard on the plastic around me.

My fist clenched, I bang over and over again. It hurts but I don't fucking care. I bang on my right side, behind me, on my left side, on the bottom, which is more plastic covered with hard rubber, and in front of me, over and over. Pain radiates over my fingers, my bones are cracking, my fingernails chipping. I pant and heave.

"Don't hurt yourself, Maia," the voice says coldly.

It's Professor Milborn.

I pant, "Please, just let me go." I cry and heave. "Please. . . I didn't do *anything* wrong."

"Maia, you must be delusional."

"What the fuck are you talking about?"

"Do you not remember what you did?"

I crouch on the ground again, sobbing, heaving. "What are you talking about? Please. . ."

"You killed Chaz Raymond."

"Who?"

"Your instructor at the Intro Session. Where you just were. Don't you remember your session with him? We hired him to analyze your urges, and to trace their causes, and to formulate a means for getting rid of them."

Oh. Him. Everything comes flashing back to me. His words, what he wanted to make me do, his assault. . . I threw a chair at him and bashed him with an iPad. That might have left him injured, but surely not dead.

"You're wrong. I couldn't have killed him. . . I just. . ." What? Resisted an assault? Knocked him cold? What's the term?

"You killed him. The blows from the chair and the iPad were brutal indeed. His brain was bleeding internally. And you left him to die."

"You're just saying this. It's just part of your treatment, your *program*. You are saying this to test me."

"No. We are not. The doctor pronounced him dead an hour ago. We saw the footage from the security camera. Maia, you killed him."

I don't believe him. I don't. I don't. But I remember his body, his cold, unmoving body. I didn't check his pulse or anything, but he wasn't breathing... his chest wasn't moving... Maybe... but I know it in my gut, in my soul, he was dead when I left the room. He was so dead, and he's dead because of me... "NO! It was self-defense! Did you hear what he said to me? What he did to me? I was fucking defending myself."

"Yes, he did say and do some things he shouldn't have said and done, but—"

Oh, fuck the buts.

"His technique is unique. He was recommended by many experts in this field, not to mention political elements at the highest level, and they did say his methods are unorthodox, but he does have a 100 percent success rate. So, that's why we hired him. You should feel lucky to have received at least a bit of his treatment plan. You might yet find yourself cured, in the fullness of time, if you play your cards right."

My eyes grow bigger and bigger. "What the fuck is wrong with you people? What the fuck is wrong with you? He made me tell him *private things*. Things no one should ever have to say to a stranger! He wanted me to..." I stop for breath; I forget for the moment that I'm naked and vulnerable and who knows what the fuck else. "He wanted me to touch myself in front of him." I squeeze my eyes. I remember the violation. I was there. I was fucking there. I witnessed it because it *happened* to me. TO ME. "He touched me, he fucking attacked me... I can't take this anymore." I go on my knees, as if I was praying. "Please, I can't handle this anymore. I'm only seventeen. You can't do this to me."

"Yes, Maia. We can."

I stand up so fast that I probably pull a muscle. My legs ache. "Fuck you. No matter how much you do to me, I will never give in. You fucking hear that?! I will always be fucking gay!"

"What you don't understand, Maia, is that now, now that you have killed someone, your case has become much larger than yourself."

My eyes widen. "What. . ."

"Word of your case has *reached the very top*. And as a consequence, you shall be granted a choice between two options. This choice will determine your future."

"What are you talking about?"

I am sitting on the floor. My throat hurts from all the yelling.

"You murdered a man, Maia. You murdered him in cold blood. You could have tried to get help; you could have said that this was a mistake and called for help. Maybe then he would be alive. But you wanted him to die, Maia. And so, you left him and ran."

"I. . . I just wanted to get away."

"And you didn't think about him! That's selfish, Maia."

"Bullshit! This isn't fair!"

"Fair?" Dr. Milborn laughs softly and goes on: "I have been in consultation with authorities at the very highest level! You have every reason to be grateful to me for this, believe me! For I have explained to them that the disease has eliminated your ability to differentiate good from evil. Nevertheless, they still want to take action. They want to hold you accountable in court."

"What?" I croak.

"Yes, court, Maia. All the evidence points against you. There's security footage. On that evidence you will definitely get time."

I sink deeper into the floor; I just want to melt away.

"You could try your hand in court, try to make the jury pity you, but I can tell you for sure, that *they* will not pity you."

I don't respond. I don't know what to say.

"A lot has changed, Maia. While you were in your own little bubble, the world moved on."

My chest feels like crumpling.

"The law, the courts, the justice system, all that has changed. The jury is not randomly picked anymore. It's picked by officials who deem which person is best fit for each case. . . If the right payments are made, you could have a selective jury of people who hate your kind. You will go to juvenile prison, and when you turn eighteen, you will go to an adult prison and stay there for life, if you *can survive* that long. And neither prison will be a regular prison; they will be dedicated to those that have the disease. And they are strict and harsh. They use techniques that some would call inhumane, horrific techniques. In the adult prison you will not be under the state's or the government's protection anymore; you will be in an institution that is under private management, led by a man who is certainly the leading authority in his field, a truly eminent man. It is true that some have called this man a sadist, a psychopath. That is not for me to judge, but I feel it is only fair to warn you. . .

"Okay, then, that is the first choice."

I gulp. There's more. . . .

"And now for the second choice." I can hear him smiling.

"In the second alternative, which I do strongly recommend, you admit to the world that the disease made you this way and that you are going to voluntarily stay here for treatment. During your time here you will follow our instructions and do what you're told.

"In this scenario, no one will press charges. You will be considered not guilty by reason of insanity. You won't have to go to court. When in due course you are *cured*, you will be free and can go home."

What. The. Fuck.

"I'll give you some time to decide,"

"What about my sister?!"

"She's going to the Junior Camp as planned. Nothing can change that, I'm afraid. We still need to see if she *got* your *disease.*"

My heart sinks.

"Now, Maia," he says, "you are going to receive a little taste of punishment now. Oh yes, just a sample."

As if this wasn't punishment enough.

"It is necessary to provide you with a taste of what is in store for you should you opt for the first choice. After you are tried and convicted. I told you things can be worse than the glass box, Maia. And yes, you are being recorded to show the rest of your kind here. I'll see you in a bit."

And then his voice is gone. I try and claw my way out from the plastic closet but of course I can't. All I see is my miserable, fucking self, and then a big object like the lower half of a black ball gets placed on the hole above me. It fits perfectly so the ball doesn't fall through, but it's still there, tight. A red dot blinks from it. It's a camera.

I sit on the floor and I notice there's a tiny hole in the plastic that I hadn't seen before, on the wall right next to my head. A metal tube pokes through it, fitting perfectly as well.

I look at the camera again. What the fuck are they doing?

And then something spurts, and cold water comes splashing on my feet. I move away, banging my head on the other side, and the cold water pours from the metal tube that pokes through. Pouring hard and fast.

*Are they going to drown me?* I stand up. I don't care about everyone seeing my naked body anymore. I don't want to die.

I'm not going to die in a plastic closet.

The water keeps pouring and pouring. I am staring at my own reflection, hitting the plastic hard. Plastic must break. Plastic must break. *Plastic must break.*

The cold water is rising, reaching over my ankles. It's cold and I shiver.

I bend down and put a finger in the mouth of the tube, stopping the flow. It works for several seconds, but then the water pumps harder, faster than before, pushing my finger out.

I am dying. I am dying. I am going to die. I am going to die. And I can't feel I can't feel. The water is at my legs.

The professor's words ring in my mind. He was offering me *a choice*. Any sane person would agree to the second scenario. But I can't bear to be propaganda for these evil fuckers.

But I want my life back. I want to choose the easier path, the path with less pain, with less discomfort. The path where I can go home.

If I go to prison, who knows how long I'll be there? Will it be life? Will I be tortured for the rest of my life?

Never to see my family and my loved ones ever again.

How can I put myself through that?

The world feels like it's ending.

I can't be a hero. . . I can't. . .

# 42

My lungs are tight and sharp. I feel the water circling my neck, as if the water had hands and were choking me to death. My mind and body turn on alert mode and I try to keep myself afloat, but nothing works. The water rises around me. My head bangs on something hard. I try to squeeze my head in a corner, where there is still a pocket of air, but the water doesn't stop.

I no longer care anymore that I'm naked.

I no longer care that people are watching.

All I can think of is life or death.

Life or death.

My vision blurs: everything becomes liquid, blue, and white. My heart beats in my head. I am in the water, banging helplessly on the plastic. I am floating aimlessly, losing strength as the seconds tick by.

My lungs are hard and solid, screaming for air.

Maybe this is when I die.

# 43

I am weightless, like a cloud, like a cloud made of smoke and whispers. I don't know what this place is. I don't know where I am. I am made of nothingness. It's cold and hot and chilly and warm at the same time. All I see is gray mist evaporating in and out of my vision, spots of light gray, all different densities of color. This doesn't make any sense; this does not make sense. It does not. Where was I before?

I was drowning, or almost drowning, or something.

*Am I dead?*

"Hey there!" I hear a beautiful voice, such a soft, beautiful voice. I swim to the voice, moving my arms and legs, and then I see a figure made out of silver butterflies with black marks on them.

A figure, a human figure. A bit shorter than me, hair flowing, her breasts small, her legs long and tender. My eyes widen.

"You. . . You're. . . You're here!"

I don't see her face, I don't see her features, but I know it's her.

I look down at my body. My skin glows. I'm naked, but not naked at the same time. I swim closer. She's here. She's here.

Which means I must really be dead.

Because she died on that night so long ago, maybe she's been waiting for me. . . "Maia," she whispers. "Do you believe in me?"

"What are you saying?" I swim closer to her, but she drifts away, farther away from me. "Of course I do. Of course I do!"

"Do you believe in us?" Her voice is urgent.

"Why are you asking?" I swim closer, but now she's even farther away from me.

The silver butterflies glint in the sun, shimmering with kindness.

Tears well from my eyes and mingle with the water. "Where are you going?"

The tears seem to form a bubble around me, collecting more tears. They are building a shield around me. A barrier. I try to swim, but the tears give me a zap of electricity. "Where are you going?" I can see the butterflies flying away.

I am losing her.

I can't lose her again.

"NO. Don't leave me again. Don't leave me."

"You won't lose me, Maia," she whispers. "You will never lose me."

"What. . ."

"Believe in who we are, Maia."

"What are you telling me?"

"You. . . know. . ." Inside the bubble, it becomes cloudy. I lose sight of the butterflies, they go off into different directions, drawing a line between dream and reality. "You know. . . what I'm telling you, Maia."

I don't want to be alone anymore. She filled me up. I don't want her to leave.

The solitude of my heart is crushing enough.

"No, I don't, please. . ." I start to lose breath inside my bubble of tears. My vision spots. "I love—"

\* \* \*

My hair is wet; my lungs burn. I am covered in just a light pink towel, shivering, teeth clattering. My body is falling apart. I just want to die. My head is clear. I see my target; I just have to pull the trigger.

My hands and elbow are rewrapped in new, clean, white bandages. Tight and snug.

I am facing Professor Milborn in his office, naked under the towel, my lips blue, my eyes red. "Just kill me, all right?" I whisper. "I give you permission to kill me."

Professor Milborn sighs. "Maia, Maia," he tut-tuts.

"I killed someone else, so it's fair, okay? You can just do it quick and easy. Or I'll do it myself."

"Do we have to put you on suicide watch?"

"This isn't. . ."

Is this what my life will be? Will he just force me to live for the rest of my life in humiliation, degraded into a piece of dead moss by the side of the road?

"Your family misses you, Maia."

My eyes dart to his eyes.

"I had to inform them of your. . . condition."

"Did you tell. . ."

"Yes, but they would have found out anyway. . . it's all over the news, Maia. You made headlines." I smile in my head. I guess I'm famous now.

"They want you home as soon as possible, and they are willing to do whatever it takes to get you there."

I gulp.

Why the fuck does he have to burden me like that?

I love my family so much, but they are now a weight. I can't die because then they'll be miserable.

I have to live and be miserable in order for them to be happy and content with life.

I open my mouth and close it again.

"Did you make your decision?"

Ah, right, the decision. I have to choose going to court and prison for the rest of my life OR admitting to the world that the disease made me like this, giving them more fuel to keep catching people like me and converting them to what they think is "right."

Will governments in other countries start adopting the methods used here in the U.S.? Will that be the cost of my freedom?

My freedom can't be at the cost of many thousands of lives. . . but prison for the rest of my life?. . .for killing a man who deserved to die? Who fucking deserved to die. I know the law is not in my hands . . . but it's good he died. He probably abused many people before, and I stopped him from abusing many more after. It was self-defense, but it was more than self-defense. I could have stopped when he was on the ground, but I didn't. I kept on killing him over and over again. Am I willing to go to prison for the rest of my life while people are still sent to camps and *converted?* How will I be able to help them? I might make things worse if I tell the world lies, though. People will think my lies are the truth. After everything they saw of me, my so-called truth will be a weapon—a weapon against my own community.

My mind races. My eyes are moving rapidly, back and forth, faster and faster.

Professor Milborn sighs. "Maia, we can't wait all day."

"Will it be a live broadcast?" I question.

He shakes his head and smiles. He has thought of everything. "No, it'll be prerecorded. . . in case you decide to go off script."

"Fuck," I mutter to myself.

I don't know what to do.

I do know what to do.

I want to see my family; I want to go home.

I don't know what to do.

I see the silver glint of the pen on Professor Milborn's desk.

Silver. . . Silver. . .

Something drifts in my mind. I'm not sure what it is.

It's like a soft dream that flips and flurries in my vision, something that I can never catch no matter how hard I try.

"Believe in who we are, Maia," I hear—from where? The inside of my head? I'm not sure where it's coming from, but I know her voice. I can recognize her voice in a crowd of a thousand voices.

"Let's make this quick, Maia." He pulls opens a drawer and takes out a pile of papers clipped together. The ink is black, and the font is tiny. He flips through and finds the right page. "You know what the right choice is. All you have to do is sign here, and you won't go to trial. You will stay with us and finally go home." He smiles.

He thinks I've already made the decision.

He takes out his silver pen and flips the page toward me, placing the pen on top.

I look at the print. A bunch of lawyered terms pop up, this and that, things I cannot and will probably never understand in my entire life.

I see a blank space above a black line; I assume I'm supposed to sign there. I look at Professor Milborn and squeeze my eyes.

I uncap the pen. It has a big, black rollerball tip, perfect for writing a bold signature—or a bold message. I put the pen's fat, juicy tip to the line on the document and I write, watching him, watching him watch me.

I shove the paper to him and wait for his reaction.

As he looks for my signature, I deftly slip the pen inside of my towel, clipping it under the fold. And his face turns red, as if it's bubbling with fire and blood. He looks at me. "You are *incurable!* IN-CURABLE!*"

I smirk as he rips the piece of paper from its packet and starts to crumble it, crumbling my message, my words to these fucked-up people. My words, my own words, that I will always shout and yell and protest. . .

* * *

I am shuffled into the back of a police car, the doors locked from the outside, still wrapped in the light pink towel, my feet dirtied and bruised from the walk through what was once a college campus.

The guards were going to clean me up and change me into prison clothes, make me presentable, but Professor Milborn wouldn't hear of it. He was in a foaming rage. He wanted me ejected immediately, like a piece of trash.

And I want it that way too. This is my choice.

The windows are blacked out, and there's a screen blocking me from the front of the car where two officers are taking me to my temporary prison, where I'll await the trial that will determine my future.

I am alone in the back of the police car. They must think I'm so weak I won't try and escape. Anyway the doors are locked.

But I'm done escaping.

Escaping does no good.

I don't have to escape. I have what I need.

I believe in us, I believe in "we."

There are no cameras in the back of the car, and I quickly get to business.

# 44

Once I'm done, all I do is wait.

Wait and think of Aimee. . .

*We are in Duane Reade, buying candy. Aimee had a sudden craving for something salty and chocolate.*

*And the music changes from classical music to: "Pocketful of Sunshine" by Natasha Bedingfield. It starts blaring through the speakers.*

*Her body starts moving to the song. And there aren't a lot of people in the candy aisle. She smiles.*

*"Let's dance."*

*I look around. People are here.*

*I shake my head.*

*"Oh, come on. No one cares what we do. They are involved in their own lives."*

*I look at my shoes.*

*"Seven, do you trust me?"*

*I look at her beautiful, shiny eyes and nod.*

*And she grabs my hand, and we both start dancing—like half freestyling and half standard dancing technique. And we move our hands together and sing along.*

*"Take me away. . . a secret place."*

*And others look at us and smile with us.*

*We don't care what others think.*

*No one sees this as abnormal. They just see two teenagers having fun, belonging in this world, comfortable in their own skin, free to do what we want.*

The beauty of love is that there are no rules to it.

We love each other.

It's just love.

\* \* \*

After several hours, the car stops for good, and I hear the shuffling of feet. The door opens.

I wrap the towel tighter around me, and the officer takes me by the arm and pulls me out.

I stumble behind him and immediately I smile at where I am.

It's a small prison by the looks of it. A silver chain fence surrounding a yellow building with several floors.

Temporary gates surround the car, only leaving space to enter the prison.

Behind the gates are reporters, pointing their cameras—their cameras with zoom lenses that can see everything so clearly—pointing the cameras at me, shouting at me, trying to ask me many questions, in a flutter of voices, on and on and on, filming me, recording me, watching me.

I feel the towel slipping, from my body, and my smile widens.

# 45

In the White House, and oh so very white it is, President Doug Miller sits on his plush garbage-green chair like a soldier. Parallel legs, 90 degrees, feet on the floor, fists clamped on top of his knees.

A striped red and white paper container with buttery popcorn and M&M's lies by his left foot. A glass cup with non-alcoholic beer next to his right foot.

In his mouth is a red lollipop, which he sucks diligently.

He stares at the TV screen in front of him, showing the news report of the infamous, *diseased* Maia Robinson as she rides in the back of a police car, on her way to prison to await her trail.

She murdered his young friend Chaz Raymond. Chaz and his parents would come to dinner with him and Mother sometimes, always bringing the juiciest chicken breast in the world. Chaz's papa was a major, major contributor to the victorious Miller Campaign. *A delightful young man, Chaz, and, they tell me, a brilliant therapist, so very effective at curing the you-know-who.*

Doug sucks more on his red lollipop, cherry flavor, *the flavor of the medicine Mother gives me when I'm unwell.*

The police van arrives in front of the prison, stopping at a chain fence surrounding a yellow building.

Reporters are on the scene, recording every moment.

The police officers get out of the front of the car, and remove Maia. *That thimble, that dirty bird, that nobody girl. Her hair is a mess, and she's covered in nothing but a towel. She will learn her lesson, for sure!*

But then. . .

Doug's eyes widen at the TV screen. He stands up, knocking down his popcorn and non-alcoholic beer, and he spits out the lollipop, which lands on the carpet.

"*Mother!!!*" he shrieks.

# 46

The officer has a grip on my arm, while the other cop stands by the entrance, watching.

I have only one shot at this.

I yank up my arm, bend forward, and bite into the policeman's hand. I taste blood and he lets go. He staggers back from me, clutching his other hand over the injury.

I run to the gate, facing the reporters and TV cameras on the other side, and I let the towel fall. I don't care about others seeing me naked. I don't care anymore.

I twirl like a dancer.

They thought they were punishing me, locking me in that glass box for all to see, but all they did was help me get used to watchful eyes on my naked body.

And now they have given me the biggest glass box in the universe—the global TV network that the whole world is watching at this very moment.

My body. It's just a body.

We all have bodies. We all have parts we like and don't like.

The towel is at my feet, and there are more cameras and more yells and screams, and the officers are coming toward me.

I'm not showing my body to the world. I'm not showing my vulnerabilities to the world.

I'm showing the truth.

Etched on my body, ink on my skin, on every inch of body that I could reach: words and phrases, direct from my soul.

I won't stop fighting.

# I am gay

Gay

I love women

I like girls

Love is Love

I kiss girls

You cannot change us

I flirt with women

I have sex with women.

I fuck women

I adore women

we

are

united

we are

everywhere

My love, my passion.
Our love, our passion.

We are one

You cannot change us

You won't change us

We were born this way

I was born this way

I will always
be
gay

# ~Acknowledgments~

Writing a book takes a lot of work. Publishing is another journey. First off I'd like to thank IngramSpark for printing my book and helping me bring it into readers' hands. I'd like to thank Caitlin B. Alexander, my cover artist and designer, for the amazing covers! Thank you Margaret Diehl for your amazing edits and critique. Thanks, Reedsy, for helping me find a terrific cover artist and editor!

I began writing this book in July 2019, the summer I went to my first Pride March and came out to the world. I'd like to thank my amazing family for always supporting me and dealing with the crap I sometimes give them. Thank you Kaya, for your silly enthusiasm and for always believing in me. Pada, for your harsh yet charming criticism. Mom, for your backbone support, loving self, and beautiful insight into life. Last, but not least, thank you Dad for always being my first reader, editing my work and always giving me thoughtful advice that I'll carry with me forever.

Thank you to my other family members all across America, Canada, and Korea. I send my love!!!

Thank you to all my friends, especially Victoria and Sam. Victoria, for going with me to my first Pride March, which gave me inspiration to write this book. Thank you for having my back. Sam, for your thoughts about my book and your ever-growing support.

Thank you to all my friends I didn't mention. You know who you are, and I thank you for believing in me and my book. Thank you my friends from Elementary, Middle and High School, my new friends I met on the dating apps and at the No More Lonely Friends event.

Thank you my fellow actors I met on set and thank you my followers on all social media platforms: you made this possible.

Thank you to my teachers I have had an honor to learn from. You know who you are. Thank you specially to Joy Tomasko, who recognized my writing talent before I knew it myself. Also special thanks to Emily Harstone!

Being an artist, being a human in general gives me a lot of mental turmoil, so I'd like to thank my therapist for always listening to me.

Thank you my beautiful cats: Rexy, Ziggy and Tiger. Rexy, you warm up my papers and climb on my laptop which brings joy to my day. Ziggy, you have always been there for me with your bright eyes and cute face. Tiger, you may always constantly ask for food every time I stand up, but you always have an abundance of sweetness.

To my ghosters and non-believers, I have nothing to say to you.

Also: Thank you dear reader for deciding to take a chance on Maia's story. She is forever grateful.

*Photo by Val Schaffner*

**Lia Athena** is a young, biracial, queer writer in New York City. This is her debut novel. As well as writing multiple novels, she is a background actor for film and TV, in shows such as Gotham, SVU, and Billions. She is inspired daily by the world around her and can embrace her creativity and emotions to write stories that feel real and pull you into her imagination.

visit her online at
liaathena.com
find her on
Instagram, TikTok, Twitter, and Spotify

subscribe to her newsletter at: liaathena.com/newsletter